DANGEROUS PLAYTHINGS

DANGEROUS PLAYTHINGS

Cover Design and Typesetting by FormattingExperts.com

ISBN 978-0-578-87737-2
Published by NouvelleNoir Publishing
NouvelleNoir.com

PAUL ANTHONY WERNER

DANGEROUS PLAYTHINGS

The true man wants two things: danger and play.
For that reason he wants woman, as the most dangerous plaything.

Friedrich Nietzsche

And he arose, and went into the house; and he poured
The oil on his head, and said unto him, Thus saith the Lord
God of Israel, I have anointed thee king over the people of
The Lord, even over Israel.

And thou shalt smite the house of Ahab thy master, that I
May avenge the blood of my servants the prophets, and the
Blood of all the servants of the Lord, at the hand of Jezebel.

For the whole house of Ahab shall perish: and I will cut off
From Ahab him that pisseth against the wall, and him that is
Shut up and left in Israel:

And I will make the house of Ahab like the house of
Jeroboam the son of Nebat, and like the house of Baasha
The son of Ahijah:

And the dogs shall eat Jezebel in the portion of Jezreel, and
There shall be none to bury her. And he opened the door, and fled.

II Kings 9:6-10

PROLOGUE

She says, "It's my hands. In the dreams, it's always my hands I'm looking at. They're shaking almost uncontrollably, I'm scared out of my mind and I'm desperate to make them be still. I'm sure my life depends on it."

He says, "I see."

"I'm not sure you do. The thing is the curtains would not close all the way, and I had to hold them together with my hands so he wouldn't find me. We lived in this crappy little apartment, the best my mother could afford, and her bedroom closet didn't have an actual door. Just these curtains that I'm holding together, terrified."

"And when you say 'he'?"

"I mean my mother's lowlife live-in boyfriend. He came in drunk and pissed off that night, which was a long damn way from being unusual for him. He'd heard a rumor down at the neighborhood bar that mom had been with another man, which could have been true. Probably was, actually. Mom was a player. Anyway, we're just talking, the two of us, but when he came through the front door yelling and cursing and crashing into the furniture she told me to hide, and then pushed me into her closet."

The man and woman sit in a richly appointed room, the elements of which reflect much effort to create a sense of serenity and safety. A low gas-fired flame flickers in a brick-framed fireplace. The two are seated to either side of it, facing each other, in extremely expensive and extremely comfortable leather wing chairs. Above the fireplace hangs a gilt-framed oil painting of a very lovely pastoral landscape, possibly English countryside. Against the opposite wall, next to the door, stands an elegant period piece writing desk, over which are hung several framed diplomas. The diplomas have been granted by prestigious institutions of medical learning. To either side of the fireplace are cherry bookcases that run floor to ceiling and extend around their respective corners to fill both end walls as well. They are the repository of a significant portion of the accumulated wisdom of the psychiatric industry. The carpet is plush. The lighting is subdued. The man is sixty, thin, gray and formally dressed. The woman is late twenties, brunette, casually and somewhat provocatively dressed. She smokes a cigarette as she talks, to the well-disguised irritation of the man.

He says, "And then?"

"And then he came into the room and began to attack her. I mean savagely. I wasn't watching, of course, but I could hear it all. The beating went on for what seemed like forever but was probably five or ten minutes, and then I could hear the bed creak as he jumped on top of her and I heard her making choking sounds. He was strangling her, I could tell. Finally the noises stopped. She was dead."

"That must have been a horrifying experience for a young girl."

She says, "Well, thank you for that profound piece of analysis, doctor. And here I was afraid I might not get my $300 an hour money's worth from this session."

"I understand that this, this process is a stressful one for you, but if we are going to do ourselves any good here we really need to eliminate any hostility between us, all right? Sarcasm is not really conducive to a healthy doctor-patient relationship."

"Yes, I see that. Sorry. Of course I was terrified. I was scared that he would discover me and kill me as well. The fear for my own life even made me forget about my poor mom."

"That's perfectly understandable and one hundred percent normal. I wouldn't trouble over that. And then what happened?"

"Either I made some sort of noise, a gasp or whimper maybe, or my shaking hands betrayed me. Either way, he realized I was there and came for me. He didn't have it in mind to kill me, though. With me he decided to take out his frustrations in another manner. He'd been leering at me ever since the day he moved in, and I guess he figured what the hell, good a time as any to make a move. He dragged me into my own bedroom, where he stripped my clothes off and raped me. After which he passed out."

"And, refresh my memory. You would have been how old?"

"Fifteen."

"Forgive me for asking, but may I assume you were a virgin then?"

"I was."

"My God," he says. "A girl of fifteen in one terrible violent night is a witness to her mother's murder, and then loses her virginity to forcible rape. It's unavoidable that such a traumatic episode is going to lead to serious and lasting psychological problems. We're going to have a lot of work to do, to help you finally process it all."

She says, "You don't understand. I've dealt with it. I dealt with it long ago. I'm fine, except for these dreams. They are driving me crazy. That's why I'm here, to get rid of the dreams."

"I'm sorry, but I have great difficulty believing you really are fine. Perhaps you are in denial? Are you able to enjoy healthy relationships with men? Sexual relationships, I mean."

"I know what you meant. Yes, absolutely."

"No problems with the enjoyment of sex, then? I must tell you, orgasmic issues are seen almost universally in cases such as yours."

"I enjoy sex. I adore sex."

"That's really very surprising. And you've had absolutely no professional counseling?"

"No. Psychiatry is an art, whether or not you care to admit it, not a science. You shrinks like to think you can analyze every last bit of human behavior and understand everything about it. You can't. You think you can predict what we're going to feel or what we're going to do, like we're all just pieces of machinery. Wind us up and away we go, right? Wrong."

"Fair enough, but I must tell you that we shrinks do know the statistics, and if you've really come through an experience like this unscathed, without the benefit of any therapy, you are in line to be a significant case study. So tell me about your self-healing process, please."

"Of course. I began by taking a hard look at my mother's lifestyle. She was not a beautiful woman, as I am not, you can see for yourself, a beautiful woman. But she had a gift for attracting men. She understood, in a way that very few women do, the right buttons to push. Men are pathetically simple, she used to tell me, as easy to manipulate as children. They have two things that require constant stroking, she taught me. One was their ego, and I'm going to leave the second to your imagination. She must have been on to something, because in fact she always had any man she wanted.

"The problem with her was, she always wanted the wrong ones. She went through an unbroken string of losers, and I mean serious losers, until it finally caught up with her. She was always being used by men.

"I learned from that, doctor. After she died, I swore I would always be the one doing the using. It was the rejection of victimhood that healed me and set me free. My mother taught me all her tricks once I was old enough to understand the rules of the game, and I'll tell you without boasting that I can pretty much seduce any man I choose. That said, however, I choose wisely. I choose men who have something to offer, which is usually money, and I use them. It really is great fun. I'm like a kid with a new toy when I meet a man I like. And I'm going to tip you to a little trade secret, doc, free of charge: The way to a man's heart is not through his stomach."

She gives the man a quick wink, to which he smiles slightly and nods. "Well, that really is remarkable, I must admit. And this boyfriend, the one who murdered your mother. Was justice done to him?"

"Oh, yes," she says. "I can assure you of that."

"That must have been some help to your peace of mind. How long did it take the police to arrest him?"

"They didn't. As a matter of fact, they never found him."

"Now I'm confused. Explain, please."

"To be honest, it wouldn't hurt my feelings a bit if we were to drop that particular subject. It was a long time ago. It doesn't matter."

There is a moment as the man shifts in his chair, momentarily puzzled. Then suddenly he understands, and nods. "Very well, I believe I see your point. I promise you, though, that I maintain doctor-patient confidentiality absolutely. I regard the protection of your privacy as my highest duty. You can rest assured that everything that is said within these walls remains here."

There is a long silence while she considers this last remark. Then she says, "All right. Since you asked. Like I said, he fell asleep after he had sex with me. So I called this friend of mom's. Name's not important. Big guy, scary-looking, not the brightest, but a real sweetheart. He had a thing for her, but she wouldn't give him a tumble, probably because he wasn't handsome at all, plus he was way too nice. Anyway, he came over and trussed this asshole up while he slept, and took him and threw him into the trunk of his car. We drove into the middle of the woods outside of town, dragged his ass out of the car and tied him to a tree. I then proceeded to beat him to death with my friend's tire iron. Slowly. Listening to him whimper like a bitch and beg for his worthless life. Now that, doc, was therapeutic, I promise you."

He struggles to conceal his shock at this revelation. He's accustomed to dealing with comfortable upper middle class suburbanites and their comfortable upper middle class neuroses. He says, "Yes, I can imagine that it was."

"When it was done my friend dug a hole and threw him in. He drove me home, I went to sleep, and in the morning I called the cops. As far as I know, there's still a BOLO out on the prick."

"I see."

"Does that make me a bad person, in your professional opinion?"

"That's a judgment I'd prefer to leave to others. Actually, you were right. This is a conversation we never had. If we may, however, revisit the subject of men and your romances with them. What I very much fear is that you are missing out on the real joy that can come from a truly loving, deeply committed relationship. I mean a relationship based on mutual respect. You are living, I would say, a very superficial life."

She leans forward, toward him, and a flash of anger crosses her face. "Doctor, if you would be so kind, spare me the concern for my love life. Trust me, I am happy. Just please help me get rid of these goddamn dreams."

CHAPTER 1

ME

The road from Prescott to Vegas is two lane asphalt threaded across the high desert of northwest Arizona, hot and sticky in the warm summer night. Friday night. Top's down. Air burbles noisily off the pillars of the windscreen. The tires sing against the pavement with a high keen, like a well-cast fishing line racing crisply off the spool. Sweet, husky V8 music trails in my wake.

My Mustang's on autopilot, cruise control locked in at eighty and the nose tracing the twisting highway faithfully as if of its own volition, just the occasional nudge from my fingers, resting lightly and tapping on the leather-wrapped wheel. A rattler warms itself on the roadbed, which still holds the heat of the day's sun. It senses my approach, it's frozen for an instant in the oncoming cone of my headlights, it slews off into the shoulder brush just in time.

I love the desert because it's real. I'm troubled by the superficiality of the modern world, a media-driven show-and-tell in which image is everything, in which perception has a thousand fathers but truth is an orphan, in which form no longer follows function but subsumes it. Like the colored sand and sculpted stone around me, my crime is no less real for having been beautifully executed.

Between twanging guitar riffs a dead Stevie Ray Vaughan warns that the sky is crying, and damned if he isn't right. Only tonight the tears are stars rather than raindrops. A thousand galaxies shine brightly in the clear air, arching in an immense dome and falling to a horizon that stretches black and gray in the pale light.

Over my left shoulder the moon hangs low in the southwestern sky against an iridescent backdrop, nearly round, cold light the color of bleached bone.

It's the intimate view of the sky that's done it; it always does. Something about being so close to the infinite expanse, able practically to reach out and grasp the enormous thing, to physically squeeze the ether in my fist, somehow puts me in a philosophical mood. That and the isolation I feel in the vastness of the desert. Plus the flask of Johnny Walker from which I take the occasional throat-searing pull.

It's when I'm utterly alone like this that it comes. The guilt. Slowly at first it washes over me, building in intensity like ever larger waves of nausea. Most men have never come up against the agonizing choices I've faced, I tell myself, have never had to deal with the untidy aftermath or the paralyzing doubt.

The saguaros are black and stark in the pale moonlight, along with randomly scattered boulders the only landscape feature, fields of them by the thousands like the risen multitudes on Judgment Day, stiff arms raised in supplication or exultation or both, take your pick. On a hill to my left, a small stand forms a fleeting scene that could be Calvary. Three shimmering crosses; no waiting.

Jezebel. Life would be so simple if our paths had never crossed. Can I lay the blame wholly on her? Can we just agree, ladies and gentlemen of the jury, that she made me commit this unspeakable act? What the hell. At the end of the day it matters little.

The atmosphere is beginning to lighten around me, almost imperceptibly. The coolest time, now, daybreak almost here. Though still quite warm, and a rosy glow begins to breathe around me.

I come to a long straight stretch of road, I press the gas, my car accelerates effortlessly and settles in at 120. The pavement slides blurred beneath me, I'm a bird in flight, yet the guilt remains. I'm no longer sure whether I'm fleeing it or chasing it, but either way it remains my companion. It's become a real and growing problem for me these past few years, a wound that's not looking like being healed by time. If anything, it's worse as I age. Schopenhauer once remarked that life is a useless interruption of an otherwise pleasant nonexistence, and I'm beginning to believe that he may have had a point.

My car tops a ridge line and drops into the sprawling basin west of the great canyon, a mountain-ringed valley where my destination lies. To my right a pair of red-tailed hawks swoop in formation toward the earth, in pursuit of a road-warming reptile, perhaps, or low-flying avian prey. I realize, watching them, that daylight has come while I dreamt. Toward the horizon to my right the unearthly white glare of Meade is a signpost.

The lake is blue now, a rich morning hue glimpsed in quick patches as I twist and turn down the hill toward the dam. Its surface is flat and unruffled in the airless dawn. The sun is still below the mountains to the east.

Another philosopher, Camus, alleged less famously that the soul of a murderer is blind. Not this murderer. This murderer is as wide-eyed as they come, and not at all caring for what he sees when he looks inside. For this murderer has devoted the better part of his longish life sworn to the administration of justice, the last dozen alone given in service to the civil security and general peace of mind of the good people of Prescott, a nice little town in the middle of Arizona, neighbor and poor cousin to the celebrated Sedona, where this particular murderer presently does duty as Chief of Police. And when you've lived your life as a basically decent man, or tried to, taking a life as I have is to cross a line into a lonely and fearsome territory, to take a step that can never be retraced. Poppy would be grievously and inconsolably disappointed.

I ease down onto the top of the dam itself, lugging along at a walking pace with my foot off the accelerator. The heat is a living thing. I feel it stir and it has big plans for today. Gonna have to put the top up. I swerve to the side and stop. Unimaginable volumes of water to my right, perfectly at rest after eons of scouring a five-thousand foot canyon artfully into the desert's heart. Below me, an immense weight of concrete deployed in a visually simple but mathematically powerful opposing arc. Within, hundred ton steel turbine shafts rotating with eternal precision. Surely here at the nexus of all these colossal works of God and man, the pain of one lousy human being can be metaphysically reduced to insignificance. I lay my head against the seat back. The sky shows off its morning rainbow, pink to blue to black. It seems smaller now, yet still vast. I push a button and with a mechanical whine it disappears. A hidden vent softly exhales chilled air across my knees.

I glance at my reflection in the rear view mirror and hardly recognize the man looking back at me. By some wholly unexpected process, the better-than-average-looking Philly teenager with the full head of hair and cocky attitude has morphed into a man pushing sixty, and looking every day of it. For God's sake how did that happen? He's looking worn around the edges, the man in the mirror. The eyes are tired, the skin is drawn, the hair is thinning and graying.

I reach for the ignition and twist the key. Viva Las Vegas.

It is the city's vulnerable hour. The bright tinkling circus noises of the casinos are hushed, the flashing lights subdued. Everybody moves as if underwater. Ashtrays are being emptied. Buffets restocked. Massive air-conditioning units work overtime to get a head start on the day's advancing heat. The whores have all grabbed taxis and are home asleep in their own beds. The gamblers have given up and will get even some other night; the day folk have yet to arise and reclaim the streets. I steal into town, a Visigoth here for the sacking.

The metaphor is apt, for I swing into Caesar's Palace and idle up to the valet parking stand. The great Palace. First, unfortunately, of a long series of theme hotels lining the Strip. Where, arguably, it all began for me. Or rather ended. Prologue meets epilogue. Before, say hello to after. Youthful innocence v. virtue lost. Good morning.

CHAPTER 2
CLEOPATRA

Why have I come to Las Vegas? Entertainment is the short answer, which will do for now. A convenient place for a break from the tedium of crime-stopping in a low-crime city. I awaken at 1400. Shower and shave and throw on some casual clothes. A headache is setting up a beachhead just behind my left temple and Mr. Walker has left a fuzzy little ball of nausea in my stomach. Coffee is required, quickly.

I ride down the elevator to lobby level. Through the long hallway past the tony boutiques, nothing less than a month's salary, thank you, and out into the lobby casino. If money is a religion, welcome to the Vatican, boys. No, we have no Pope. The Vicar of Christ is presently pursuing other opportunities. But we have sacraments by the dozen, you name 'em. Blackjack. Craps. Roulette. Keno. Drive-through matrimony. We have rituals and pageantry, we have marble and nifty artwork, some of it real. And Christ, we have churches, pardon the blasphemy. More churches and chapels and temples than the periodic table has elements, rendered in every fanciful color of the rainbow. Faith? My God, that's our specialty, the whole town was built on it was it not?

I look to my right and I can see the blackjack tables. Not just yet, Jezzie, it's too soon. I plow into the battalions of slots and fight my way through to a bar. Trying not to see the rows of liquor bottles as I drink my hot black coffee down nor to hear the scientifically annoying noises emanating from the machines around me, as slowly I pull myself together.

Partially restored, I head for the main entrance. I cross under a cascade of frigid air, step through a set of automatic doors and onto the surface of the Sun. 1600 PDT, the absolute peak of a suffocating unrelenting desert heat that instantly penetrates my entire being. My eyes are assaulted by intense levels of sunlight, reflected and redirected off of any number of prismatic glass surfaces, of endless variety of shapes and shades. I'm pretty certain that I would be totally unable to cope without my Ray Bans; I pray thanks I've remembered them.

The first thing I notice is that the last decade's democratization has brought volume to this enterprise. That's where we're making it now, off the proletariat. Great volumes of traffic inching along Las Vegas Boulevard. Astonishing volumes of humanity jostling and bumping their way along its sidewalks, a Brownian motion rush to nowhere and everywhere simultaneously.

I move off down the Strip, northward. I pass a man-made volcano and a replicated pirate battle. Cross the street. Eat a gelato and watch a pair of newlyweds gondola their way down the Grand Canal. Head south. Take a Gallic ride to the top of a truncated Eiffel Tower. Lunch in a New York New York deli. We're slowly but surely assembling a replica of the entire globe here, minus the untidy bits, and it's so damn shamelessly American and so damn easy to bounce off of I don't have the heart to comment on it further. Here represented is every city or cultural milieu on the planet worth mentioning, plus a few that aren't. Any day now some entrepreneurial visionary is going to venture out into the solar system for inspiration.

I have an early evening shooter at Bellagio. I enjoy the Italianate opulence inside and the computerized water dance outside. After perhaps thirty minutes, I head back to Caesar's. The long dusk is ending and the insufferable temperature has faded just a tad with the light, but after all the walking I'm feeling very sweaty and looking forward to another shower.

Back in the lobby, I swallow hard and decide it's time. The table is there, right where we left it, under the watchful hawkish eye of a buxom Queen Cleopatra, resplendent in her faux gold barge as she cruises eternally down an imaginary Nile. There are two people playing. I join them and toss a twenty-five dollar chip onto the felt tabletop. I turn to my left, and there she is, my Jezebel, sitting just where we first laid eyes on one another. Jezzie. Femme most assuredly fatale. Mistress of the known universe. Giver of transcendent pleasure. Taker of my soul. She hasn't changed a bit, not even her dress, she looks as if she's wiped away the thousand yesterdays since the night we parted. The dealer is asking with impatience if I need another card. I glance down at a Queen and a six, look at his three, and decline with a short sideways wave of my hand. And of course when I turn back, she's gone. The spell is irrevocably broken, but suddenly I understand why I'm here.

It's the futile hope that somehow, by hovering on this very spot, the exact physical location where it all started to go wrong for me, I can make it unhappen. In concert with this epiphanous moment, the dealer goes bust. I let my winnings ride.

It's just a subconscious notion, of course, and an unrealistic one at that. Still, the people who do advanced thinking about the cosmos for a living believe that we may occupy one of a large number of parallel universes, each with its own unique history. According to quantum mechanics, this is for a fact the case on a micro scale. Just maybe it's true on the macro. And just maybe, here at the intersection of a hundred different realities, if I wish it hard enough I can jump on one that's headed in a happier direction.

Or maybe I'm simply losing my effing mind. The dealer deals himself blackjack. Back in my room, I have a quick shower and flip on the tube. I draw the shade across my window, preparatory to falling into bed, and notice yet another high rise in the skeletal steel stage of construction, a block over, night lit in an orange sodium glow. Mars World, probably. Or Venusville.

CHAPTER 3
JEZEBEL

It's been nearly a decade, I'm astonished to realize. Still, it could easily be ten days, my memory of it all is so clearly intact. I hesitated for just a moment at the entrance to the sports book. Do I walk through and check out the craps tables, and then move on to the next casino? Or do I turn around and work my way through the blackjack wing? Option A and I head home, probably, my mission a failure and live happily ever after. Regrettably, option B is the one I chose.

She was seated at third base, which is to say the last position to the dealer's right. One seat is open, immediately to her right. I take it. We exchange the briefest of nods and I get my first glance at those outsized brown eyes that will haunt me for a long time to come. She's dressed in a very chic little number, a fashionably simple black dress that in front rises all the way to her neckline, but that in back is open in a *V* that descends to the lowest point good taste, or for that matter municipal code, allows. Seated as she is, the hem comes to mid-thigh. She has a very lovely pearl necklace around her throat and an equally lovely gold Rolex watch on her left wrist. She is wearing a wedding ring. Not really my area of expertise, but it appears to be a very nice one. She is clearly one spoiled girl.

I bide my time. The group is betting fairly large; I see nothing but bumblebees on the line. I go along, just trying to hang for the duration. To my right is one of these jerk kids, two years out of business school, big good-looking bastard, Ivy League from the top of his head to the tips of his Bally-shod toes, just in from the East Coast to treat us all to a dose of his arrogance, obviously raised spoiled and installed in some overpaid sinecure, likely as not in his daddy's business. He's playing like a moron, to my great satisfaction. To his right is a nicely turned-out middle-aged lady with a New York or New Jersey accent, I can never tell which, dressed in an evening gown and a very serious jewelry collection, assuming it's not CZ. Somebody loves her. Beyond her is a latter day cowboy, just blown in from Texas or maybe Prescott, complete down to the Tony Lama snakeskin boots and turquoise-studded bolo. What the hell, we are in Nevada.

A couple of uneventful hands go by, during which I manage to get up maybe a hundred and a half and work myself into a state over this asshole next to me, drinking too much and talking too loudly to a group of guys and gals, fellow spoiled assholes I assume, kibitzing from behind him. We're all impressed at the sangfroid with which he's managing to drop thousands of dollars he never earned.

I notice that there hasn't been a lot of paint on the table for a little while, so I figure it's time to jump in. I've been betting twenty-five, but I decide to quadruple my bet. The dealer is laying out everything but his hole card face up. This tends to be off-putting to some, but affords him absolutely no advantage, given the rules of the game. Cowboy draws a ten and a Jack. Miss Zirconium, as I'm coming to believe may be a relevant moniker, receives a nine and a six. The genius to my right, a queen and a three. For me, a five and three. And for the lady to my left, with one very long, very thin leg poised over the other and her skirt hiking up another notch with every round, a pair of eights. Dealer's hole card is a lovely little four.

Cowboy, obviously, is done. Glitter gal hits, unwisely, and is blown away by a swatch of that missing paint. The kid hits, fool that he is, and is promptly busted by yet another face card. I'm a study in mixed emotions, happy of course to see him get his stupid ass kicked but pissed that he burned my ten. Nevertheless, I do the right thing and double down. A seven. What the hell, with any luck that'll be good enough.

It's time, I understand, to make my move. I lean over to my left and say to her, "It's none of my business, I realize, but if I were you I'd split those ochos."

She says, "Really? And then do what?"

"Double down on both sides. You're working against a four."

She takes my suggestion, effectively changing her original two hundred-fifty dollar bet into a grand. She now gets only one card per side. First, a king. Bingo. Second, an ace. Excellent. The dealer flips over his hidden card, and it's another king. And then he draws a jack and I'm looking very smart. Cowboy gives a little western-style hoot of joy at this face card roundup, and my girl gives me a wink and says with a nod of her head, "I owe you a drink."

I return the wink and say, "At a minimum."

She scoops up her winnings, tosses a chip to the dealer, throws the rest into her handbag, grabs my arm and steers me to the nearest cocktail lounge.

That's how we came to be chatting in a Vegas casino that night, so many years and so many uncharted miles ago. The thing that I would hope to make you understand about Jez, so that you may forgive or at least sympathize with the extent to which she led me astray, is this: she was simply the sexiest woman I ever dealt with. She was an illustrative example of a fact that we men know well, but that most women will never grasp, that sex appeal has little to do with looks. She wasn't unattractive, but she was far from beautiful. Her face was a trifle too thin, her nose just that much too large, her lips not full and sensuous as modern practice dictates. Her hair was an everyday shade of brown and its styling perfectly ordinary. She was too thin even for the day, with little to offer in the way of breasts, though here again we have an aspect of feminine charm sadly overvalued by America's Cosmo gals. Show you a photograph of her, the point is, and I promise you'd not give it a second glance.

But ah, Jez, she wasn't operating in two dimensions. The fully-realized three-dimensional version would, if you were a man she cared to have, simply burn you down. Some of it was the aforementioned eyes, big and brown and intense, and fixed on you from the moment you entered her presence as if you were an avatar whose splendid sight transfixed her, hanging on your every word as if your wisdom guided the planets in their celestial orbits. She made you feel, I'm saying, like the center of her world and that's about 90 percent of the battle with most of us men.

A part of it is much harder to verbalize. There is to some women simply an ineffable something, a mixture of the proper pheromones, the right genetic chemistry, a subliminal connection with some epochal touchstone of male desire, some shared tribal sense memory, some synaptic tether to the most ancient and primitive reptilian shell of the male cortex. Sex appeal, plain and simple and inexplicable.

That's for starters. In the boudoir is where she really pulled out the stops. Being thin, she looked better the more clothing she removed. Naked, her body had a vulnerable girlish quality to it, A-cup breasts budding demurely above a belly flat as Kansas and a cute little butt riding atop a long and nicely formed pair of legs. And she went at you. I'm no expert, but I had never seen anything like it. She was a man-pleasing little piece of machinery in bed. She made damn sure you enjoyed screwing her like nothing you'd ever enjoyed before; but more importantly, she herself enjoyed lovemaking, noisily and with great abandon. Jez adored men and adored the act. Nothing sexier than that, I'll tell you for nothing.

"So where did you learn to play cards so well?" she asks, fixing those eyes of hers on mine for the first fateful time.

"Misspent youth," I say.

There was a lull then, which I found to be uncomfortable but with which she was quite content. In the interim, the waitress sidled up and we each ordered a scotch rocks.

"Listen," I finally say, "I'm sorry, but patter is not really my thing."

"That's fine," she laughs. "I'm an expert." Then, "What's your name, my friend of the misspent youth?"

"Carlo. Carlo Jardina."

"You don't look like a Carlo, no offense. I mean with the blue eyes and the brown hair. You're not traveling incognito now are you, Carlo?"

"Not hardly. The name I got from my Italian father. Everything else comes courtesy of my fair-skinned Scottish mother, God rest her soul."

"Well, she did all right by you. You're not too awful-looking. I've given my heart to worse."

"Thanks for those generous words. And you?"

"Me what?"

"What may I call you?"

She gives me a look that says first names are just fine for this evening's purposes. "Jez. Or Jezzie, your choice."

"Jezzie. That's an interesting one."

"If you say so. My given name is Jezebel."

"Nice. Very original. Why not use it?"

"I've never wanted to give men the right idea." This is enormously funny to her, and she breaks out laughing. "Wrong idea, I meant." I join her self-consciously. She lights a Virginia Slims menthol, not bothering to ask.

"So," she asks, "What brings you to Vegas? Have we segued into a misspent adulthood?"

It's my turn to laugh. "Hardly. Just here for a little R and R. I was lost as a young man, but I am now well and truly found. Actually, I'm a cop. Been a couple years with the force in Prescott, Arizona. Just made lead detective, as a matter of fact."

This intelligence galvanized her. She leant across the table toward me, a feral glint in her eyes. "Really?! You're just the man I've been looking for."

"Don't get yourself too excited. Prescott is a very small town with a very small police force."

"That's fine. I only have a very small problem."

"Is that a fact? Well, Mrs…?"

"Call me Jez."

"That being the case, Jez, I have to wonder. Here you are, clearly a very well-tended woman, a woman of means you might say. Your jewelry is tastefully understated and quietly expensive. That little dress you're almost wearing is obviously designer *haute couture*, I'm thinking four-figure *haute*. Then there's the Italian purse and footwear."

"I see you have an eye for fashion. It's always nice to meet a man with good taste."

"I'd say it's your husband that has good taste."

"You would, would you? Thanks for the compliment, but trust me, you'd be surprised how undiscriminating he can be when it comes to the fair sex."

"Is that so? That's a pity. Anyway, I'm asking myself why you're getting yourself so excited about an obscure rookie detective from Prescott, whom you've known now for all of five minutes. Like I'm the guy you've been looking for your whole life. You're a rich sophisticated city girl with access to rich sophisticated city detectives and lawyers and what not. Like I said, Prescott is a very small town."

"No worries. What I have in mind is a very small crime."

"Excuse me?"

"What I'm thinking, Carlo, is who better to help me kill my husband than a cop? Who would know better how to get away with it? A *detective*, no less. One with a low profile at that, which is actually helpful. I consider myself a good judge of character, and I can tell you're a serious no bullshit kind of man, a man I could trust to do the job and do it right."

"Jez, where I come from premeditated homicide is not considered a small crime."

There's a moment of silence while she considers her response, during which she burns another cigarette and drains her scotch. "Well, Carlo, it depends on your perspective, I suppose."

"If you say so...anyway, I guess I would probably have a better chance of getting away with murder than most. Hypothetically speaking, that is, and the operative word being chance. Nothing is 100%."

"True, of course. But I believe I'd be comfortable rolling the dice on you, Carlo."

"And you would want to...eliminate your husband why?"

"Because he's a dumb boring self-centered fuck who can't keep his dick in his pants."

"So leave him."

"Problem is, he's a *rich* dumb boring self-centered fuck."

"Where you live?"

"California. Why?"

"Community property. I hear they're very generous as a rule to divorcées in that particular jurisdiction."

She blows a stream of mentholated smoke my way, a look of sincere regret on her face. "Prenup," she says, enunciating the word as if it were an obscenity.

"Prenups are made to be broken, I'm told."

"I said my husband is dumb. I didn't say his lawyers are."

I say, "I see. That's a drag. Jezzie, you are either a very careless lady, or you have a strange sense of humor. I'm gonna lean toward the latter, if you don't mind. Bearing in mind that I *am* an officer of the law and all."

There was a weird interlude involving probably a full three minutes of absolute silence. And then she smiled and said, "Don't mind me, Carlo, I was just letting off some steam. Inadvertently giving voice to my internal dialogue, you might say. The prick is off chasing showgirls as we speak, which is damaging to a girl's self-esteem, you know? But I was just playing with you."

"Good."

"So where are you staying?"

"Why?"

"You don't expect me to take you back to *my* room, do you? Roger could return any time, which would be awkward."

"Oh. I see. Actually, I have a room here, at Caesar's."

She frowns. "Hmm. Convenient, but not really very discreet, do you think?"

"Now that you mention it, no, I guess not. There's a place I use to stay before I was promoted. The Oasis. Dive a couple blocks east of the Strip. What I could afford on a patrolman's salary."

Her smile reappears. "Perfect," she says. "Take me to your camel."

Thus Jez and I spent our first night together, and I will tell you it was beautiful. I was pretty badly out of practice at that point, but it mattered little. She was a lover with whom you could just let go and enjoy the ride, stress-free. Only I will tell you further that I fell in love with her right there on the spot, and I don't mean some adolescent brand of puppy love. I mean our-souls-are-merged-forever, never-before-attained-spiritual plane, two months' salary diamond be-my-mate-for-eternity love. She was that good. During the following months I sank into the quicksand that much deeper, without a struggle, but I was hooked from the first.

Afterward, we lay together naked on the bed enjoying a quiet afterglow moment. As she lit another cigarette she evidently decided it was time for a spot of biographical research on me. Out of the blue she asked, "So how does a juvenile delinquent grow up to become a cop?"

"I never said I was a juvenile delinquent."

"Sorry. You're right. I inferred."

"That's OK. Actually I was. A serious JD, you don't want to hear the half of it."

"JD?"

"Sorry. Juvenile delinquent. My parents were pretty much useless, so I lacked discipline and structure as a child and young teenager."

"Aha. So what turned you around?"

"I met this man. He became a father figure to me, which was something I'd never had. It may not surprise you to know that studies demonstrate time and again that the single factor shaping a boy's outcome in life is the presence or absence of a father."

"Really? And what do studies demonstrate about what happens to little fatherless girls?"

"I hear they tend to become promiscuous. Other than that I can't say for sure, but I guess that's not a good situation either. How could it be? Anyway, this guy took me under his wing, as they say, and showed me the right path."

"He must have been a very good man."

"You would think so, wouldn't you?" I said, shaking my head. "Actually, he wasn't. He led a pretty bad life. I don't really want to go into it, but he was involved in a lot of bad stuff and did harm to a lot of people. By the time I met him, though, he'd come to a point where he realized it had all been a horrible mistake for him. Sort of a midlife reassessment. And he wanted to steer me away from making the same mistake. Which good deed he accomplished. He and his wife. They gave me love and guidance."

She said, "Hmm."

We got out of bed and pulled a couple of miniatures out of the minibar. Sitting on the edge of the bed, sipping scotch neat, I tried to get her to return the favor, to tell me a bit about her own life. I said, "And how about Jezebel? What's she been doing my whole life?"

She was in no mood to play. "Nothing worth discussing, Carlo. My life has been pretty unexceptional."

"Yeah? Why do I find that hard to believe?"

Suddenly she turned to me, put her arm around my neck, pulled me toward her and gave me a long, deep kiss. "I have to go, baby. It's been great."

She started to dress.

I asked her, "Will I see you again? I must."

She answered, "We'll see, won't we?" She went downstairs and had the guy at the desk call her a cab. It took me many hours to fall asleep.

* * *

I slept in late the next morning. Jezebel didn't. I found a note she'd slipped under my door sometime early in the morning. It read:

You know that thing we talked about, last night? Actually, I was sort of serious. Last night was just great. Thanks. Perhaps we'll speak again. Love you, J.

I didn't know whether, that morning in the desert, to be happy or sad. Falling in love had not actually been part of my plan.

CHAPTER 4
THUMPER

Driving back to Prescott after that improbable evening, I remember that Thumper was much on my mind. Thumper, AKA Joey Taccolini, AKA Joey T., who started the ball rolling. Thumper, the policeman's friend. Considering some of the elements of my encounter with Jezebel, it was natural enough, in view of a story he once told me, that he became the subject of my lonely riding-down-the-highway musings. I jammed a Bob Dylan CD, *Blood on the Tracks* it must have been, into the dash and as the miles unrolled beneath me and my mind's eye danced over visions of him and of Jezebel I tried to sort through the possibilities.

Now days my trips to Vegas are in the summertime, when it's hot and the air is clear as French crystal. But that fateful weekend it was winter, and a violent sodden weather front had just lumbered in from across the Pacific west of Baja, battered Southern California with heavy downfalls and was sorting itself out across the desert, organizing for an assault on the Rockies. Heavy black rain clouds stalked the skies ahead of me, like huge machines of war searching for targets of opportunity. They came with sudden agitated bursts of wind intent on blowing me onto the sandy shoulder, dropped solid shafts of water at me a hundred feet across, and just as quickly left me completely becalmed and sunlit and struggling with the wheel to regain my track along the wet but newly windless pavement.

And between storm cells, Thumper. When I moved to Prescott from the East Coast and hired on as an officer with the police department, patrolman of lowest describable rank despite my experience with other departments and still damn glad to be in the West, Thump was already installed as a sort of local cop groupie. He liked to hang where we hung, loved to hear the stories, share our doughnuts, listen to our radio, even toss us a tidbit from time to time he'd picked up on the street, for despite our affection for him

Thumper had a serious record and no regular means of support since he'd sworn off crime, and the street was indeed where he dwelt.

Although he was more or less homeless, or at least had no permanent address, he was no bum. He supported himself by performing various odd jobs and by being our occasional snitch, for which big-hearted Carlo compensated him in an absurdly generous fashion.

Thumper was a very nervous young man, with the restless energy of a caged monkey. When forced to remain in one spot for more than a few moments he had this distracting habit of tapping his foot on the ground like the cartoon rabbit, and thus of course the unusual handle.

He was a tall and scrawny kid, with unwholesomely pale and freckled skin but surprisingly muscular arms. Despite his circumstances Thumper was no dummy. He was college educated and well read. It was a mystery to me how he'd found himself with a rap sheet rather than a resume. I never asked, but I figured his life must have taken a pharmaceutical detour somewhere along the way. He grew up and spent most of his life on the East Coast, as did I, and so there was that bond between us. Then, as now, Prescott was a fairly placid little berg and so we frequently had time to talk.

One day we were sitting at the local coffee shop, Louisa's, where we often met, and I asked him on a whim about his renunciation of the criminal lifestyle and what exactly had turned him around. Over a couple cups of coffee and maybe five Marlboros he told me a story he swore he hadn't told anyone else since coming to Arizona.

"You know I've done time, right, Carlo?"

"Sure, Joey. I am aware of that unfortunate fact."

"Serious, hard time I mean. Different places, different beefs. Last was a situation in Harrisburg, PA."

I knew this part. A collection of auto parts of questionable provenance was discovered in his garage, and the authorities leapt, very rashly in our mutual opinion, to the conclusion that he was associated with a large auto theft ring they were rolling up at the time. Long story short, he's a guest of the state in a nice secure facility thoughtfully located in a scenic rural part of western Pennsylvania.

"So here I am in the joint, Carlo, and for my amusement and like, edification, I'm given a cellmate, name's Brad. Brad is a very nice young man, very well-built body builder type, blonde hair, if we were in California I'd think surfer for sure. Now as likeable as this dude was, you gotta know he was not at the time entertaining job offers from NASA or JPL. Ask Brad about the last book he read, and he's gonna like, unroll it on the spot and tell you about some guy in a cape or something, you get my drift. Real dumbass."

Thumper's narrative is accompanied by the rhythm of his left foot tapping frenetically against Louisa's linoleum floor, and punctuated by pauses for drags from his cigarette. Both activities increase steadily in frequency as he gets more deeply involved in his story.

"What Brad is doing is life imprisonment for murder one. Being this kind of heavyweight criminal usually makes a guy pretty cocky in environments like of which we speak, but Brad was always extremely nervous, I'll go so far as to say fearful. Terrified, actually. All the time.

"With good reason, it turns out. See, in his previous life Brad was working for this pool service company. And he had a client, name's Paul Agnelli, guy has a beautiful big house in a fashionable neighborhood. And said client has like this young wife, Rochelle, who must have also been very beautiful, 'cause before you know it Brad's servicing both Mr. Agnelli's pool and Mr. Agnelli's bride. Who, by the way, is a real little firecracker, the wife I mean. She has two passions in life, gambling and screwing strange men. She's caught the old man sort of on the rebound and he is unfortunately unaware of her character flaws. In addition to the obvious bad aspects of this scenario there are two less obvious but very unfortunate circumstances. The first is that this cuckolded gentleman happens to be like a fairly important figure among the OC crowd, in fact he's a made guy, a boss. Second is that this little beauty Brad's banging convinces him that they are an item for all time, and that he needs to whack her old man so that the two of them can live happily ever after."

The thing about Thump is he's very talkative, the kind of guy who can make a short story long, and consequently I often find myself listening to him with just one ear. However, this little tale strikes a chord. I'm finding it absolutely riveting, and I am at this point leaning forward against the edge of the table, both ears tuned in. I said, "At which point Brad says what?"

"At which point Brad eagerly signs on to a supposedly foolproof plan. Rochelle provides him with a very effective high-powered rifle, poached from Mr. Agnelli's own collection, very clean and guaranteed untraceable. With which one evening Brad drills Mr. Agnelli accurately and fatally, right through the poor man's windshield."

Now I had to feel a great deal of sympathy for the poor guy, despite his unfashionable resume, getting capped as he drives his expensive automobile home after a hard day's work through the lovely secluded lane that leads through the wooded patch between the lesser sections of suburbia and the privileged enclave containing his own beautiful house and beautiful wife, who by the way has conveniently gone off to Atlantic City for the weekend. Set up in a blind, was Brad, in the brush just back from the pavement at the head of a nice stretch of long straight roadway.

"So like the plan at this point called for Brad to drive home and wait for Rochelle to return and come by, take the weapon off his hands and dispose of it, and proceed about the business of rounding up the late Mr. Agnelli's largesse, so that the two of them could begin a life of enjoying it together.

"Except, wouldn't you know it? The new widow changes the plan without consulting my friend. With the late great still in the cooling off process, she's already busy breaking into his inner and supposedly impregnable sanctum at the *casa*, helping herself to millions in cash, jewelry, bearer bonds, you name it. And, oh yes, his collection of black books. And off she goes to the authorities, where she's warmly received. Of course they know she was behind the hit on her husband, but what the hell do they care? She has enough info to give them to shut down a huge and continuing criminal enterprise and generate months of salutary headlines. Big friggin' show. For her part, she knows the cops are going to seize the house and all the bank accounts, but she has a small fortune in liquid and easily transportable assets. She sends the police around to pick up Brad and the still-smoking gun, and dances off into the sunset courtesy of the witness protection program. And it's not until like after his half-day trial and his fifteen-minute appeal denial and he's packing his bag for the getaway of a lifetime that the poor bastard wakes up from the ether and it dawns on him how badly he's just been screwed."

"Man," I say. "That's a tragic and cautionary tale."

"It's just getting started being tragic, Carlo. For one of the other things that dawn on Brad is that Mr. Agnelli probably has a bunch of pissed-off friends, thus accounting for his paranoid mindset from the moment I met him. And sure enough, it took over a year, and we became really good friends during that time. But one night during the designated hour I go to the latrine to grab a shower and there's Brad, lying on the floor under a spray of water just like the chick in *Psycho*, what's left of his lifeblood gurgling down the drain mixed with shower water in this really disturbing barber pole swirl. The problem being that Brad has like, this ice pick, planted firmly and deeply into his left ear, right up to the bloody hilt. And that, my friend, is the moment when I knew that a life of crime was no life for me."

If you're guessing that the moral of this story is that women are dangerous playthings, congratulations.

CHAPTER 5

TANYA/MARY

Tanya Bergstrom was an actress/model/entertainer/stripper/escort. What I'm saying is she was a beautiful young girl of twenty-seven years, with a killer body, D-cups probably plastic included, and a pretty face, looking to capitalize on her assets in whatever manner might present itself. She waited tables and danced at Rick's Player's Club, a gentlemen's establishment located in one of the less discriminating neighborhoods of Prescott. Only she was to blame for stirring up a major shitstorm for me to walk into when I returned Sunday night from my Vegas cum Jezebel weekend, by virtue of getting herself brutally murdered the Friday night I left town and having her badly mistreated corpse discovered by a girlfriend and fellow entertainer on Saturday afternoon. Incidentally, Tanya turned out to be a stage name, real name Mary.

My answering machine was blinking at me when I let myself into my apartment. In my experience that's rarely a good thing. "Detective Jardina," my then boss and future predecessor is talking in his mock-formal voice. "It's Max. Call me when you get in, any time day or night. Afraid we got a customer for you, and it's a really nasty one."

Max's Sarah answers the phone and hands it right over. "Hey, Chief. What's up?"

"Welcome home, Carlo. I'm gonna guess you haven't seen the paper?"

"No."

"Take a peek. No sooner do you make detective and we have the crime of the century right here for you. One of our local exotic dancers got herself killed two nights ago in a most vicious and ugly manner. A sex killing, I guess you'd call it. We are dealing with a very sick fuck, sorry Sarah, who did this, my boy, a real sociopath and possibly worse."

"Jesus." I contemplate this happy news for a few moments and then ask, "You want me on it tonight?"

"Get a good night's sleep. Nothing to be done now. ME has the girl, he'll start on her tomorrow afternoon. We've done preliminary interviews with her neighbors at the apartment complex. Eric wrapped the crime scene last night. Autopsy results will be available not later than close of business Wednesday. He'll brief you first thing and you can get at it. Congratulations, Carlo, this is your baby. Good luck."

Easier said than done, of course, the part about getting a good night's sleep. I grab the morning's paper off the kitchen table where I'd tossed it, unread. Already we are beset with lurid headlines and I'm confident we'll be seeing lots more. The seamy nature of the victim's lifestyle and the prurient elements of her death are going to combine, I fear, to make a very high profile situation. Between the gruesome images of the poor dead girl dancing in my mind's eye and blissful memories of my evening with Jezebel I toss and turn for God knows how many hours.

* * *

Brief me first thing he did, Eric De Leon, resident egghead of the department, the only member of the force with a graduate degree in criminology, courtesy of the University of Arizona, Tucson. I arrived at the office at 0730 and he came hurtling through my door as was his habit, skinny little Mexican kid dressed like myself in casual civilian clothes, oversized cup of coffee in one hand and a fat manila folder in the other. Only he had an expression on his face I'd never before seen there, and I found it disquieting.

"Good morning, amigo," I said. "Que pasa? How was the water in the Rio Grande this morning? Not too cold, I trust?"

"Good morning, paisan. It was just right. And how's your day been going? The old lady you mug this morning on your way in have anything good in her purse?"

"Nah. Turns out it was your mom. I didn't have the heart to take her food stamps and welfare check."

He laughed and said, "Fuck you, Jardina. Actually, a lot's happening. None of it good. It was a really busy weekend."

"So I'm told. Run it down for me, por favor."

I sat and rolled my coffee mug back and forth between my hands and watched his face as he plopped down across from me and huffed himself up to read me the litany. I still didn't care for the look in his eye.

"OK, first, the simple facts. On, we believe, Friday night one of our local citizens, a Tanya or Mary Bergstrom we have yet to figure out which is right, was murdered in her apartment over on the southwest side of town. Her death was the result, again we believe, of strangulation that occurred as the culmination of a fairly involved sadomasochistic ritual. Grand finale, you might say. You will not be surprised, I'm sure, to hear that she was raped and sodomized. A friend discovered her body Saturday afternoon, so we are guessing at TOD just now, but as I say most likely Friday evening late. She was bound and posed with the various instruments of her torture and murder. This is a behavior, the posing, common to serial killers. But I guess you know that. There's a complete set of photos in the folder but if you're wise you'll save it for after breakfast. It ain't pretty, believe me."

He laid his file on my desk and pushed it my way. Before saying anything else I played with the edges for a minute or two and collected my thoughts. "Eric, you say she was raped. So did whoever it was who killed her ejaculate? And did he use a condom?"

"Copiously. And no," he said. "There was semen all over the place, which he made no attempt to clean up. Plus a bunch of hair pubic and otherwise and fingerprints to beat the band. Plus every bit of his paraphernalia. He was making a statement to us here, Carlo. Catch me if you can. Another behavior of serial killers."

"I see. Well, whatever else this sonuvabitch is, he isn't as careless as you may think. That's pretty well thought out, leaving all his stuff. That way if he just happens to get pulled over afterward in a random traffic stop, for example, he has nothing on him to tie him to this."

"Never said he was careless. Said he was taunting us."

"This is a fact for certain. So have you had a chance," I asked, "to chat with Rick and company?"

"Who?"

"Miss Bergstrom's employer of record."

"Oh. Yeah, some. Rick is a DBA, but we talked to some of the people from the club, whoever we could round up at short notice. The shift manager, the bartender, a security guy and two dancers, one of whom was also the friend who discovered the body. Tanya left with a customer who wandered in about two, two and a half hours before closing. This was not unusual in her case. He had her do a lap dance for him and she spent the rest of the evening sitting and drinking with him, between her stage performances. He was quiet, she seemed to be smiling and laughing and generally okay with the guy. White, maybe mid-thirties. Everyone agreed he was a very average-looking dude in very average looking attire, no distinguishing characteristics at all. They left together at two. Nobody knows for sure if it was business or pleasure or both."

I opened the folder and gingerly began to peel away the layers of paperwork atop the photos. Preprinted crime scene report forms, completed in Eric's undisciplined scrawl. Numerous stacked pages of transcripts, typed, of interviews with the victim's apartment complex neighbors and strip club coworkers. Inventory of all items removed from the room. A receipt from the coroner's office for the remains. And then I'm looking at the top photo and she's looking back at me with unseeing eyes.

The shot is from the foot of the bed. She lies spread-eagled across it, supine, her still lovely body completely nude. The bed is stripped of all but a fitted bottom sheet. Her arms are stretched behind her head in what must have been a very uncomfortable posture, and though they disappear in this view behind her head they are apparently bound together at the wrist and affixed in some way to the headboard. Her head is propped up by a pair of pillows in a very unnatural attitude, through the arch of her arms and at almost a ninety degree angle to her chest, her hair carefully arranged in a platinum corona across the pillows.

Her legs are held in a widely splayed position by what bondage enthusiasts refer to as a spreader bar, her ankles fitted into leather cuffs attached approximately three feet apart along the length of a wooden rod. This device in turn is equipped with eye screws protruding from each end, by means of which said bar is affixed with nylon cord to the bedposts. Between her legs are displayed three items. To the left, a coil of piano wire with crude dowel rod handles on each end. To the right, a neatly looped length of extension cord with its female end removed and replaced by another section of wooden dowel, perhaps six inches in length. Placed precisely between these two, and neatly bisecting the angle formed by her outstretched legs, a leather riding crop. Resting on her sternum, just above and between her breasts, a bondage shop ball-gag of black rubber, shiny black leather and chromed metal.

Her skin is a ghastly white, shading toward morbid lividity where it meets the mattress and gravity has pooled her blood. Spider webs of purplish welts curl up from the backs of her legs. Her nails have all twenty been recently, perhaps post-mortem, painted a bright and glossy shade of red, disturbingly inappropriate to present circumstances, and lip polish to match reflects the camera flash.

There are three crude letters, made in some fashion I can't immediately fathom, inscribed in a descending column beginning just below her breasts, across her abdomen and ending just above her pubic mound. *S-A-D*. They are written in short segments of reddish-black streaks of varying thickness and intensity, twin jagged tracks scrolled half an inch apart in a looping block-letter script, the sections punctuated occasionally with pairs of ugly scorched circles of perhaps a quarter inch radius. The effect is as if the letters have been *burned* into her flesh.

I could feel Eric squirming in his chair. I peeked over the edge of the folder and his brown choir boy's face was screwed up into a pointy fierce expression of concentration. His gentle mestizo soul was having difficulty processing this level of brutality. I figured maybe giving him a chance to talk would help. "So, Eric, break it down for me."

He was ready. "Here's the way I figure it, Carlo. She leaves voluntarily with this guy to take him back to her place. Maybe he was a John, wouldn't have been unprecedented, maybe it was love at first sight. This we'll never know. They arrive at her apartment. Somehow he manages to get her into this bondage position. Perhaps he drugs her and she wakes up like that, or maybe she's freaky and she volunteers. Koz will tell us for sure." By which he refers to Dr. Kozlow, medical examiner.

"You can't tell from the pictures, but her hands are tied to a large eye screw that's been drilled into her headboard, which makes me lean toward date rape drugs because I can't imagine her letting him mess up her nice furniture like that voluntarily. Rohypnol possibly, or GBH. Combined with the spreader bar for her feet, this makes it easy to flip her over either way without untying her. Just undo the bar from the bedpost, turn it over and retie it. Done.

"He starts with her on her back, has regular missionary intercourse with her, who knows could still be consensual at this point. He doesn't ejaculate, though. At some point, he gets bored with this, over she goes. Now the fun starts. In goes the ball gag, nice and tight, so we don't disturb the neighbors.

"He goes to work on her with the riding crop. No photos for you of her back, figured the autopsy would cover it, but believe me it was flayed to a pulp. After which he sodomizes her. It was during this act that he actually killed her. Looking at the ligature marks, it's clear she was garroted from behind. You'll notice on the close-up the multiple impressions made by the wire. Sick bastard played cat and mouse with her. He took her to a point very near death, probably to unconsciousness, multiple times, releasing the pressure at the last possible moment and giving her time to revive. This guy is angry, this guy has issues with women. Must have been a horrible way to die."

There was a pause, during which I turned to the next photo, the head shot, and nodded a brief confirmation of his analysis.

Eric continued, "After she finally dies, he returns her to her back and goes about setting up the little scene he left for us, including writing those weird letters on her. At least I hope that occurred after she was dead. See what he's done? He's taken the end of an extension cord, stripped off about six inches of insulation and fed the two wires through holes drilled in a length of dowel rod, with just the tips protruding. An electric flesh-writing utensil. Beautiful."

Eric is feeling it, Eric is taking this very hard, and as the senior man I need to say something at this point to pull him back. Unfortunately, I'm paralyzed by the photo, the second one, taken close up of her face and her poor mutilated throat. Her lips part slightly in what in other circumstances would be an alluring glamour pose. She stares at me with frozen dead eyes, the whites red-starred by strangulation, the irises a crystalline testimony to the horror of her final moments. She died, it seems she's telling me, looking straight into the gates of hell. I was forty-seven years old, back then. But until that moment I'd always assumed the phrase "involuntary shudder" was just a literary construct. I took a pass on the rest of the portfolio.

CHAPTER 6
AMY

Amy Racine is my best friend on the force. She's smart, tough and beautiful. Were it not for the difference in our ages I might well have pursued her romantically. It's probably better I never did. Platonic relationships are less fragile and significantly less stressful, and I've enjoyed playing uncle to her little girl Shannon, the light of my life.

As soon as Eric left my office that morning, I put out a call for her to come see me before she left on patrol. She was the one I most wanted to talk to just now.

Like everyone else in my life, it seems, Amy has a story.

"Amy" is short for *America.* She was sixties-bred and came by the name fair and square courtesy of a pair of starry-eyed tie-dyed flower-children parents. She grew up in the fertile central valley of California. Amy is all apple pie and freckles and strawberry blonde bangs and porcelain smile cheerleading girl-next-door. Predictably, she married her high school sweetheart. He became a CHP officer and they bought a house in Bakersfield and had Shannon and generally settled down to live happily ever after.

Except that one awful night Brian pulled a guy over on highway 99, just a random speeding stop, but it turned out the driver had very recently knocked off a liquor store and was stoned and scared and nervous and congenitally stupid, and rather than show Brian his license he showed him the business end of a Saturday night special. The love of Amy's life fucked up and let this guy get the drop on him, and as often happens in this cruel world was never given the opportunity to correct his error.

They rounded this character up fairly quickly, and it seemed for a long while that at least justice would be served and Amy would have that fact, the pitiless meting out of punishment, to comfort her and her four year old daughter, the fact that this worthless asshole would be heading for the gas chamber or at an absolute minimum life without parole. However, out of the blue, some sage solon of the bench decides the cops have in their prosecution of this piece of excrement egregiously failed the cause of the endlessly accommodating and infinitely tolerant lady justice.

Maybe they got confused while giving him his rights, and gave him a few lefts. Maybe the date on the search warrant that allowed them to recover the still-smoking murder weapon with his fingerprints was wrong. I don't know, maybe he embraced a different, though equally valid culture that doesn't view blowing a cop's face off in as dim a light as we. Whatever. One hates to be judgmental in these matters. The judge released him for some reason, this much we know to a moral certainty.

And we know that our plucky little Amy was waiting for him, right there in the courthouse hallway, when he walked out. We can only guess how long it took the smug grin on his face to evaporate when he saw her assume a very well-trained squatting shooter's stance, watched her, probably, bring a hefty little Glock 10mm automatic loaded with some manner of diabolically contrived flesh-rending ammo to eye level, her left hand holding her right, her left eye shut in deference to her right, take quick but steady aim, and with one lowlife attorney and about half a dozen reporters diving for the deck put a nice tight little group of four rounds into his chest. God, the sound that must have made in that narrow stone-lined and vaulted passageway. History does not record, though I am reliably informed, that in the pulpy mess of his heretofore thoracic cavity there was nothing a surgeon could even identify as heart tissue, much less restore or repair.

The PA made quite a stir about it, of course...he had to, I guess. Amy was eventually brought to trial. The jury found her not guilty by reason of being not guilty. Little Amy, who'd have thought? You had to love her.

Which circumstances all make it easy to understand retrospectively why she would have wanted to change her life venue and throw herself into a career. For Shannon and herself, she chose the lovely and untroubled Prescott, Arizona, apotheosis of small-town America. For Brian, she chose law enforcement as her own life's work, applying for a position with our idyllic little force about two years after I'd done the same.

Then, as now, police recruits in the smaller cities of Arizona are typically trained in academies run by the sheriff's departments of the various counties. Yavapai County's is right here in our town, the county seat, where Amy distinguished herself mightily, attacking the course with a crazed zealotry that landed her honors as the top graduate of her class of eighteen. So when she showed up at the department, it wasn't without some fanfare despite the fact that the events surrounding her husband's death were withheld from us by Chief Max Coulter and his personnel staff until long after she'd made her bones unburdened by gratuitous sympathy.

Amy was the first uniformed police officer of feminine persuasion hired by the city, and to be honest we made her life more or less miserable from the moment she walked through the door. I was as bad as any of them, not being one of those liberated types who are thrilled at the notion of women moving into areas traditionally considered male enclaves, for reasons good and bad, logical and otherwise.

Trouble was, she just refused to let our boorish behavior deter her. She didn't complain, she didn't explain, she just went without whining about the business of quietly proving herself, all five-foot three of her, of putting up such a good performance record that even dolts like ourselves could not continue to cling to the myth of her unsuitability. Slowly but surely, as the saying goes, she won our hearts, mine particularly.

I became her number one fan and cheerleader. As our friendship blossomed I came to think of myself as her mentor. Still, her instincts were often better than mine, and I also came to value her opinions and advice. Thus the genuine smile spreading across my face as my little sunshine stepped into my office later that morning.

"I'm here," she announces for the benefit of the assembled faithful, leaning with arms widespread across my desk and reciprocating my grin. She's up on her tippy toes, pixie face hovering in front of mine, her green eyes bright and quick and reading me as if we've just met. "How ya doin', Carlo?"

"Good now you're here, sweetie. Radiant this fair morn, as ever." She's looks trim and girlish in her patrolman's uniform. Just a slight pudginess amidships, but what the hell, she has a right; she's on the cusp of thirty. "How do you manage to make street blues look so sexy?"

"Lots of gym time, big guy." She leans farther toward me and pats my paunch, saying, "Maybe you should join me."

"Indeed. And the princess?"

"Spoiled as ever. Other than that, doing great."

"It's about to get worse, I fear, the part about her being spoiled," I say, reaching into my bottom drawer and handing the princess' mother a gift-wrapped package.

"Picked it up in Lost Wages."

Shannon collected antique toys at the time, a hobby she shared with her mom. I'd managed to find her a little something in a shop off the Strip, a porcelain marionette made in Europe, dressed as a harlequin. Cost me a small fortune, but then nothing was too good for my Shannon.

"Uncle Carlo, how nice of you. She'll be thrilled."

"So have a seat, Amy. We need to talk. I have myself a small problem."

"You're telling me. Have you been reading the newspapers? Prescott's in a state of near panic. They'll be looking for quick results on this one."

"Yeah. Which is exactly what I'm guessing they won't be getting. This is gonna be a tough one, I think. You up to speed?"

"Just what the papers have. Fill me in."

I recounted my conversation with Eric, then asked her, "So what do you make of the fact this guy left so much personal biological information lying around?"

"Clearly he has no connection to the victim, no way for us to work backwards to him. He's not a friend or a former lover or customer or relative or ex-relative. I'd bet any amount of money that before Friday night they had never laid eyes on one another."

"Precisely." I say. "Of course we're gonna run down every male who was ever in her life in whatever tangential capacity, and we're going to invite them to leave us DNA swabs and blood samples and fingerprints, no matter what they look like, on the off chance that the guy who killed her isn't the same guy she left the club with, and that's a damn slim chance. And of course we're gonna draw a big fat blank."

"I'm afraid so, Carlo." Amy has too much energy to sit for long in a chair, and she's already prowling around the perimeter of the room as we speak. "I bet this guy came into town from a long way away, very far, with the sole purpose of doing this murder. And then went straight back to where he came from."

"If that's true we're never gonna catch him."

"Maybe we don't have to by ourselves. Guy like this, he could be popping up all over the place. You been onto NCAVC yet?" By which she refers to the National Center for the Analysis of Violent Crime, a computer database run by the FBI to cross-reference crimes committed by same party or parties in different jurisdictions.

"That's the next item on my list. Also, I'm faxing the fingerprints down to CID for them to run. I thought I'd ask them to send a sketch artist up also, so we can get some flyers out on this asshole." CID being the Criminal Investigations Division in Phoenix, the state law enforcement agency.

"This guy has no record, Carlo, no military service and, you heard it here first, no prints on file. Guarantee it."

Following her lead, I had by this time without realizing it left my own chair, and was staring out the window behind my desk. "I know, Amy. I know. Love the way you always cheer me up when I'm down."

She comes over to me and lays a hand across my shoulder. "I'm sorry, Carlo. Just telling you like I see it."

"Of course you are, and I appreciate it. I was just kidding. So we get the artist, we get a likeness, and we put it out to every hotel, motel, bed and breakfast, hostel, camp site, bus station, gas station, car rental agency and pet shop within fifty miles of here. Maybe we get lucky."

"Never know."

"So what do you think the deal is with the letters? *S-A-D*. What's going on there? What the hell is that supposed to signify?"

"Very interesting twist, isn't it? With a pervert like this, it could be anything. Could be his monogram, I guess, though I doubt it. That would be all too easy."

"Yeah, I agree. We're not going to get that lucky. Sure, he's looking to sail close to the line with us. He's looking to maybe get a little thrill from messing with our heads. But he doesn't want to get caught, at least not consciously and at least not now. So we check it out anyway. We take a peek at the Prescott phone book and we ask the travel-related industry to look especially for transactions with a man whose name fits those initials."

"Of course, *S-A-D* could also be short for sadist, or sadistic, which certainly fits. I just don't know."

"One thing I do know for sure. The paper's going to be out for blood.

The people are scared, and the people are pissed off. They're looking for results. We have a very short window before they lose all patience with us."

"Yeah. Glad I'm not Max."

"Me too."

After Amy left to retake the streets of Prescott from the anarchists, I made a mental note to myself to ask the chief to let me have her assist with my investigation. There was going to be a ton of grunt work, lots of road time, lots of time flogging the artist's sketch around to the local business community. Note to self also to put a bug in Thumper's ear, a long shot for sure but you never know.

After making a quick call to the ME's office, I logged the case into the NCAVC and checked for any record of similar crimes elsewhere in the country. Lucky us. As it happened, Prescott was the only town currently featuring a young man who liked to carve random letters into dead girls' bellies.

CHAPTER 7

MARY BERGSTROM, R.I.P.

I very much dislike autopsies. It's not as if I haven't seen my share of death. I've been a cop for more than two decades, and God knows along the way I've seen enough guts and gore to last me a hundred lifetimes. But nothing slaps you in the face with the pitiful, tragic transience of life like seeing a human body cut open and methodically taken apart. To be honest, these are things I prefer not to think about.

Nevertheless, Mary Bergstrom's postmortem was one event I simply had to be there for. As lead investigator into her murder I owed it to her to make sure that there were no clues that the crime scene photos, as thorough as they were, failed to reveal. Also, as crazy as it sounds, I felt like she needed someone there with her in her final intact moments. Someone to honor and dignify and validate her life, as short and pitiable as it had been. Dr. Kozlow is a clinician, the sort of man who has no emotional connection with his subjects. This is no knock on him; detachment is pretty much part of the job description for a coroner. But she deserved more.

In her employment paperwork from the club she had written "none" for next of kin, which did not surprise me. You have to figure that a girl who ends up in her line of work most likely hasn't much of a family behind her. Nor had a significant other worthy of the name stepped forward. Therefore, I was pretty much the guy.

The Yavapai County Medical Examiner's office is in the basement level of the county hospital, a ten or fifteen minute drive from my office. The procedure was scheduled for 1300, and I'd arranged to meet Koz at 1230. I left the station right after finishing a quick lunch.

The trailing edge of the winter storm I'd run into on my way home from Vegas still lingered over Prescott, but most of its energy had dissipated overnight and this morning we were left with a steady drizzle and solid low overcast.

I pulled my unmarked cruiser out of the parking lot and into traffic, which was light but moving slowly in the diminished visibility. My wipers were set to intermittent and cycling slowly, perhaps once every five seconds or so. I left the radio off. With the windows rolled up against the weather, the rubber blades scrubbing across the glass made the only sound I could hear. The rain and gray sky that filled my windscreen between wiper sweeps complemented my mood very well.

Prescott is basically just a small patch of suburbia spread horizontally across the Yavapai Valley in the high country of northwestern Arizona. There are no high rise buildings and no well-defined city center. The civic offices, including the police station, are grouped around an area of tree-lined streets, along which sit private homes mixed with small businesses. My drive to the hospital took me past cafes, drugstores, the occasional bank, a few insurance and law offices, a couple of parks and a school or two. All very small town, heartland of America scenery.

Most days of the year around noontime the sidewalks are filled with people moving about with energy and enthusiasm and mostly smiles on their faces. They are going to be looking to grab lunch, get in a little quick shopping, jog a couple of miles or maybe just enjoy a few moments of sun and relaxation.

The rain had changed all that today. This part of Arizona isn't as dry as Phoenix, which receives only eight inches of rain a year, but neither is it Seattle. We ordinarily get around twenty. This year, though, we'd experienced an especially wet and cold winter and people were beginning to take the lousy weather personally. The overall mood was definitely not festive. The few citizens I saw scurrying in and out of cover or dashing across the street in front of me wore pained expressions, as if the deluge itself was at hand. The way in which colors were washed out by the flat light and the grim faces distorted as in a funhouse mirror by the sheet of water on my windshield created a funereal atmosphere, which I found completely appropriate.

Still, I had no illusions of solidarity with my own emotions. None of these people had any idea that Mary Bergen's autopsy was scheduled for today. But even if they had, few if any would have cared about Mary personally. Her murder was big news, the biggest to hit Prescott in years, topic

A of most every conversation in town. But the public could pretty much be divided into two camps at this point, those who followed the story out of interest in its prurient elements and for whom the whole situation fell into the category of entertainment, and those who had a collateral concern for their own safety, either because they were themselves young women her age or had daughters who were.

No, it was the bad weather killing everybody's *joie* today, not the fact that Mary Bergen was lying in a drawer at the county morgue. Police detective Carlo Jardina cared, professionally and personally, but he belonged to a very small club.

I found Koz in his office, just down the hall from the morgue. He waved me in and motioned me to take a seat. He unfolded his 6-3 frame from the chair and reached across his desk to shake my hand. There was a wide smile plastered across the lower half of his mug, which is a more or less permanent feature in his case. Whether this is due to the nature of his job or in spite of it, I cannot say.

Under his medical smock he wore a dress shirt and tie, and I said, "Jeez, Doc, here you're about to slice and dice a corpse and you're dressed like you're going to dinner at a five star restaurant." Myself, I was wearing jeans, cowboy boots and a western-style checkered shirt.

With a vertical sweep of one long arm he indicated my outfit and said, "Remember, detective, I grew up in Poland. We are a little more formal on that side of the pond. We have no cowboys."

I said, "That's too bad. You should get some. You could have yourselves a couple of rodeos. It might liven the place up."

"Hah. We let our hair down with best of them, I promise you." He rapped his knuckles against the side of his bare head. "At least those of us who are lucky enough to have any left."

"And so but seriously, I'm sure that back in the Old World you guys go absolutely crazy rolling out the beer barrels and dancing the polka, but you've been in Arizona for, what, ten years? Right here in Prescott, the Cowboy Capital of the World. When you going to join the party, Doc, and go country?"

He simply shrugged in answer, and after a moment said, "Old dogs and new tricks, partner."

"Okay, I give up."

"So you ready for this, Carlo?"

"Not really, Doc. I feel like a goddamn ghoul. I'd rather be elsewhere, any elsewhere, I'll tell you for nothing."

"Ah, well. Maybe it will be not so bad."

"So what am I in for?"

Another shrug. "Standard postmortem protocol for homicide victims. We do a complete external exam. We take some pictures and samples of hair and nails. Then we take a look at her organs. We do toxicology on her blood and urine, of course, and her stomach contents. Don't worry, there won't be much bleeding when we open her up. The heart doesn't beat, we have no blood pressure, see? But still you might not want to stick around for that part. I must cut her pericardial sac open and take a blood sample for analysis from the inferior vena cava. Then her stomach for its contents, and same for the bladder. By the time I'm done I going to have her parts strung out like the Saturday laundry."

He gave me a big toothy grin, happy with his little joke, and I managed a weak smile in return. Gallows humor was not really what I needed just then. "Tell me you're not going to cap her skull."

He said, "No, I see no need for that. There's no reason to expect brain abnormality. Also Eric collected vaginal swabs for us at the scene, so we can leave her feminine parts alone."

Which news made me feel a little better. I felt the poor girl had suffered enough abuse, and that this entire procedure, though required by law, was an unnecessary insult. We knew how she died and we had all the evidence we needed to identify the man who killed her.

I said, "All right then. Let's do it."

And so we walked on down the hallway.

There are few environments less inviting than one afforded by the fluorescent lighting and polished stainless steel of an autopsy room. Adding to the ambience is a pervasive smell of some chemical or mixture of chemicals I cannot identify, but which is not pleasant. It does not smell like victory.

When Koz and I slide open the refrigerated drawer she is in, Mary is still in the body bag they used to remove her from the crime scene. He starts to unzip the full length, but I signal him with upheld hand to stop when just her face is visible. I want a moment before seeing the rest.

I am struck at how young and innocent she looks when seen in detachment from her body, which is anything but young and innocent looking. She is angelic. Indeed, in death her skin is the color of Carrara marble and I'm reminded of the stone figures of angels that adorn the vestibule of St. Francis of Assisi Church, where as a boy I attended mass.

After a moment or two Dr. Koz pulls the zipper the rest of the way and I help him extract her, slide her onto a gurney and thence onto the metal autopsy table. For no logical reason, I recoil at the thought of her being placed naked onto the cold steel.

They call it a table, but it's really a shallow tray, with a drain to carry away body fluids. Above it is an articulated high-intensity lamp that can be maneuvered to any position along the length of the deceased. At its foot is a wheeled rack of shelves filled with surgical instruments and other assorted tools for disassembling cadavers.

At the opposite end is a body block, across which we lay her upper back and shoulders, so that her head tilts back and the ligature marks of strangulation on her poor violated throat become plainly visible. Cause of death in this instance is going to be a pretty easy call. Her eyes, thank God, have been closed by some kind soul at the crime scene.

The binding bruises evident on her wrists and ankles are an ugly shade of purple, and the letters burned into her stomach black, but elsewhere her skin is as white as her face. Hairline scars are visible just beneath each breast, the result of implant surgery.

I lift her left hand and examine her fingernails for signs of her attacker's skin, but there are none. She obviously never had a chance to put up a fight. It mattered little, I suppose, as we already had plenty of his DNA.

"Doctor," I say, "do you mind if we turn her over for a moment?"

He says, "No problem. Take your time, Carlo."

We flip her onto her belly, revealing the dozens of marks left from the riding crop he used on her. There is a colorful tattoo of a butterfly about six inches across on her lower back, just above the cleavage. There are still faint traces of dried ejaculate spattered across its wings. Otherwise her appearance is unremarkable.

Basically, there is nothing to be found that Eric's photos don't show. Of course, seeing her in the flesh has a much more profound effect than any picture could possibly produce. It can't help but make one think. If you overlook the desecration she's suffered you can see that Mary was a really beautiful woman. Just days ago she made roomfuls of men go wild with lust by simply removing her clothes. Now she's just a lifeless collection of decaying organic matter. Christ, what a depressing thought. Rest in peace, Mary Bergstrom.

Before returning her to a supine position Koz begins his external examination. He photographs her from several angles and goes over her body slowly, using a handheld ultraviolet lamp, all the while dictating an oral record of his observations. He performs the same routine after we turn her back over, working from the head down. His posture and movements have a precision that suggest military training, though as far as I know he has none. His head is clean shaven except for a pair of outsized salt and pepper eyebrows, and his scalp glistens in the overhead light. The bald pate and his thin, beakish nose create an effect as he bends over her that is oddly avian, as if some giant bird of prey is picking over her remains.

His visual exam complete, he begins to collect hair and fingernail samples. After a while my attention wanders and I'm just sort of aimlessly looking around the room, but suddenly he says, "Jezus Madia! Detective, take a look at this. I nearly miss it."

I say, "What is it, Doc?"

He has spread Mary's legs apart as far as the sides of the tray allow. He says, "Here, Carlo. See this. There's a piercing on the anterior portion of the left labia minora."

"I'll be damned. That's one Eric missed."

The ornament is a silver wire circle with a five-pointed star inside, perhaps 8mm in diameter. I say, "Well, that's not so unusual for a girl in the sex industry, right?"

"I suppose maybe not, but this was not hers, detective." He holds the magnifying glass to the area, and says, "If you look very closely you will see signs of trauma and very slight bleeding where the flesh has been pierced. This is a fresh wound. Her attacker must have done that. Interestingly enough, on the opposite side there was another piercing, no doubt her own. You can still see the hole where it was removed."

"Man, that's weird. Why would he do that, and why not just use the existing hole to insert the new piece?"

"Why pass up an opportunity to inflict more pain?"

"Yeah, right. Why give her a break. So what do you think the significance of the circled star is?"

"Finding it, that's my responsibility. Explaining it, detective…that's yours."

While I ponder that little puzzle, Dr. Kozlow resumes his examination. When he finishes, he takes a marking pen from the pocket of his smock and draws a Y-shaped pattern on Mary's chest and abdomen, extending from each shoulder to the sternum and thence downward to the pubic mound. He takes a scalpel from the rack and with it poised above her chest looks me in the eye and raises his eyebrows in a questioning gesture.

I take the hint. "Well, Doc, thank you for the hospitality. However, I just remembered that I have a hair appointment. Think I'll be going."

He laughs at my joke for a moment, and then turns serious. "Find this man, Carlo. He is a monster. This girl will not be the last."

"God knows I'll try, Doc. God knows I'll try."

CHAPTER 8
THUMPER AND ME

Monday evening. I sit alone in my town house, which is located in the northwestern part of the city, close to the edge of the suburban sprawl. My living room window faces north, away from the city lights, so that I have a decent view of the stars. It's a moonless night, and the stellar disc shines brightly as it gradually rotates westward over the high desert. It's only seven in the evening, but it's wintertime and the sun's been down for nearly an hour and a half. The plastic tray from a frozen dinner sits on the table next to me, as does an empty bottle of Fat Tire ale. Across and down the street a block is a city park, and I hear the occasional voices of teenagers talking and laughing.

I walk into the kitchen and grab another bottle of beer, and then return to sit in my big easy chair. The TV is off. It's the photos on the wall behind it I'm looking at.

May you live in interesting times, goes the ancient curse. Suddenly I do.

There are four of them, the photographs. All four are blown up and professionally framed. The first is a shot of Poppy, Celeste and me at my high school graduation. Hard to say which of us looks the proudest, but for Celeste, who was never able to have her own children and thus thought of me as her son, it was clearly a glorious day. It was a day to forget her failing health for a few hours and recapture some semblance of a healthy glow, if only for a while. I hadn't seen her look that good in a year. For his part, Poppy is attempting to look serious and stern but he too can hardly contain his pride. The corners of his mouth betray the hint of a budding grin.

Next to this photograph is one taken at my graduation from the police academy. Sadly, it's just Poppy standing by my side in this one, as Celeste had long since died. I wear my newly won uniform and Poppy is sporting an expensive hand-tailored suit, bespoke especially for this day. Neither of us smile; our faces tell the camera that this is a solemn occasion.

Next to these two photographs are hung a couple more. The first of these is of another academy graduation, but the subject this time is Amy Racine. She stands alone, somehow looking very businesslike yet very cute at the same time. The other is my favorite of all, a picture of Amy, Shannon and me at her daughter's First Communion. She's a tiny angel, my princess, standing between her mom and me and dressed beautifully in white lace gown and white satin shoes. Her hair is in braids, a crystal rosary is draped across her little hands, which are clasped as in prayer, and an ethereal smile lights up her face.

The subjects of these four photographs comprise the people who are, or have been, important to me in my life. Each of them is, in his or her own way, a lodestar.

Since establishing myself in Prescott I'd lived what can only be described as an uneventful, even boring existence, both professionally and personally, and frankly I liked it that way. There is something about the prosaic that I found at this time in my life quite charming. Police work is much less exciting day-to-day than a civilian might suppose, and that is, if you think about it, a very good thing. But all that had changed in the last few weeks, unfortunately. Suddenly Carlo's comfy little world had been turned inside out and upside down and he had some serious decisions to make. Am I right, Poppy?

To begin with there was, of course, Jezebel. As I've said, when I set out for Las Vegas the last time it was not with the intention of falling in love. Of this much I am certain. Yet here I was, smitten like a teenage boy with a summertime crush. This was a situation that presented a serious dilemma for me, an unwelcome conflict of interest that would take some real hard thinking to resolve.

Then, as if that was not enough, there was poor Mary Bergstrom. No dilemmas there, of course, no moral ambiguity to wrestle with, but rather what promised to be an extremely tough case to crack and a poorly-timed distraction I really didn't need.

* * *

Speaking of the Bergstrom case, I'd decided to see if I could scare Thumper up on my way home earlier this evening. I figured I might catch him at the Sidewinder, a downtown saloon just a few blocks from the station.

The beer is cheap, the company's agreeable and there are a couple of pool tables in the back. He likes to hang out there and maybe hustle up a few bucks to supplement his income.

It's a local landmark and a charming little spot, the Sidewinder, particularly if you enjoy the smell of fresh cigarette smoke and stale beer. It's patronized for the most part by some of Prescott's less industrious citizens. There was a decent crowd of them that evening, maybe a dozen customers, all of whom gave me the once over when I stepped inside.

In the front room the bar runs the length of the side wall to the left, and on the opposite wall stands a vintage Wurlitzer jukebox box that pumps out a steady stream of vintage country and western music. It's flanked on either side by red Naugahyde booths. The rest of the room is filled with half a dozen tall Formica-topped tables. The walls are decorated with sepia-toned photos depicting the Wild West Prescott of a hundred years ago, and posters of comely lasses celebrating the many fine beers and spirits available for purchase on the premises. Suspended against the inside of the front window is a bigger-than-life rattlesnake fashioned in polychrome neon.

The back room, which is really just a section partitioned off by a curtain of strung glass beads, is filled with two pay pool tables, a pinball game and a quartet of vintage arcade machines. The walls are decorated with fading centerfolds of women who by now are middle-aged or worse, framed in black plastic.

It is here I found Thumper, sitting in a corner with a cigarette in one hand, a beer in the other and a pool cue tucked between his legs, one of which is working up and down nervously off the ball of his foot. He's waiting for his mark of the evening to finish shooting.

I waited politely for the two to finish their game, which ended in victory for my friend and left him richer by enough money for maybe a pack of Marlboros and another couple rounds. While he was collecting his winnings I walked into the front room and bought us each a bottle of beer.

Handing one to Thump, I said, "What do you say, amigo, you wanna do a rack of nine ball?"

He nodded his head and I crammed two quarters into the slot to release the balls. He began arranging them on the table. No bets this time; he knows better. We lagged for break and he won. He chalked up his stick and powered the cue ball hard into the diamond-shaped rack, blowing it wide open. As it happens I shoot a better than average game of pool, and this is a very risky move playing against someone of my skill level. There's little chance of sinking the nine that way, as it's buried in the center of the pack. Meanwhile he risks giving me an open table I may very well run before his next turn comes around.

He got lucky and dropped the five into the side pocket with his opening break. Unfortunately for him the one ball was buried behind the thirteen and seven down in the corner. He managed to play safe, just kissing it and nudging it even further from a position in which I could make a play on it. I had to bank the cue ball off the cushion just to make contact with it, the one ball, and in so doing exposed it for Thump. He had a tough shot though, a table length attempt into the far corner pocket with the cue and object balls separated by only a few inches.

He just missed, leaving the pretty little yellow ball a cripple in front of the pocket. I knocked it in with a stroke that had heavy backspin on it, and the cue ball rolled halfway back across the table toward me, coming to rest in a perfect position for the two ball in the side. I was off to the races.

"So, Carlo," he said as I was working my way through the table and he was standing against the rear wall blowing smoke my way and banging the butt end of his stick against the floor, "you just drop by to give me a lesson?"

"You know better than that, Joey. Thought we could discuss this murder we have on our hands. Maybe you heard about it."

He pulled a face to let me know my sarcasm was unnecessary.

"Thought you might be able to give me some insight is all. Like for instance, what's the buzz on the street?"

"Oh man. Big news, very big news. Lots of chatter, but it's all sound and fury. You know this was no local, right, Carlo?"

"Don't know it. Strongly suspect it."

"Trust me. Nobody in Prescott sick enough to do this shit."

"Well, maybe whoever did it interacted with a local during his visit to our little town. He must have. If he did, if anybody saw or dealt with a guy who fits the basic description, maybe word will get around. I just wanted to remind you to keep your ear to the ground. Anything you hear, anything at all."

"You got it, Carlo. You can count on it."

"Thanks."

While we chatted the balls were falling in rapid numerical sequence. I dropped the last one remaining on the table, the nine, into the side pocket and put my cue stick back on the wall.

"Buy you a beer, Carlo?"

"Thanks, Joey, but one's my limit. I'm driving. Wouldn't do for me to get a DUI in my own cruiser, right?"

"Guess not. Man, I tell you what. Whoever did this, he wasted like a really beautiful piece of ass, no disrespect to the dead. You ever see her? Alive, I mean?"

"Afraid not."

"Well, I did, a couple times. One of the bouncers at Rick's is a buddy. Lets me in sometimes without paying the cover. I'm here to testify, brother. She was a smoking hot little lady."

"Yeah, it's a damn shame all right. Tell you what. The rest of the girls from the club are extremely scared and extremely angry. You manage to help us break this case, I can guarantee you there's a free lap dance in it for you. Or more."

CHAPTER 9
MAX

It's not as if we had no homicides in Prescott. We did and do, of course, but we're talking run-of-the-mill stuff pretty much, and not many of those. Maybe a guy gets knifed outside a sleazy bar at 2:00 AM after a pointless drunken brawl. Or somebody puts a round or two into the significant other or whatever in a nasty domestic dispute, again usually in the small hours and invariably involving alcohol. You get my drift. Low class behavior by low class citizens. Below the fold news. Nothing really stylish.

This thing with Mary Bergstrom, though, this was an interesting challenge. Despite my initial reaction, after a few days I was beginning to warm to it. Unwelcome as it was at first, I began to realize that in a perverted sort of way the prospect of tackling the investigation was energizing me.

That and the pressure the city fathers and press were bringing to bear on my poor chief, Max Coulter. Around town there were two schools of thought regarding Mary's murder. The first held that the killer was obviously targeting girls of some disrepute, and therefore "nice" girls had little to fear from any further attacks. The second, and at the moment much larger, school of thought held that the first was dangerously delusional and that everybody better double-lock the doors and law enforcement had best get a move on rounding the bastard up. To the public, Max was the face of law enforcement and he therefore was on the receiving end of the latter group's collective wisdom.

As for myself, I agreed completely with Amy's thoughts on the killer and his willingness to leave prints and DNA at the crime scene. What might at first take seem a break was actually very bad news. Clearly it indicated complete confidence on his part that he could never be connected by circumstance to the crime, which meant almost certainly that he wasn't local. The silver lining to that particular cloud was of course the probability that if he struck again, it would be in another jurisdiction.

At any rate, I threw myself into the task at hand with all the energy I could muster. I commandeered an office that wasn't being used, and in the following days we set up a war room dedicated to tracking down Mary Bergstrom's killer. We brought in a special phone line for tips and put the number out to the public. We had the staff from Rick's sit down with the sketch artist CID sent up and cobble together a likeness of the guy Mary left with. Eric drove the batch of evidence he'd collected from the crime scene down to Phoenix personally for processing at the state lab. He brought back the splendid news that Amy was right about the fingerprints not matching any on file. Our one big hope for a quick resolution was gone.

The Chief agreed to pull Amy off of patrol and let her work directly with me. We put together a flyer with the sketch and tip line number, which we distributed by the hundreds throughout Prescott. We started working our way down the list of motels and hotels, starting with the cheapest and seediest first, checking guest registers and running our flyer by the clerks. I figure this project alone took over a week to complete, working every day. After that we started on the gas stations, convenience stores and fast food joints.

Meantime I had asked the strippers, bouncer and bartender from Rick's to put together a list of the men they were certain were at the club the night of the murder. They came up with around thirty names, regulars all. Questioning the married among them required some discretion, obviously, as I couldn't see any reason to embarrass them with the wives. This meant I had to catch them alone, which took some planning and time. It was a futile exercise, at any rate. They weren't at Rick's to check out the other customers, were they? Most didn't recall anyone in particular being with Mary, and the few who did could only confirm that he looked like the guy on our flyer and that they had never seen him before.

We re-interviewed her apartment complex neighbors, none of whom had seen or heard anything out of the ordinary. This particular property catered to singles and tended to be noisy on Friday nights. Nevertheless, I found the fact that the crime was executed totally unnoticed amazing under the circumstances. I was beginning to realize that whoever we were looking for was very good. We found a couple of guys in the building with records, and we invited them to give us cheek swabs, which they did willingly, along with solid alibis.

Mary had no relatives in the area, but we did identify half a dozen old boyfriends, all of whom also volunteered for polygraphs and DNA swabs. We identified a couple dozen registered sex offenders citywide that fit the basic description we were after, but none turned out to look anything like our friend, though we dragged them in for questioning and swabbed them to be safe. Eric made another trip downstate with the DNA samples we collected.

At the end of three weeks the war room had developed that lived-in look. One wall was covered with photos of the victim and her various associates, plus a selection of the less disturbing crime scene shots. The long wall opposite the door bore a large framed map of Prescott, marked by pins with various sites of interest including Rick's, Mary's apartment, and all the places of lodging clustered along the highway in and out of town. The other end wall had about a hundred post-it notes stuck to it documenting the random thoughts and ideas of Eric, Amy and myself. In one corner stood a metal end table with fax machine and multi-line phone. In the opposite corner an identical table with a coffeemaker stacked on top of a microwave oven. A large collapsible table sat in the middle, surrounded by folding chairs and covered with stacks of evidence files, legal pads full of bogus tips and an impressive collection of used Styrofoam coffee cups and empty microwave popcorn bags. We were not, as far as I could tell, an iota closer to identifying the killer.

It's a Saturday morning, and I'm sitting in the corner rereading interview transcripts, when in walks Max, or rather in limps Max. Max was a sailor in the Korean War and was working the deck of an aircraft carrier one night in the Pacific when an aircraft arresting cable snapped and shattered his left leg below the knee. They put it back together as best they could but the injury still requires him to use a cane.

He carries in his free hand a brown lunch bag, which he hands to me. "Chocolate chip cookies, compliments of Sarah. Good morning."

"Morning Max. Be sure to thank her for me. How you doing?"

I open the bag, take out a cookie and hand it to him, then grab one for myself.

Between bites he points his walking stick at me and says, "You tell me, kid. How am I doing? Fucking city council and sons of bitches at the *Sentry* are all over my ass. I need some good news. Got any for me, Carlo?"

I shake my head. "Such language, Chief. I'm gonna have to have a talk with Sarah. But no, sorry. We're all out of stock on good news. I sent out for more, but it's on back order. I am seriously butting my head against a brick wall here."

With his white hair and the sort of thick-lens glasses that make his eyes look larger than life Max has the appearance of a banker or maybe a college professor, but when he's unhappy the air tends to turn blue and you get reminded of his nautical past.

I will state here for the record that Max is a great cop. He's tough and he's got street smarts. The thing about being Chief, though, is that it's basically a political job. It's about keeping the people who run the city, the councilmen, the businessmen, the fifth estate and other assorted power brokers happy, which means kissing some very distasteful ass. Max is maybe not really cut out for the job, which, believe me, I mean as a compliment. Cutting your teeth as a navy NCO tends to leave you with an allergy to happy talk and other assorted bullshit. This is probably why he hit it off so well with an ex-hoodlum like me. He has three more years until full retirement, and I know he's counting the days.

"Max," I say, "I do understand the pressure you're under. I wish to God I could give you something. Anything. We're busting our asses, Amy and Eric and me. You know that. Twelve hour days. Seven day weeks. Amy has even flown grandma in to help take care of Shannon. But this prick, he has just not given us anything to work with."

Max sighs, nods his head and smiles. "I know, Carlo. Just keep plugging away. Maybe we catch a break."

"They're really busting your balls out there, aren't they? So are you okay? How you feeling?"

There's a long moment of silence, and then Max says, "You know, Carlo, in 1948 Thomas Dewey was running for President of the United States against Harry Truman. It was his third shot at the brass ring. Going in, the poor guy was looking solid in all the polls and was being touted as a mortal lock. He goes to bed on election night and his chief aide says 'Good Night, Mr. President.' Sadly for him, the pollsters and pundits were wrong. When he wakes up he learns Truman has won.

"So later that day he does a press conference, you know, to congratulate Truman and what not, and some reporter asks him how he's feeling.

He says, 'I feel like the guy who woke up in a coffin. If I'm alive, he asks himself, what am I doing here? And if I'm dead, why do I have to go to the bathroom?' It's like that."

CHAPTER 10
SEDONA

Mary Bergstrom had knocked Jezebel off my front page temporarily, but hardly made me forget her. You don't forget Jezebel in a hundred years, much less a hundred hours. So as the days passed by, satisfyingly chocka-block with futility, dead ends and subtle but increasing pressure from my chief and the aggrieved citizenry as represented by the press, my nights were given over increasingly to thoughts of Jezzie and bittersweet memories of our passionate night together. Separation was indeed making my heart grow fonder; I admitted to myself that I loved her as much after a week, and then two, as the morning after we met.

This realization made that much more painful the other, dawning with shattering ineluctability, that I was never going to see her again. She was married, she was in California, we were a one night stand, and all these truths put the ball squarely in her court. It was my duty, and I knew it, to reconnect with her. This simple fact sat in a lump perched on my chest every night I lay awake in bed. Excuses, though, are so easily had to avoid one's duty, once morning arrives and sunny Arizona daylight reclaims the realm and girls like Mary are demanding justice.

There it lay, and most certainly would have lain forever, only that on the third Tuesday after my return from Vegas I received an envelope at the station, addressed to Detective Carlo Jardina, Prescott Police Dept., AZ, no return address, no zip, the lazy girl. The envelope and the single sheet of notepaper inside were of extremely fine paper, expensive Wilshire Boulevard stationery shop fine. To my amazement, the notepaper was embossed in gold leaf with the name Mrs. Roger Waterhouse, and appeared above a tony-sounding and presumably authentic Westlake address. Below it in the same hand that wrote the note she slipped me in Vegas, the message read:

God I've missed you. I'll be in Sedona next weekend. I'll stay at L'Auberge. You won't, please. Come into the lobby lounge at ten. This hotel is popular with my Valley crowd, so you never know. Please don't act like we're acquainted. I'll slip you a cocktail napkin or something with my room number. Come see me after thirty minutes, I'll make the drive worth your while. Can't wait! Love you. Jez.

There was also an index card in the envelope with a PO Box address, for the benefit of my response. And of course once again I don't know whether to be happy or sad. My heart leaps at the thought of being with her again, that's for sure, but the dilemma I've been avoiding, the cruel choice I've been wishing desperately to finesse, is seriously reactivated. It's going to have to be dealt with. Jezzie, Jezzie, Jezzie.

Meanwhile, back at HQ, our little festival of forensic fun was still spinning its wheels. What the hell was I supposed to do? Amy and I had interviewed countless known associates of the victim. Endlessly revisited the various stories told by everybody we could find that admitted to being in Rick's that fateful night, plus a few who denied it on their mother's graves. We'd shopped around the sketch we'd put together of the man Mary left with, to every conceivable establishment with which an out of town visitor might have reason to deal. For good measure, we'd rousted every male inhabitant of Prescott who'd ever so much as been cited for a parking violation, all to no good effect.

The autopsy report validated Eric's theory about the date rape drug, by the way. A small quantity of flunitrazepam, trade name Rohypnol, was found in her blood, along with generous amounts of alcohol, a little coke, and a pinch of marijuana for the road.

Mary Bergstrom was consigned to the earth on Wednesday, the day after I received Jezebel's note. I was there to show the flag for the department, with Amy at my side for reinforcement. The interment was a sad little affair, with just a smattering of weird characters from the club, mostly her fellow dancers, which troupe was well-outnumbered by the nearly dozen reporters who trekked in from all corners of Arizona for the prospect of a morbid scoop. No family. Mary died the same way she lived, with nobody caring much one way or the other.

The week passed too slowly, and the sad fact was that I was getting no closer to identifying a suspect. I knew it. The Prescott Sentry knew it along with their readers. And so too apparently, Max, who'd subtly begun to attenuate that understanding tone in his voice that had so comforted me these last few dark days. The killer had come from nowhere, and returned.

One may easily imagine, then, the unrestrained joy with which I rolled out of town late Friday evening for the ninety-minute trip to Sedona, pushed by Mary and pulled by Jez. I'm in my unmarked cruiser, a perquisite of the rank, two tons of Detroit iron, Chrysler or Dodge I can't remember which, of eminently forgettable design painted an uninspired color somewhere between brown and white previously unknown to mankind by any name I can recall. But under her dowdy hood she has a 426 hemi, souped up by the factory boys for the benefit of law enforcement, and when I punch the gas she squats down on her iron haunches and leaps down the highway with a soul-satisfying rumble howling out the tailpipe. I'm pressed into the back of my genuine imitation leather seat with a relentless acceleration and amazing quantities of Arizona real estate stream by as the speedo hits three digits. At which point the steering wheel gets squirrelly and I lose my nerve.

God did Northern Arizona when He was in His red period. Or She, in Her red period, if you prefer; I'm not looking to step on any toes. Wind, water, tectonics and unimaginable eons of time have combined to carve a complete impressionistic gallery from the sedimentary layers of rock, rendered in a subtle palette of reds, pinks, desert browns and mauves. Most notably, of course, the Grand Canyon at the very northern line. But there are more: the Painted Desert, Monument Valley, Canyon de Chelly and, just south of Flagstaff and, eroded into the foothills of the San Francisco Mountains by a tributary of the Colorado, Oak Creek Canyon. Here lies Sedona, arguably the jewel of the entire enterprise, superior in every way but scale to the great canyon. Also, unfortunately, irresistible magnet for every New Age charlatan, every snake charmer, every leftover unwashed hippie, burned-out drug case, dope-smoking tofu-eating visionary, would-be artist and wannabe poet, every RV-dwelling sunbird and slack-jawed tourist west of the Rockies.

The night is clear in a way only desert night can be. Waves of rainstorms have beset us in the weeks since the murder—poor Mary left us during a light rain, her virginal white casket slipping into a muddy maw—and they have scrubbed the air of dust and smoke. Luminous curtains scatter-shot with stars hang in all four points of the compass. A full white moon clambers up the eastern sky, washing the mountains to the north with pale light. Gray cotton swaths the sodden valleys. Eerie shadows of desert flora populate the landscape to either side of the road. Country music spills plaintively from my cruiser's tinny speakers. Love and sublime sex await me, and for a few precious moments I allow myself reverie.

I made great time until I joined Highway 17 and the weekend traffic streaming up from Phoenix. One can fly into Sedona, but the airport is located precariously atop a narrow mesa; only spendthrifts and thrill-seekers need apply. Few do. I hauled my car down to a walking pace and slipped into the glacial river of red lights creeping northward. I made Sedona with just minutes to spare, my pulse rising as I parked and strolled into the lobby of L'Auberge, the finest hotel in town.

She is there. Her back is to me as she sits at the bar working very fastidiously on a scotch rocks. I take a place about ten feet to her right, not daring to glance in her direction. I order a drink of my own. Eventually she sweeps the room with a turn of her head and I see her register my presence. My heartbeat accelerates further. An uneventful quarter-hour passes, after which my peripheral vision detects her rising to leave. As she walks toward the exit I turn to follow her with my eyes, and I notice that she's let drop a cocktail napkin, which now lies on the floor beneath her stool. It's fine, it's not going anywhere. I time out another quarter-hour. I finish my drink, I get up to leave and on my way out bend over and scoop up the paper. Her room number's on it. I go to the men's, I loiter in the lobby, I time out another fifteen minutes and head for her quarters.

When she answers my knock, not a word passes between us. She places an arm around my neck, she drags me unceremoniously into the bedroom of her very expensive suite, she rips my clothes and her own off our bodies, pulls me greedily onto the bed and we commence rolling around like a couple of deranged lovesick weasels.

This pretty much describes our weekend together. We came up for air just occasionally. We had to go out for food, as Jezebel didn't want a record of two people in the room such as using room service would leave.

We took one short drive to Bell Rock and did a little hike. But mainly, we made love. Or recovered from making love. Or talked about what we'd do the next time we made love. Amazingly, the entire period passed without Jezzie once mentioning her husband or her desires for his future disposition. I was braced for it, I expected it, I would have put money on it. When we kissed good-bye late Sunday afternoon, though, it was a subject that never passed her lips.

Except that when I opened the door to my own car to leave, after having dispatched her in her expensive German luxocruiser, she somehow had managed to leave yet another note for me, perched innocently enough in the driver's seat.

> *Carlo, baby. I didn't want to say or do anything to spoil our weekend. It was super. And believe me, I don't want this thing to get in the way of us, or make you think somehow I don't really love you, or just want to use you. So I'm going to say this just once, and if you wish we can forget it forever, and I still love you. You should understand, though, that Roger is worth a lot of money. Huge amounts. Enough for two to live any way they wish for ten lifetimes. Money that won't be mine while he's alive, but that much of is set aside for me in his will. People die every day, Carlo. Thousands of them. Wouldn't it be something if just one of them just one day were Roger? I know I don't have to tell you to get rid of this note. Love You! Jezzie.*

* * *

I shake my head and grin to myself, standing as I am about fifty yards off the road about ten miles south of Sedona, cigarette lighter in one hand, flashlight in the other, and Jezzie's note in ashes on the gritty desert floor at my feet. That's the thing about Jezebel. She was truly without question a pisser and a half.

CHAPTER 11
POPPY

It's the winter of 1965-66. Philly. The gritty unfashionable South Side. The streets are blanketed in white and swept by a stinging blustery wind. In the lee of the buildings, fat wet snowflakes zig zag silently to the ground. From the jukebox the Castaways are belting out *Liar, Liar*, one of my favorites that year, with an enthusiastic falsetto chorus. I am a skinny seventeen year old punk, full of smug self-importance, dressed in Levis and a woolen Pendleton shirt I boosted from Macy's. Hair's down my collar and a half-smoked Marlboro hangs jauntily from my lips. A bottle of Rolling Rock sits on the edge of the pool table. Next to it is a filthy ash tray and a stack of crumpled bills. The game's straight pool, nine ball's for pussies, and the wager is a dollar a ball. The money's my stake now, but it started the day in the purse of the old Jewish lady I mugged at the bus stop. Or was bullied for protection out of the old Polish guy who has the bakery down the street. Or Mr. Kim at the corner liquor/deli, who can know for sure? My life is a one-man crime streak on a penny-ante scale.

The sign on the big window says "Spanky's," written in shadowed gold block letters arched in a semi-circle, enclosing "Bar and Pool Parlor" in smaller black font. Except of course that my memory must be taking literary license with me now; the writing would have been reversed when viewed from inside. I'm looking at a difficult table-length shot, with a seventy degree cut or so on the twelve ball, hard against the far rail a foot and a half from the corner pocket.

Pocket pool is a straightforward matter of steady hands, a basic knowledge of geometry, and a keen eye. The prime rule is simple: draw an imaginary line from the center of the pocket through the center of the object ball. The cue ball must kiss the spot where this line emerges from the opposite side of said object ball, plain and simple.

Now comes the rasping sound of leather cue tip twirling in the chalk cube, the selection of the line, the studied crouch, the drawing of the cue stick, the practiced squint, the pause, a suck on the cigarette and into the ashtray it goes, the breath taken and held. The soft thump of tip on cue ball, the hollow sound of ivory rolling on felt-covered slate, the sweet satisfying click as the balls kiss on the appointed spot and the twelve rolls gently along the rail and plops into the pocket. More to the point, I've imparted just the proper amount of backspin and just the right momentum to the cue ball so that it rebounds off the cushion and sets me up for an easy shot on the six into a side pocket. I'm gonna run the table, kiss my ass.

My triumphant march is interrupted, however, by a cold blast of air as the door is opened and I see the man who will be Poppy, looking turned out in a white suit with maroon shirt and tie, black hair slicked back, flanked by a couple of salty-looking goombahs in cheap black suits, Carmine and Guido-types big enough to be fitted with OSHA horns in case they back up unexpectedly and probably neither with an IQ larger than the temperature outside. The Man himself is a solid-looking dude, a squared-off bull of average height but impressive muscular heft. He's a fairly good looking middle-aged guy running just a little to fat at the waist and the jowls, but with the sharp dress and improbably tanned skin for this sunless corner of the world he makes an impressive picture.

Poppy, it turns out, owned Spanky's and kept a small office upstairs where he stored records for his many various businesses, a couple of which were actually legitimate. He was taking his sweet time closing the door, he was talking to somebody on the sidewalk, and I was getting annoyed and like the fool I was I gave verbal vent to my pique. "Hey, fat man," I yell across the parlor. "You wanna close that door? It's fucking freezing in here."

At which brilliant move the mouth breathers set out for me, only to be restrained by Poppy. "Hold your water, kid," he yells back at me.

"And who's gonna make me?"

He chose to ignore the question and continued to take his time concluding his conversation with whomever it was, hidden behind the door. Everything seemed to stand still for the moment, my fellow pool enthusiasts in a frozen tableau around the table and adolescent anger rising in a hot flush inside me while the room filled with the bitter outdoor air. Finally my impatience overcame me and I yelled to him again, "I said close the fucking door, man."

The door closes, slowly. All movement ceases. Total silence throughout Spanky's. He smiles and walks unhurriedly across the room to me. To this day I can hear the soft sound and rhythm of his expensive shoes on the wooden plank flooring of the hall. He almost whispers the question, "What's your name, kid?"

"Carlo."

"You got balls, Carlo, I'll give you that. I wonder if you got any brains, though, like sense enough to respect your elders."

"I don't take shit from no one, man," I announce to the room at large, but I have without thinking about it turned the volume way down, to match his own quiet manner of speaking.

"That's a policy you might want to reconsider, my young friend. You know who I am?"

I say, "Don't have a fucking clue, don't give a shit, just back off," and grasp my cue with both hands on the business end, baseball bat style, step away from him and brandish the fat tail in his general direction. Some people say I was quick-tempered back then, I don't know. At any rate, I've backed myself into a corner now and need to show face for my buddies, five wide-eyed deaf mutes who are presently standing with their backs pressed so hard against the wall behind me, trying to create space between themselves and Poppy, that I think any minute it's gonna go over and they'll all be lying in a heap on their yellow butts in the alley on the other side. Unfortunately my own heart's pounding and it's begun to dawn on me just what a dumbshit I am and suddenly I'm not feeling so tough.

Cat-quick Poppy snatches the stick from my grasp, snaps it in half over his knee, and he's on me and administering a skillful beating. It was the funniest thing, I remember, that day. Through the pain of it, I felt a weird sort of pleasure. No adult had ever cared enough before to lavish this much attention on me. And of course he took it easy on me. Hell, he could have killed me. I learned a major lesson, the first step of my reeducation, and it only cost me a couple of bruises and a laceration or two.

So about two days later Carmine and Guido came around in the big car to take me to see him. Such a prospect might have made some people nervous, but I figured, what the hell, he's gonna give me a follow-up lecture on what a big shot he is and how I have to show him respect. They took me to his house and disappeared after leaving me at the front door. Big spread in the country, long driveway past the gate, lots of trees, white columns and brick, I'd never seen anything like it.

Poppy greeted me like I was his son, home for the weekend from college. He was having me for dinner, I'm damned if he wasn't. His wife came rolling into the foyer in a wheelchair, an ashen-faced and obviously very ill lady who at that time looked more like his gray-haired mother and who would be dead in less than two years' time. Cardiomyopathy it was, her untreatable affliction. Set into that ravaged face, though, were a pair of intensely alive eyes, and they burned passionately with a quality I'd seen very little of in my short life, human kindness. Such never graced the eyes of my shiftless drunk of a father or my copped-out, zoned-out welfare queen mother. That he loved her, Celeste, his wife, with a grand love was immediately obvious even without my ever having seen such affection between two adults, for example my own parents.

We had a fantastic dinner, a meal cooked and served by hired staff, which was another new experience for me. After dessert, Poppy waved me into his study. A nurse wheeled Celeste away.

Alone now, the two of us, and he hands me a Montecristo and as he's helping me fire it up he says, "So, Carlo. Now we talk."

I think to myself, oh shit, here it comes. I say nothing, waiting for him to fill the silence. The study is paneled in polished oak, the walls are filled floor to ceiling with books, there's a monstrous desk, burgundy-colored leather chairs and sofa and a fire going to town in the fireplace. It's a scene almost beyond my imagining.

"Carlo, I been askin' around about you. For some crazy reason I like you. Maybe it's your moxie, maybe you remind me of myself at your age, whatever. You have on occasion made some pretty savvy moves on the street. I even checked at your school. They say you do okay on the rare days you show up. Seems you're a smart kid. Not as smart as you think you are, that I believe is an impossibility…but still. Trouble is, my friend, you're going down the wrong road. I know, trust me, it's the road I went down."

I can't believe what I'm hearing. "Look at you man. What are you talkin' about? You're doing more than just fine, I'd say."

"You like the place?"

"Hell, yes. Who wouldn't?"

"Yeah, you're right. Who wouldn't? I have a beautiful house, nice car, good food, money in the bank."

"Exactly."

"Carlo, would you believe I'd trade it all for a clean conscience?"

I take the cigar from my mouth and stare at him, dumbfounded.

"It's the thing with Celeste, her sickness, that's made me take another look. I grew up on the streets like you, and I fought my way to the top any way I could and time was I was proud of that fact. No more. Now I look around and my Celeste is going to be dead soon. I'm no longer a young man, I'll be dead before you know it too, twenty years maybe, or thirty, what the hell difference does it make. When I do go, you think I'm really gonna be cashing in those indulgences I've been buying from the Church? Can my dirty money really wash away my sins? I wonder. 'It's like this, God. Sure I whacked half a dozen people in my lifetime, but I built a fancy new rectory for the bishop, so we're square, right?' Sound reasonable to you, Carlo?"

I took a draw on my Montecristo and continued staring at him wordlessly.

"Most people have pleasant memories to keep them company in their old age. You know, family stuff, maybe, Christmas dinner, a picnic in the country, a little league game, a graduation. I've been too busy looking over my shoulder for that stuff, kid. I have instead pictures of a lifetime of victims dancing in my head. I get to think about the rackets I've run and the pain I've caused and lives I've destroyed, stuff I'm trying hard to forget.

"And there's friendship, Carlo. God, what I'd give to see a smile that's genuine. Regular people have *friends*. I have associates, who are with me today but may or may not be tomorrow. The thing is, when you're in my line of work it's like running with a pack of wolves. And that's maybe being unkind to wolves. As long as I'm strong I have their loyalty, the pack. Let me show any weakness, and suddenly they're circling with a hungry look in their eyes. Everybody wants to sit in the big chair, is the problem, and you can't figure them to be sentimental about it. Heavy lies the head that wears the crown.

"It's no good, Carlo. A young man like you, you have a quick mind, you can make something real of yourself. You can give instead of taking. You can build something, Carlo, and at the end of the day I swear, I know you're gonna have a hard time believing it, but at the end of the day that's where real pleasure comes from."

I wasn't at all sure this wasn't a load of preposterous bullshit, but the astounding sincerity of the man was not to be denied and from that evening forward he was my father. He was Poppy. They took me completely under their wings, he and Celeste while she still lived. Saw that I finished high school, with honors no less. Fed me. Clothed me. Supplied me with unconditional and unending emotional support. Then college, all expenses paid, and steered me into a career in law enforcement, his way I think of somehow making up for the damage he'd done.

* * *

It is years later now, and I hold in my hands the letter informing me of his murder. Karma, some would say, but I always prayed he'd die in bed. I have never in my life before cried for any human being, yet now I blubber like a baby, the tears flowing uncontrollably. Good-bye, Poppy.

My headlights sweep around a turn and across a coyote standing at the edge of the road, its eyes bright red in the sudden illumination. It's frozen. I snap out of my dream state, slam on the brakes, jam the wheel to the left and miss him, barely, while almost sliding off the other side of the highway. My cruiser and I regain our equilibrium and here it is, almost midnight and I'm slinking back into Prescott. I pass the sign warmly welcoming all and sundry passersby to our fair city. I wonder if they mean to include homicide detectives on major losing streaks.

CHAPTER 12
PATIENT 5436

The room, which is a conference room, is quite large, perhaps 30' by 40'. The wainscoting along the perimeter is fashioned of cherry wood, as is the coffered ceiling. The long exterior wall is composed principally of tall leaded glass windows with wooden mullions, also cherry. The upper half of the opposite wall is painted an institutional shade of mint green and is hung with large oil portraits of long-dead men. At one end is a seldom used fireplace with massive limestone mantel and hearth. The opposite end features wall-to-wall built in cabinetry. At the center of the room stands a mahogany table, sufficiently large to seat twelve. The floor is slate. Three men sit at the table.

The building on the top floor of which the conference room is located is a baronial structure three stories in height, with gabled roof covered in gray ceramic tiles. It is constructed of umber-colored brick complemented by granite quoins and a thick growth of clinging ivy.

Beyond the long expanse of windows lie extensive and carefully landscaped grounds. Paved walkways are interspersed with small lakes, flower gardens and greenbelts shaded by elm and sycamore trees. In one of the lakes a flock of Canadian geese have taken up temporary residence, resting and feeding for a while before resuming the journey northward.

The property is surrounded by ten-foot high brick and masonry walls that match the building. The complex could easily be mistaken for an English manor or exclusive East Coast university, save for the fact that the walls are topped with coils of razor-studded concertina wire.

Beyond the walls lie the rolling hills and farmland west of Springfield MO. It's the spring of 1974, a time of political convulsion in America. Gerald Ford is just eight months into his accidental presidency. The Viet Nam war is in its final chaotic phase. The Arabs are boycotting oil exports and there is a gasoline shortage, which is the most traumatic of all America's many problems. There is much unrest in the land. Except that inside the brick walls all is tranquil.

The oldest of the three men is the facility's director, and as such sits at the head of the table. His two colleagues flank him, one on each side. He is in his late sixties, the Director. He wears thick glasses, is more or less bald, and his features are vaguely Slavic. He is dressed in a three-piece suit which was probably bespoke and expensive when new; however, it's been a while since said ensemble was new. His face bears the slightly bored and put upon expression of an individual with long experience being in command.

In front of him, on the table, is a stack of five medical folders. Next to this stack lies a single folder, which is noticeably thicker than the rest. The tab on this one has the typed label: BMH-JM-5436.

"And so, gentlemen," he says, flipping open its cover, "We come to our final subject. Patient 5436. Thoughts, if you'd be so kind?"

The man to his right is perhaps fifteen years his junior, with ruddy complexion, strawberry hair and large pale blue eyes that have a permanent sort of shocked look about them. He wears a white medical jacket over white collared shirt and dark brown dress pants. He says, "I am just very pleased with the progress this young man has made. In all modesty I consider him my star patient. Therapy has been extremely effective and I am prepared to say at this point that his issues have been successfully dealt with."

The Director turns to the man to his left, who is younger and more casually dressed in cardigan and slacks. He has a longish face and a blonde crew cut and is the tallest of the three. He is slumped in his chair in a posture of studied insouciance. "And you, Doctor Andreessen? Do you agree with that assessment?"

"Well, I would please like somebody to refresh my memory. Did this young man hack his mother and stepfather to death in a very savage manner just five short years ago or not? And am I now supposed to believe he's back to being perfectly normal? Just another bright-eyed teen with maybe a bit of a mischievous side to him and low impulse control, is that what you'd have me believe? Like maybe he was just going through a phase, is that the theory?

For my part I have to wonder if this situation doesn't warrant a slightly longer stay with us, if not a fully paid-up lifetime reservation. Yet you propose to let him simply waltz out of here, Harold, no harm no foul?"

Doctor Tomlinson, to whom these antagonistic remarks have been directed, is clearly irritated. He's butted heads with the younger man on more than one occasion in the past. The two belong to quite different camps of psychiatric philosophy. Tomlinson is old school Freudian, whereas Andreessen is a tough love modernist. He replies, "Nobody is suggesting the subject waltz, as you put it, out the front door, Nicholas. He has an aunt, his late mother's sister, living in Colorado who has expressed a willingness to take him in, become his legal guardian and finish raising him. She's already had custody of his sister ever since the event. She has absolutely no misgivings.

"As for the killings: I'll remind you that the subject and his younger sister were being subjected to unspeakable abuse. His mother was married to a pedophile, a deviant who regularly beat him, brutally, and molested the girl. There is even some indication that this monster may have sodomized the subject. Meanwhile, the late lamented mother of the year in question not only refused to intervene but actually assisted and enabled all his depravity. Frankly, as far as I'm concerned the subject's actions were perfectly understandable and even quite courageous for a boy of twelve."

Doctor Andreessen leans forward in his chair and says, "Which brings us to the manner of killing. There was a loaded pistol in his stepfather's nightstand, you will remember. He admitted that he was aware of this fact, and that he knew how to operate said pistol. So why not simply give each of them a double tap to the head while they slept? No muss, no fuss. They are gone and he and his sister are safe. Instead, he chooses to attack them with a hunting knife, which he plunges into stepdaddy's heart and then uses to slit the man's throat ear to ear. Then the same for mom. Then stab them viciously and repeatedly in the chest as they bleed out. Now that, my friend is some serious anger."

"Righteous anger, to be sure, would you not agree?"

"Yes, of course. No one ever claimed the kid wasn't provoked. As far as I'm concerned he did us all a favor ridding the world of these two pieces of garbage. They had it coming, there's no argument. That isn't my point."

"Then what is your point?"

"My point is simply that however justified the subject's actions might seem to you, the combination of the abuse that drove him to murder, plus the trauma of actually having to commit such a violent act, has just necessarily got to have left deep and abiding psychological scars, the sort of scars you don't fix in five years or maybe ever. After all, he was basically abandoned by his mother. Do you really imagine that the hurt and disappointment and rage that failure of duty engendered is not going to be transferred more generally to all women? I'm very much afraid he is concealing a pathological and thoroughgoing hostility to women of every description, and this hostility is inevitably going to surface and quite possibly manifest itself in further acts of violence, except that the next victim or victims will be innocent. Clearly, he's demonstrated that he's capable of homicide. That's the very real risk you're taking if you release him into the population."

"My analysis finds absolutely no evidence of such hostility. We've worked through it. He seems an exceptionally normal and well-adjusted young man at this point."

"Which is precisely what bothers me. Does that even seem possible to you? I say he's a very clever patient, and he's either fooling you or you're fooling yourself. Perhaps you can't see past that big bleeding heart of yours."

"You're one to talk about hearts. Sometimes I wonder if you even have one. Perhaps you're content to see a perfectly good human life wasting away inside this hospital. I am not. This young man has tremendous potential. I'll remind you that his IQ tests north of 140.

"At any rate, whatever issues he may or may not have are not of his own choosing. He's a victim here, remember. Is it fair to punish him with what amounts to life imprisonment for a situation he did nothing to create?"

"You know, Doctor Tomlinson," Andreessen answers, "In the more remote areas of India they have these tigers. As you probably know, your tiger is usually a reclusive beast that stays as far away from humans as it can get. But every once in a while one comes along that likes to wander into the villages and eat the occasional villager. Now, from its standpoint the tiger is not doing anything wrong. It's simply acting according to the nature it's been given, right? Does that mean the good folk there shouldn't trap the tiger?"

"That's a ridiculous analogy. We're not talking about an animal here."

"No we are not. Nor are we dealing, in my opinion, with a normal human being. What we are doing, or rather are supposed to be doing, is using the trust we've been given to balance the safety of many against the convenience of one. I happen to come down on the side of the many, thank you. That always seems to be a difficult choice for you to make, Harold, because you're always falling in love with your patients and losing every last shred of clinical objectivity."

At this point the Director intervenes in the discussion. "No use becoming personal, gentlemen. Let's bear in mind that we are colleagues. You've had this disagreement before, and you'll have it again. We're not building rockets here. We just have a very difficult but very simple decision to make. Is the subject fit for release, or is he not?"

Andreessen waves a hand across the table and says, "Right you are, Doctor. So shall we put it to a show of hands?"

The Director says, "Indeed. Voting in favor of release?"

The Director's raised arm joins Doctor Tomlinson's. He says, "All right then. It's decided. I'll contact the subject's aunt and give her the welcome news. I'll prepare papers, as well, for the court. As per standard practice with juveniles we will arrange to have all criminal and medical records in this matter sealed. Patient 5436 will begin a new life, with a clean slate and, one hopes, brighter prospects."

Doctor Andreessen says, "And also, one hopes, we live in a world where fairy tales really can come true."

It's early afternoon, and beyond the room's high windows the heat and humidity are beginning to build. On the western horizon, just visible at the moment, a long gray squall line drifts steadily eastward.

Down on the grounds, below the three men, the geese lift off the lake and climb in a widening circle. As they gain altitude they assemble into their customary echelon formation and head north.

CHAPTER 13
STEPHEN

The next morning I slept in late, figuring to hit the office around 1000. The moment I awoke I began to experience Jezebel withdrawal pains. It was such an intense experience just being around her, she burned so brightly, and my feelings for her remained so strong that the aftermath of our weekend was like coming down off a drug high, hard. Yet the Jezebel situation presented an obvious dilemma for me, and such was my ambivalence around her that I longed for her next communication yet feared its coming.

I had a chat with Max when I first showed up at headquarters, which conversation I dreaded though it turned out the chief was becoming resigned to slow going on the Bergstrom file.

"Any luck with the big case, Carlo?" he asks. "Haven't heard from you in a couple of days."

"Believe me, Max, I get the smallest break I'm going to shoot the word to you first. Fact is, I'm still getting nowhere fast. I've done everything I can think of, I swear, I've been walking the soles right off my shoes. This type of case is tough, you know that. Girl doesn't know the killer, he's a guy probably lives nowhere near here, picks his victim and maybe even the town totally at random. He's a phantom. He has no record. He has no prints on file. Realistically he's going to probably have to make a mistake to get caught."

"Meaning some other poor girl's got to die."

"Sadly, yes. That's a distinct possibility. Let's just hope not here in Prescott."

"Christ, please. Fact is the media's finally beginning to let up on this one, more interesting news is coming along, people are forgetting. So the heat's off a little bit. But say we have another one on our watch… Jesus, I don't want to think about it."

So I was doing his thinking for him, with horror, as I had been for weeks, when of all people Eric De Leon stuck his head into my office and tossed a manila business-size envelope onto my desk.

"Hey, Carlo," he says. "Que pasa?"

"Nada, dude. I was just sitting here reading my latest issue of *Yachting*. Trying to decide between the eighty or ninety-footer. What do you think?"

"You know what they say, dog. Go big or go home. You owe it to yourself. What's another mill or two?"

"Excellent. Thanks. Believe I will. So anything new with forensics? You need to give me something, anything to get this investigation untracked. Any ideas?"

"Not really, amigo."

"Come on, Eric, what are we paying you guys for? You've been through the final report state sent up, right? The killer spent a lot of time in that apartment. CID didn't find anything, any little shred that could maybe tie him to a specific geographic location? Cloth or carpet fiber? Soil from his shoes? Anything? I am seriously desperate."

Eric shakes his head sadly in commiseration with me. "Can't help you, Carlo. We've covered every base there is to cover. I've got a catalogue of physical evidence so fat my grandmother could prosecute this guy, once you find him. Including fibers we're pretty sure are from his clothing because they don't match anything the girl owned. It's all very generic though. He could have blown in from anywhere. And with no record of his fingerprints…we just need to get lucky."

I say, "Luck and I haven't been the best of friends, lately, my friend."

"It'll happen, Carlo. Trust me, this isn't the last girl he's going to kill."

"Yeah, I know. That's what's troubling me."

"Not a thing we can do about it at this point, except maybe hope next time he makes a mistake."

"Yeah, in another jurisdiction."

"Right. So keep your fingers crossed, and like they say, *buena suerte*."

With which he departed down the hall, and I gave a look to the package. It was addressed to Detective Carlo Jardina, no return address. My heart momentarily skipped a beat until I settled down and realized the writing was a man's, not Jezebel's. I remembered also that I'd given her my home address when last we met, for any future correspondence. Finally, I noticed that the postmark was Tulsa, Oklahoma.

I ripped it open. Two sheets of typewritten paper and a folded square of bubble wrap. I shook the latter loose and out fell a couple of locks of hair, platinum blonde, and a gold genital piercing ornament consisting of a ring with one small bead, obviously the one Mary's killer removed and replaced with his own. My heart was beating fast again as I gingerly unfolded the letter. It read:

Dear Carlo,

I hope you will forgive the familiarity, but it appears we're destined to be adversaries in a very high stakes game of hide and seek. The stakes, of course, are quite literally life and death. I warn you, you'll have to be mighty good to catch me, Carlo. Please don't think it's rude of me, but I won't be able to give you my real name. So call me Stephen. I've sent you some souvenirs, just in case you think I'm kidding you about who I am.

Carlo, from this point forward our fates are inextricably linked. To be honest, I don't think you or anyone else can figure out who I am. By the way, don't bother being careful with this letter or the envelope, spare the tweezers, my prints are all over it, they won't help you. The thing is, I'm anonymous. I've been anonymous for thirty-five years, and I'm quite good at it by now, believe me, I can just fade into a crowd without a soul noticing me. I'm also very well prepared. I've approached this thing with great care and planning, believe me.

I suppose you'll think I must be sociopathic or psychopathic or whatever fancy word you care to use for crazy. But I would discourage you from going too far with that. The fact is, Carlo, if you could have been there, if you could have experienced what I experienced, you'd understand, I know you would. That night, in the club, talking to Tanya, laughing with her, spending money on her for lap dances, spending like a drunken sailor because I know I'm going to take it back after she's dead anyway. To have the knowledge, while she's sitting there smiling at you and inside her pretty head figuring out how much she can take you for, to know that as far as her fate is concerned you are God to her, because you will absolutely determine the time and manner of her death. To have that kind of power, Carlo, I swear the thrill is beyond imagining.

And then of course the exquisite sex, the delightful torture, the prolonged and beautiful act of execution. Carlo, there's something in all of us that just naturally takes pleasure in these things, you won't convince me otherwise, though most of us are never able to muster the courage or righteous anger required to surmount our inhibitions. If you could have been there with me, my friend, you would have been caught up in the excitement yourself.

The whole experience was so exhilarating that it's actually inspired my muse. I've prepared some poems, Carlo, just for you, in case you're blue. They're in haiku:

Once so alive! yet
Wide lifeless eyes, cold flesh, now
Just a memory

Tanya, she'd tease us
She used to strip to please us
Now she's with Jesus

Not bad, do you think? And so what do you think about the SAD business, Carlo? Any thoughts? Don't go wasting your time thinking it's my initials, I promise you they are not although I trust you will check anyway. I'm just trying to be helpful. And the S doesn't stand for Stephen, okay? Stephen's a name I just pulled out of my ass, as I believe a policeman might say. You are a crude lot, admit it, now, no offense. But I will tell you that those letters are a powerful clue. Properly understood, they might help you. They are also the only damn clue you will ever get, because even now you're hoping I'll make a mistake but I won't because I'm too damn good.

One last thing, then I must go. I had so much fun with Tanya, Carlo, I do believe I'll do another one! Won't that be grand? Talk to you later.

Stephen

The text is garden-variety ink jet printer. The signature, like the address, is in his own hand. Therefore I now have an excellent sample of his handwriting in case we ever find him, which of course I won't need in the event we ever find him.

Nothing in my considerable experience with the less uplifting aspects of human nature has really prepared me to deal with this level of illness, this malevolence, this cruel insanity. Never before have I seen a young woman, or anyone else for that matter, dehumanized in the way Mary Bergstrom was. I believe at this point I'll get up from my desk, walk down the hall to the men's, and quietly get sick.

CHAPTER 14
STONER

I've now known Adam Stoner, that's Agent Adam Stoner for the record, for all of ten minutes and already I am aching to kill him. There is a certain universal quality to FBI operatives, it seems, at least the ones I've met. What's the word? Supercilious, I believe. It's Thursday. Stoner is up from the field office in Phoenix to give guidance to us poor indigenous and lift us from our ignorant ways. He sits across from me in standard agency attire, off-the-rack gray suit, steel-rimmed glasses, buzz cut. His face is round and pasty but under the suit the frame's in better shape than mine, which increases my sense of discontent no end.

Our conversation heretofore has consisted of a monologue on the superior methods of his proud organization, and the increasing hopelessness of Stephen's position, crumbling as it were under the relentless assault of the bureau's arcane tactics. To be fair, my largest grievance with the man is probably the fact that he's brought me word and photographic documentation of the fact that Stephen has made good on his promise to me.

She's another well-built blonde stripper, starring in another ghastly tableau. She's hung from the ceiling with care, the room in which she's died having conveniently been furnished with heavy beams running wall to wall along the ceiling. Into one of these Stephen has drilled a large hook and her hands are tied together with rope strung through it. Extremely elaborate and efficient-looking knots, one wonders if the man's had nautical training. She's completely naked. Her ankles are also bound with rope, and it seems that originally she was suspended at a height which allowed only her toes to touch the floor, barely, thus inhibiting her movement as she struggled, but in the intervening time between her death and discovery either the rope or more likely her arms have stretched so that her feet are cocked sideways against the floor like a broken doll's. Her left baby toe has been neatly severed away.

Like Mary, her body is a tapestry of welts from a vicious flogging, though this girl was done back and front. Like Mary, she has been posed, post-mortem, so that she greets us with dead wide-staring eyes as we enter the room, her hair having been bunched together and tied with more rope trussed to the hook, thus keeping her head unnaturally upright. However, Stephen has thoughtfully provided us with variation on a theme with this victim, for this young lady's formerly lovely throat has been opened from ear to ear, the cut gaping at me obscenely, and all the blood from her neck up has come spilling out, cascading over her breasts and belly and running down the insides of her legs to the floor, the fluid now dried to an ugly black crust. It makes a macabre contrast with her drained face, now alabaster white, and her lips and nails, freshly done in shocking pink.

On the floor at her feet, neatly arranged, a cat-of-nine-tails whip, a bloody straight razor folded carefully back into its handle, a terrycloth gag, and another homemade electric skin-writing tool. That's what's been bothering me. I knew something was missing. I look at the back and front photos again of her body as it was initially found, and I see no letters. And then I find a picture of her lying in the steel tray atop an autopsy table, where the blood has been washed away, and there they are. *S-A-D.* Only, my God, these letters are done in a very unsteady hand, they're much jerkier than the ones on Mary, and I realize they must have been done while she still lived, writhing desperately to avoid the horrible pain, struggling, screaming silently into her gag. Stephen is escalating the violence.

The one piece of good news here is that this particular young exotic dancer has never been west of the Rockies, and could not I'm sure if asked have found Prescott on the map.

"So, Carlo," asked my obnoxious guest, "guess where we found this one."

I blurted it out without thinking. I wanted to bite my tongue off the moment it was said, but I absolutely could not resist the temptation to show this smart ass up, "I don't know, Adam. Let me guess. How about, I don't know, how about Tulsa, Oklahoma?"

It was almost worth it, the look on his overstuffed federal face, except that now of course I was going to have to share Stephen's letter with him, which I dearly for some inexplicable reason wanted not to do, despite the fact that withholding it would constitute obstruction of justice.

He said, "How the hell did you know that?"

"I'll tell you in a minute. First, let me see if I have the rest right. There's semen and fingerprints and body hair all over the place, correct?"

"Correct."

"Which of course match my case but no known actual individual living in the US of A."

"Correct again."

"Not to mention the letters *S-A-D*, which you picked up from my entry in the database and which seal the deal."

"Three for three, Carlo. Unlike the Bergstrom girl, however, it looks like the sex itself was consensual all the way to its conclusion. Appears to have been conventional missionary intercourse with no sign of struggle. The coroner found his semen in her vagina. My guess is he paid her, and the party didn't get rough until after he satisfied himself. So how'd you know Tulsa?"

I opened a desk drawer and tossed Stephen's letter to him. "Had a little love letter from our boy a couple days ago. It was posted from there, so I just made a lucky guess. Don't sweat the fingerprints, they're all over it and they're all his."

He pushed a soft whistle through his lips when he was finished reading. "One sick son of a bitch, am I right? Plus he thinks he's William Shakespeare or something, with the poetry. What an asshole."

"And getting sicker by the minute, it appears, though he clearly has a high intellect, judging by his letter, and that can't be good news for us. Shakespeare did sonnets, by the way, not haiku."

"Yeah, yeah, a manner of speaking, OK? You may be right about the IQ part, though."

"He's looking mighty goddamn clever so far."

"He's looking a little more clever than two strippers, that's for sure. This could be a tough one and so here's the deal Carlo. Multiple states now, more to come no doubt, it's a federal VICAP case from here on in and we're taking over lead responsibility."

"Say what? VICAP?"

"Violent Criminal Apprehension Program, that would be. It's sort of a government-sponsored honors program for interstate serial killers. It's actually a subdivision of the National Center for the Analysis of Violent Crime, with which you are obviously familiar, but it concentrates on kidnappings and homicides, particularly those that are sexually oriented or are part of a series of killings."

"I see."

"Anyway, they've put me in charge of the investigation, lucky me. With our resources maybe we have better luck than you've had."

"Well, I certainly hope so, Adam," I said, which is not at all what I wanted to say in response to his less-than-subtle dig.

Stoner was sitting directly across from me at my desk. His arms were locked behind his head and one leg was crossed over the other, ankle on knee, in a way that suggested, I don't know, maybe an attitude of gratuitous self-satisfaction. For reasons I find hard to verbalize, he was really pissing me off.

He said, "Run it down for me. What all have you done so far?"

"You name it. We've done a very thorough professional analysis of the Bergstrom crime scene. We have hair, semen and fingerprints which will absolutely nail this prick if we ever catch him. Dozens of interviews with people connected in any way to the victim, or who were at the club where she picked her killer up, or who lived in her apartment building. We've put out an artist's sketch to every living soul in western Arizona, I believe. As now seems even more likely, we figured he traveled a considerable distance to get here and so we've concentrated a lot of effort on car rental agencies, airlines, buses, hotels and motels, restaurants, any business a man on the road would patronize.

"We were very hopeful about the club. We concentrated a lot of effort there. We figured somebody was bound to have seen the guy arriving or leaving in his car, maybe give us a make, or notice an out of state plate and give us where he lives. But we came up empty. Customers had tits and ass on the brain, they were noticing nothing else. Plus some of them were there only unofficially, if you know what I mean. We thought about forcing them to give depositions under oath, but in the end we thought, what the hell. Bottom line is do they want to be crosswise with us or the old lady? Prescott is a small town. We value our domestic tranquility."

"Right. Why rock the boat for one little whore?"

"Hey, come on Stoner, that's not fair. I don't make the rules."

"Okay. Okay. Shift topics. Pity this asshole's prints aren't in our database."

"True, which surprises me a little. You'd think a guy does something like this would have a record."

"You would, wouldn't you? Truth is, this type of offender sometimes comes along with no previous criminal history and no military service. They've simmered on the back burner for years, solid citizens to all outward appearances, and then one day out of the blue they just cook off. That's one theoretical possibility.

"The other school of thought, the one I lean toward, is that it's even or better money this character has killed before, maybe been killing for years, maybe a dozen or two girls. We've seen it before. If you're really good, and really smart, and really careful, and you spread the murders out chronologically and geographically, you work a different jurisdiction each time, you can have yourself a career that spans years and never get caught."

"You're telling me you think he's killed dozens of women and never left any DNA?"

"Not telling you that at all. Maybe he left plenty. He sure didn't have any problem leaving it in these last two we have here. I'm telling you he never left any evidence that could lead back to him or identify him in any way. Don't forget, it's been only a few years ago that no one had a clue as to how valuable DNA typing would become. Our boy might have a dozen of his samples sitting in cold case files in various jurisdictions scattered across the country. Doesn't do us a hell of a lot of good, does it?

"Of course as you know these days there is a national database, CODIS, of DNA profiles, and it's not beyond the realm of possibility that some local yokel out there might wake up one morning feeling extra ambitious and decide to type and run some old samples. But that's an expensive process, the cases are cold, and there's no way of getting a hit if this asshole's never been convicted of a crime, because that's the only way you get logged into the system."

A sudden movement flashed across my peripheral vision, and I turned toward the office window. I realized it was an alligator lizard that had skittered across the glass and was sitting on the ledge, doing lizard pushups, probably in an effort to impress some nearby female. Once drawn to the window I found I could not take my eyes off of it. It was like a portal to another world, a clean and fresh world, so far removed from the barbarity under discussion in my office. In the distant sky a hawk cruised effortlessly, borne aloft by the afternoon thermals. I would have been very happy to fly right out of the office and join it.

After a moment, I snapped too and returned my attention to the matter at hand. My eyes fell upon the one photo I kept on my desk, which was of Shannon in her kindergarten class uniform, a little angel in white shirt and plaid skirt, and I reflexively folded it face down. There was no way I wanted her to be a party to any of this sickness.

I slid the folder that held Rebecca's file in Stoner's direction as if it were on fire, across the slick metal surface between us. He caught it in one deft move just before it fell into his lap, and stashed it into his briefcase.

I said, "Right. Okay. So why the letters to me, all of a sudden? Why go public now?"

"Boredom, maybe. Maybe it stops being enough of a challenge just getting away with murder. So what do you do, you up the ante. You start the cat and mouse game with law enforcement and get the adrenalin pumping again. Or maybe it's frustration with the lack of recognition. No fun being a fucking criminal genius if no one knows about it right?"

"Yeah, I see your point. But if you're right we have a real hill to climb."

"You got that right, my friend. A damn steep one. And lucky us, we'll have the press and the public and all the bureaucratic hounds nipping at our heels all the way."

"Yeah. Lucky us."

"So how about credit cards? You check the credit card transactions around that date for a cardholder from out of state come visiting in Prescott? Maybe a guy with initials *S-A-D*?"

I flushed. Shit. Didn't think of that one. "No, Adam, I didn't. Can do, but I believe him about that not being his monogram."

"That's fine, we'll check it. We're going to need your evidence also. Maybe our lab can find something your guys missed. Our boys are the best, we feel."

Right, you smug bastard, I'm sure, I think, but I say, "All right, Agent Stoner. I'm sure your colleagues at the Bureau will be able to throw some light onto this situation for us. We just got everything back from Phoenix, along with the report of their analysis. I'm going to call Officer De Leon in and he can take you downstairs to our evidence storage facility and you two can complete the chain-of-custody paperwork and you can load everything up and be on your way."

"Thank you too much, Detective Jardina." Nodding at the folder on my desk, he asks, "Want a souvenir copy of the glossies? We have plenty."

"Thanks. I can live without them. Gonna have a permanent set right here, I believe," I say, tapping my head. "I would appreciate your keeping in touch, though. I'm still considering this a case for Prescott Police, and I understand you fair-haired boys be in charge but I'd love to play along."

"Of course you're going to be in the loop. We'll be consulting you and keeping you up to speed. Speaking of which, maybe next time you get a letter from our friend you don't take two days to get word to us, okay?"

"Didn't know the FBI was even involved till you showed up this very AM."

"Fair enough, but maybe we could have done something with our people in Tulsa, maybe given them a heads up. Maybe next time, if there is one."

"Yeah, maybe, but for my money this girl was already dead when he mailed me the letter. And we both know there is going to be a next one."

"Well, I'm sure you're right on both counts, detective. Unfortunately."

With this my new pal stood, shrugged his shoulders and casually stretched both arms above his head. He said, "Don't trouble your head about being marginalized. If this character has decided to make you his pen pal you could be an important player. Wordy bastard like this, he might just give us something we can use to find him. So far you're about the best hope we have. Here's my card. You get more mail, give me a ring ASAP."

I took the card from his extended hand, slipped it into my shirt pocket and said, "You can count on it."

"Thanks very much. Believe me, Carlo, my colleagues and I look forward to working with you."

"Likewise."

He was lying, of course, through his coffee-stained teeth, but the words made me feel better. Eric showed up at that point and after introductions were made led Stoner off to the basement of the headquarters building. Watching them walk away I was reminded of my conversation with Eric on Monday, and thought to myself, *buena suerte*, motherfucker.

CHAPTER 15
LOUISA'S

I caught a break the next Saturday morning. Thumper's call awakened me at 0700 sharp. "Hey, Carlo, can you come buy me a cup of coffee at Louisa's? Got something for you."

Thumper has his faults, but he was never one to ring false alarms. "Give me 45 minutes," I answered him. I hung up and hopped out of bed.

It took me more like an hour, but Thumper and I were in due course seated at a booth across from one another, coffee in hand and bacon and eggs on the way. Thumper's a kid with a secret this morning, just bursting to let me have it. As always he's bouncing all over his side of the table frenetically, his foot tapping out a steady rhythm on the linoleum. I say, "So what's up, Joey?"

"Heard a really funny story the other night, Carlo, sitting around the campfire. One you're gonna want to hear. There's this guy, can't tell you his name and I don't think it matters, but let's say he's a real straight shooter. Family man, wife and four kids, deacon in his church and on the side he's the choirmaster, if you can believe it."

"So?" My heart is sinking a little. I'm afraid Thumper is off on a tangent.

"So stick with me, man. The night Mary Bergstrom was murdered this guy was working late at the church. Only the poor dude must have taken a wrong turn, because instead of sitting in the loft working on Sunday's choral arrangements, like he told his old lady, our friend was actually reclining in the rear seat of his car, which was parked in the lot of Rick's Gentleman's Club, with his pants down to his knees receiving oral favors from one of Rick's girls."

"You're kidding."

"Not in the slightest. This young lady is very close to finishing the deacon off when a car pulls in right next to his very own. They hear, he and the girl, a door open and crunching gravel, and don't you know suddenly there's like this face like peering in at them, right into our upstanding citizen's face. It was a cool night, as you know, and the windows were fogged. But they were near a light pole and it was a full moon and they each got a good look at one another, the two men. It was the killer, for sure. He laughs, gives our guy a big smirky grin, and walks off."

"What did he do then, the deacon?"

"What any pillar of the community caught in his situation would do. He had the girl go back to work on him. Except with the shock to his system it took her like maybe another quarter hour to even get him back up, you know what I'm sayin', which pissed her off mightily because of course she ain't getting paid by the minute, is she?"

"You digress, my friend."

"Sorry. She finishes him, finally, and he pulls his pants up and gets out of the car, and he checks out the other car because he's like curious as well as embarrassed and he's never seen this character around Rick's before and it turns out this isn't the first time he's gotten lost on the way to church."

"I see. And the car?"

"Late model gold Camry."

"Plates?"

"Arizona, Carlo."

"Positive?"

"Absolutely. Thing is Carlo, this poor guy's like crapping his pants because you haven't rumbled him and he's afraid you will, which would pretty much screw up his life. Everybody at the club is covering for him. He's a good customer."

"Well, my friend, you can put the word around that he's okay by me. I needed the information, not his testimony. If we identify this guy we have enough evidence already to convict him ten times, plus his mother, his brother, and probably his dog."

"I thought you'd feel that way. So did I do good, Carlo?" He has his brows raised and a palm sort of wandering around aimlessly on the tabletop.

I fished a hundred dollar bill out of my shirt pocket, folded neatly and stashed there for the occasion, and slipped it to him. Around this time breakfast came, which we enjoyed together in a haze of cigarette smoke while reminiscing about old times in the crazy world of cops and robbers.

CHAPTER 16

SHANNON AND AMY

When I left Louisa's, I headed for the suburbs on the south edge of town. I was invited to a picnic lunch with Shannon and Amy, which diversion I badly needed and gratefully anticipated. Our investigation had hit a wall so fast that Max decided to put Amy back on patrol. Consequently we really hadn't spent any time together lately.

She owned a three bedroom home in a nice neighborhood near a park, with great schools for Shannon and lots of clean air and sunshine and all things good for raising little girls. I figured she must have gotten a nice settlement after Brian's death, as the place was a little pricey for a rookie cop.

She greeted me with the usual big smile at the door and we gave each other a big hug. "Morning, Amy, how's my girl?"

"Super, Carlo, you?"

"Tip top. Man, am I happy you asked me over. We have some talking to do. But first, where's the brat?"

"Where else? The toy room."

One bedroom for Amy. One for Shannon. And one for the toys, a huge collection by now, begun when the girl was three with just two rules. Nothing less than seventy-five years old and no plastic. There are dolls, of course, by the boatload, dolls sitting on shelves and propped in corners and hung from the ceiling, of every description and from every point of the globe. Mechanical toys, merry-go-rounds and miniature Ferris wheels and wind-up animals. Little trains snaking along the floor. Animated coin banks, for example one with a monkey with outstretched paw that accepts a coin and slowly tosses it into a slot on the top of its simian brass head. Replicas of famous structures: a leaden Eiffel Tower and silvery London Bridge and an ivory Taj Mahal. Marionettes in splendid abundance. An old wooden stereoscope with accompanying box of slides. Spinning tops and kaleidoscopes and games. Stacks and stacks of children's games.

Seated cross-legged on the floor in the middle of this semi-organized chaos, my sweet little princess. She wears jeans and a pink tank top with tennis shoes to match. Hair in carefully braided tails halfway down her back, darker than her mom's. She converses softly but earnestly with a stuffed Pekinese she holds in her lap.

I steal up behind her and silently place my hands over her eyes. "Guess who?" I whisper.

"Uncle Carlo!" she squeals, and squirms around in my arms to pop up and grab my neck. I stand, pulling her up with me, and she smells of strawberry shampoo and Irish Spring soap and the clean freshness of her breaks my heart after all the unwholesomeness I've been wallowing in. I want to hold her to me, I want to draw the purity from her and make it mine.

While Amy prepares our lunch basket Shannon gives me a lengthy tour, not for the first time or last, of the collection in all its magnificent detail. When it's finished we all three head out the door for the short walk to the park.

Amy and I sit at a picnic table on the verge of a long sloping green, partially shaded by a stand of young conifers. Shannon has a new friend, a girl around her age, and the two of them are trading turns pushing each other on swings. The basket between us smells of fresh baguettes, cheese and potato salad. The bottle of white Bordeaux I brought along is open and we sip it from plastic cups. It's a gorgeous Arizona afternoon, late March, unseasonably warm and the sky a lovely shade of baby blue. It's dotted with a layer of white flat-bottomed clumps of stratocumulus clouds, looking like they've just been dropped onto a sheet of glass. The birds sing and the cicadas chirp and suddenly all's right with my world. Amy is looking cute as she can be in turquoise Capri pants and a white turtleneck sweater, blonde curls spilling down either side of her rosy cheeks. She takes my hand.

"So you wanted to talk, Carlo?"

"I did, Amy. Couple of things. First, business." I describe my conversation with Thumper. "It's looking more certain this guy's coming from a long way, like we figured, Amy. Tulsa just makes it that much more likely. Probably lives somewhere in the middle."

"Which makes the Camry a rental?"

"No, I don't think so. You really can't rent a car without a credit card and I'm pretty sure this man is a cash and carry customer."

"So, explain," she says.

"Try this. I want to bounce this off you. He's coming a long way, it's pretty safe to assume. I figure he's not going to drive eight hundred or a thousand miles in one day and then do this kind of crime halfway into the night. This sort of recreation, you'd want to be refreshed I believe. I figure he comes halfway, say, or a little more, the day before. In Mary's case, say Flagstaff, where he pays cash for a cheap motel and spends the night. And where he steals Arizona plates for his car."

"Okay."

"Amy, if you wanted to take somebody's plates in Flagstaff and be certain they wouldn't be missed for a few days, where would you go?"

She thinks about this for a moment, then sits straighter, smiles and says, "The airport, of course."

"Good girl. He slides into long term parking, waits for somebody to park that has a couple of suitcases and is obviously leaving for a few days, guy on a business trip most likely, and bags his plates. Off he goes, cruising in anonymity and air-conditioned comfort right into our fair little city in search of random prey."

"And returns the plates after he's done here?"

"No, I don't think so. It's one thing to steal plates before the act; it's a very minor beef if he's spotted. But to get caught after the killing is another matter. He wants to take no chance of contact with law enforcement. Why take the risk of returning the plates? For my money, he just tosses them into the desert well off the road and they're never seen again."

"I like it. Brilliant work, Detective Jardina."

"Thank you, Amy. I'm going to check it out with DMV first thing Monday morning and see if anybody's reported missing license plates. Man would I love to one-up that cocky Stoner bastard."

There follow a few minutes of silence while we enjoy the afternoon, the sun warming our faces and the reassuring sight of innocent children at play. And then Amy asks me, "What was the other thing, Carlo?"

"Huh?"

"The other thing you wanted to discuss."

"Oh, yeah. Seems I've fallen in love, honey."

"Carlo, you're kidding, that's great!" she says, but to my ear the statement lacks conviction, and there's a look on her face that makes me regret broaching the subject. "Where did you meet her?"

"In Vegas last time I was there, a couple of months ago. Seen her since in Sedona for a weekend. Yes and no about it being great."

"Meaning what?"

"There are complications. One of which is the fact she's married."

"Oh, Carlo. Say it isn't so."

"Sorry."

"Is she leaving him, at least?"

"It seems he may be leaving her."

"I see. Well..."

"Thing is, Amy, I don't know. How do I say this? There are other things about the relationship that are troubling. Yet I really have fallen for her, fallen hard. To have her would mean to enter into her world, though, and to play by her rules, which would require...adaptation on my part. My whole adult life I've been playing by a completely different set of rules. It's exhilarating in a way to contemplate the sort of, of liberation, I guess, that I feel around her."

"So she's a free spirit, you're saying?"

"Yes, in spades. She is certainly that. The thing I'm struggling with, my question to you, I guess, is how far do I go for love? This thing has so many ramifications, stuff I can't even go into with you. Sometimes I wish to God I hadn't met her, because the fact I have just creates a very big dilemma for me. But I have met her, and she has put an arrow right through the old ticker. I can see you're confused. I'm sorry, I'm rambling along like a maniac making no sense. It's frustrating because I really would love to have your advice but yet I can't give you all the information you'd need to give me any that would be worthwhile. Hell, the damn wine is starting to do my talking for me. Forget I brought it up."

"I'd love to help. Maybe if you reframed the question?"

"Okay. I suppose what I'm trying to ask is do I reassess my whole set of values at this advanced point of my life? I mean for any reason: for love, for money, for any conceivable reason? I'm a man who's made commitments, after all, and who still has a heavy load of Catholic guilt to deal with. And how important is it, anyway, romance I mean, to a man my age?"

"Carlo, you're forty-seven years old. You're in your prime. Anyway, I've always believed love is the most important thing. I think it would be great for you to have someone in your life. I've always wondered why you didn't."

"Oh, you have, have you?"

"Yes I have. You care to clear that mystery up for me?"

"Amy, that's not easy. For starters, the fact is that I have always been shy around women, especially very desirable women. Even when I was a cocky little hoodlum back in Philly I talked a good game but it was mainly just that, talk."

"Lots of men have that problem, Carlo. Maybe most. We girls can be scary. But they still manage to hook up."

"Yeah, well, the other thing is I have very discriminating taste. I never wanted to settle. I wanted to play out of my league, so to speak, but I never had the balls to really go after what I wanted and close the deal. Sounds crazy, I know, but what can I tell you? I'm a man, and we men can sometimes let the best be the enemy of the good."

Amy shakes her head and sighs. "I guess I have a lot to learn about the male psyche."

"Probably. And vice versa, for that matter. Anyway, a funny man you probably never heard of once said it best. He said he'd never want to join a club that would have him as a member."

"Any club would be lucky to have you, Carlo. You're a good-looking guy and a decent man besides."

"That's kind of you to say, Amy. Especially the part about me being decent."

"So this girl, is she a club you'd like to join?"

"I guess that's the question, Amy. The dues are high. I'll tell you that for nothing."

"And is she out of your league?"

"As it turns out, no. Amazingly enough."

"Will I meet her?"

"Yet another difficult question, sweetie." I answer her, by which of course I mean no.

And there it lay. This wasn't one Amy could help me with. I should have known that from the beginning. There was also the fact that, given the way things were going with Jezzie, I could envision a day in which I wouldn't want Amy to know she even existed.

"Speaking of love," I say after a long silence during which we refill our wine glasses. "When are you going to start dating, Amy? You're a healthy, beautiful young woman. And Shannon needs a dad."

"She has a dad."

"I mean one that's not in the ground, Amy. Excuse my harshness, but it's the truth. A walking, talking dad."

"She has a man in her life, Carlo. You."

"Not the same. Not the same for her. Not the same for you."

"Let's not, Carlo. Not today."

"Okay. Sorry. You're right."

I called Shannon to lunch.

CHAPTER 17

SARTRE AND INGRAM

So who's killed more people? French intellectuals or all the generals of all the armies in the history of the world? If you answered that it's a toss-up, but that ambitious women have far outstripped either, you are two for two.

It's the Wednesday after Stoner's visit. A dozen days since Stephen's second kill. The FBI has gotten nowhere with its investigation, it gives me enormous pleasure to report. I sit alone in my apartment, staring at a blank wall. The shades are drawn. Lights are out. The mood is tenebrous. At my feet is a bottle of Johnnie Walker Red Label. Red is what real men drink, the Black is for pussies. I pour myself another two fingers, neat. The burn as it goes down makes me feel better for some reason. It's a rocker, my chair. My head lolls backward at an unnatural angle like Mary and her friend and like the girls my eyes are wide open and unseeing. My arms hang loose at my sides. One hand grips a cocktail glass by the rim. In the other, the next letter sans return address to darken my door, the one I've dreaded, the one I've feared would never come, the one to which I've looked forward as a kid longs for Christmas to arrive. Jezebel has struck again, the ethical calculus I'm working with is extremely complex, and it is, as they say, nut-cutting time.

She's provided, very thoughtfully I have to admit, a few snippets of critical analysis of the abstruse thinking of the great existential philosopher Jean-Paul Sartre. Notably, an explication of the ontology of *Being and Nothingness,* the centerpiece of his writing. I've found she loves this guy. She gave me his rap when we were in Sedona. She likes him because she believes, as do most people, wrongly in my opinion, that his work prefigures and somehow justifies the brand of moral relativism so popular these days. If you ask me the poor guy's been tragically misunderstood.

At any rate, the piece provides me a refresher on that sophomore philosophy course I so enjoyed, back in the day. For Sartre, I read, the key premise is that "existence precedes essence." This means we are born into a world not of our choosing, with no predetermined purpose, and therefore must define our own identities and shape our own fates by the manner in which we live. In this light, and this is the fun part, *moral values are created, not discovered.* Conveniently, our highest goal is thus to become the most authentic person possible and to live the most fulfilling life we can. By "authentic" he means one who realizes that *his own freedom is the ultimate value and the source of all other values.*

And so on and so forth until my head is spinning, emphasis by Jezebel. This the sort of twaddle, of course, which is supposed to make it okay for me to end the life of a fellow human being, violently and in all probability painfully, for the simple repugnant purpose of enhancing the convenience of my own and Jezebel's existence. A formerly unthinkable thought, it is, for a nominally decent and moral man whose pursuit of probity has been as zealous as his pursuit of happiness. That, of course, was the problem with Jezebel and her effect on me. She could make the unthinkable thinkable.

Included in her letter is a short note proposing our next rendezvous and a reminder of the private PO Box number for my response. I have a feeling the kabuki dance is over, and the hard sell is on its way.

Jesus, the gospels say, experienced a moment of doubt and angst as his arrest, betrayal and crucifixion approached, known ever after as the agony in the garden. That would be the Garden of Gethsemane, on the Mount of Olives. He was in a corner and he wanted out. "Father," he said, "if you are willing, take this cup away from me; still, not my will but yours be done." This story occurs to me, just now, for some reason, though I must have been ten years old and in the fifth grade of Catholic grammar school the last time I heard it cited. I believe I know how he felt.

I stumbled off to bed and slept. Then dreamed. I was once again in my living room, back in my rocker staring into the darkness mindlessly. As my eyes accommodated to the dim light I realized that I wasn't alone. There was Jezebel, sitting on the couch. And next to her, Stephen as I've imagined him to look. His face is a study in bland anonymity, expressionless, dead-eyed. "Get with the program, Carlo," he says to me.

"Yeah, Carlo," says Jezebel. "Get with the program." They both break into laughter and high-five each other with blood-soaked hands.

Again I sleep soundly. Again a dream comes to me. I'm in a forest on a moonlit night, a gothic scene drawn in blacks and shades of gray complete with wolves howling in the distance. I stumble into a meadow and in the lunar glow I see a couple making love on the ground in a bed of wildflowers. As I approach, the man turns to look at me over his shoulder. It's Stephen, lying between Jezebel's outspread legs. He grins and wordlessly removes himself from her, stands and by gesture invites me to join the party. However, as I kneel beside her and prepare to embrace her I realize I'm staring into the tortured eyes of Mary Bergstrom, the hand that had been reaching for her breast involuntarily recoiling at the sight of her desecrated throat. "Hey, buddy, leave her alone, she's spoken for, she's all mine," I hear a strange man's voice say behind me. Turning, I see that it's a naked Roger Waterhouse, complaining from the edge of the clearing. On the ground at his feet are the clothes he was wearing in the photo Jezebel once showed me. "They both are," he says with a demented laugh, and I realize that next to him with her right arm around his shoulder is the poor girl from Oklahoma, except that dangling from her left hand, held by the hair, is her freshly separated head.

Rough night, in other words. I wake up, walk to the bath where I towel off the sweat, down a Zantac to deal with what the scotch has been doing to my stomach, and flip on the radio on my nightstand, thinking to have some music to lull me back to sleep. It's set to an R and B station and I swear to you that the song playing when it came on was *If Loving You is Wrong, I Don't Want to be Right*, courtesy of the great Luther Ingram.

CHAPTER 18

BIG SUR

Her note asked me to meet her in Big Sur for a weekend in early May. She planned to stay at the Post Ranch Inn, a deluxe resort built into cypress and pine forest on a headland overlooking the rugged and fog-shrouded California coastline south of Monterrey Bay. This property features individual guest cottages, hot tub and roaring fire included, with chardonnay and brie all around. The privacy this arrangement would afford would be perfect for our purposes.

The two intervening weeks dragged by with very little progress in finding Stephen. Actually, no progress in finding Stephen. Nor did I receive any more letters from him, and as it appeared his first was precursor to another killing this was probably good news. I was able to confirm my theory with Arizona DMV concerning the plates, and had amazingly enough guessed accurately right down to the location of their theft. Some poor citizen had indeed lost his tags at the Flagstaff airport the weekend Mary Bergstrom was murdered.

I called Stoner to share this intelligence, and to give him my information on the make and color of her killer's car. He seemed to my not very great surprise unimpressed with the former and skeptical of the latter. FBI profilers had worked up a thumbnail sketch of Stephen since we'd last spoken. White, mid-thirties single male. Above average intelligence. Drives a mid-level sedan, probably foreign, a common vehicle either red or white in color. Has deep-seated hostility to women, reverse side of a pronounced fear of them. Quiet, most likely steadily employed, perhaps as a professional or technician of some sort. As both killings committed on a Friday night, assume he works a Monday through Friday week, nine to five.

When I hung up I could only shake my head at the thought of taxpayers putting up good money for this heroic piece of headwork. We know for a fact he's a white male, now don't we, ask about fifty eyewitnesses all told. He's already written me that he's thirty-five and I've no reason to doubt him. I trust Thumper, so I'm pretty sure Stephen drives a gold Camry, top-selling vehicle in America, which makes them right about the commonplace foreign sedan thing if not about the color. But that's really self-evident. Think about it. He's looking for invisibility. What's he gonna do, drive into town in a Lamborghini? And the part about hostility to women, a masterstroke of insight. Gee, do you think? As far as the Monday-Friday gig, there I'm not so sure. I'm convinced that he started on Thursday, as I theorized with Amy. Who's to say that the timing is work-related, though? You want to snatch a girl from a strip club without becoming famous you probably want it crowded, which means a weekend.

What the hell, by this point I was just going through the motions.

On Saturday morning I hopped a commuter flight down to Phoenix Skyharbor. From there it was a short jet ride to San Francisco, and another prop job to Monterrey. There I rented a car and headed down Highway One toward Carmel.

I've never necessarily been a fan of Northern California, but there is no question that this particular piece of real estate is about as gorgeous as there is to be found on the planet. Past Carmel the road climbs up from the sea to run along the rim of steep cliffs, snaking its way back and forth along the edge of the precipice, two lanes, through miles of unspoiled forest, firs, sequoias, cypress and gnarled and wind-bent Monterrey pines. Across deep ravines spanned by white deco arches and divided by strands of falling water. Two hundred feet below me, a black and blue Pacific pounds relentlessly at the base of towering stone walls, breaking into thousands of foamy pieces against dark rows of craggy rock. It's a soggy maritime environment, rainy and cloudy and cold and more akin climatically to Oregon, perhaps, than the Golden State of popular imagination. Beautiful it is, however, surpassingly so and romantic too, especially when it's a Saturday night and the road belongs to you alone and tonight the clouds are layered on the sea below you but above the night is clear and starry-bright, and every mile is bringing you closer to the comforting embrace of Jezebel Waterhouse.

Into whose arms you are warmly and eagerly welcomed upon your late night arrival, who husbands you into her private hot tub to ease your travel-weary bones, a steaming cauldron in the cold evening air, who pours you a slender flute of Schramsberg blanc du blanc champagne, Napa's finest, and who makes sweet soul-stirring love to you on the floor before her private and well-tended fireplace, blazing brightly. I managed for the evening to put out of mind the reason she'd summoned me, and the frontal assault I was expecting the next day.

She did not disappoint. She got to it first thing in the morning, over her crab and lobster room service omelet, "So, Carlo, did you enjoy that article I sent you?"

"Sure, Jez. It was great. Very uplifting."

"Wasn't trying to uplift you, baby. I was trying to straighten you out. You know I love you, and I want to spend the rest of my life with you, but how can that happen unless we're on the same page?"

"The same page? Christ, Jez, I don't even want to open that particular book."

"So answer me this, lover. Do you really propose to allow Roger Waterhouse to stand between you and your happiness? *Our* happiness? Cause let me tell you, he isn't worth it. He's no frigging saint, you know. He's a long goddamn way from it. He's a brutal, selfish, double-dealing lying bastard. How do you think he built that auto dealership empire of his? By dealing fairly with people? I'm not even talking about the way he treats me, which is like trash, which if you love me should seriously piss you off. He's not been faithful since the day we were married. You have any notion of the way he's run around on me and humiliated me publicly?"

"No. I don't know what he's done to you or what he's done to the auto-buying public, to be honest. I know nothing about him."

"Then let me tell you. He's screwed everybody who's ever bought a car from him. And lied to them. Some poor guy comes in and gets cheated out of a week's salary, that's like taking a week of his life, isn't it? So we're not really talking about crossing some bright line that Roger's never crossed himself... we're just talking about degrees, Carlo. For God's sake can't you see that?"

"Now that you mention God, maybe that's the problem. I don't see Her buying your line of argument, to be honest."

"Oh Christ, Carlo, grow up. You don't really think there's a God, do you? Turn on the television. Pick up a newspaper. You gonna tell me we live in a world that some deity is running?"

"Sweetheart, you must have had one scary childhood."

"We both did, baby. But we are not the products of our childhood. This is what I'm trying desperately to make you understand. We are who we choose to be."

"I'm the product of a Catholic upbringing, Jezebel. I was a charity case, on account of my being raised basically by wolves, but I did twelve years in that system. Hard to put that training behind you."

At this point she stood, threw off her robe to reveal her completely nude self, and said, "Maybe you'd rather put this behind you?"

"Oh, God, girl. You know I can't."

"Good. That's a good boy, that's much better. All I want is for you to step up and be the authentic man Sartre was talking about. Recognize that you define your own values. No one else does or should, and definitely not a weasel like Roger Waterhouse. You see what you want and you take it. Because I guarantee you, darling, no matter what the nuns taught you, there is no hereafter. There is here and there is now. A tiny slice of eternity. You either carpe this particular diem or you condemn yourself to a life of deprivation and frustration and, incidentally, not being laid by *moi*."

She has by now more or less wrapped herself around me and is caressing me in every erogenous zone I've ever been aware of, plus a few I had no idea existed. The last thing I want to contemplate just now is a life of not being laid by *moi*.

So there it is, as I figured it would be. I have a decision to make. The time for vacillation is gone.

The rest of the day was given over to an illustration by Jezebel of just how much fun it really isn't when one is not on the receiving end of her adoring attention. She wasn't angry with me, which may have been counterproductive at any rate. It was just that the thermostat got dialed down a couple degrees. "Passive aggressive" is the term, I believe, a clinician would use. She really wanted me to understand the stakes of the game we were playing.

We went wandering through the splendid headlands of Big Sur, and sat side by side at bluff's edge watching the sun go down over the Pacific. We dined on some of the finest California Nouvelle cuisine to be had anywhere at any price, and drank of the finest wines Napa County is capable of producing. We even made love. But the dinner talk was small, and the sex perfunctory. Her little demonstration had its intended effect. When I headed home the next morning, it was with a sense of having my metaphorical tail between my legs.

CHAPTER 19
REBECCA

Turns out her name was Rebecca Reichenbach, the girl Stephen did in Oklahoma, and Rebecca came from a very nice God-fearing family who had no idea that she was working her way through college by taking her clothes off for strange men. Her father was a physician of apparently substantial means, and he raised quite a fuss about the search for his daughter's killer being as strenuous as humanly possible. He and his wife eventually came over from the family estate north of Oklahoma City and called a news conference before the local press in Tulsa, where they announced a reward of one hundred thousand dollars for information pertinent to the case. The national media picked up the story and as we slid into late spring my pen pal Stephen suddenly became a minor celebrity, coast to coast. The "Strip Club Killer," no less.

I hadn't heard from Stoner in a week, so I decided to give him a call and rattle his cage a little. "Agent Stoner, your buddy Carlo from Prescott."

"Hey there, Detective Jardina. Call me Adam, please. What's new?"

"All right, Adam. You tell me. How's the new case going?"

"Pretty much the same story as the old one, I'm afraid. Plenty of people saw Rebecca and her killer together at the club, sitting together between her shifts, and a few remember seeing them leave together. They seemed like a very happy couple, everybody says. Very plain vanilla white dude, no distinguishing characteristics. We haven't been able to turn up any traces of his comings and goings so far. He used cash at the bar, naturally. Nobody saw his car. They left hers in the parking lot. Nobody saw or heard a thing at her apartment. He's a phantom.

"All the witnesses agree the sketch your artist did matches very well. We're circulating it all over town of course, but no luck so far."

I said, "I don't get it, Adam. What's a girl like Rebecca Reichenbach doing prostituting herself to complete strangers? I mean, she's a beautiful young lady and apparently didn't need the money. Why isn't she dating nice young guys from school or going to fraternity parties in her spare time?"

"Well," Adam said, "to be fair we don't know that she was turning tricks. Could have been a regular non-commercial one night stand. Granted, she was for a fact stripping, which is kind of in that same area lifestyle-wise. She had issues for sure."

"But she came from such a good family."

"A wealthy family. Not necessarily a good one."

"What do you mean?"

"I mean our background investigation has turned up some unpleasantness in the Reichenbach family saga. The Doctor, Rebecca's father, is a very successful and very well-respected orthopedic surgeon, but behind the scene things haven't been going all that swimmingly for a while. He has plenty of jack, that's for sure, he has the big house in the country, the fancy cars, the European vacations etc., etc. But if you believe the local gossip he also had maybe a tad too much enthusiasm when it came to being attentive to his daughter. If you know what I mean."

"I see."

"Meanwhile, back at the ranch, Mama's been carrying on with another lover for the last decade, guy by the name of Gentleman Jack."

"Huh?"

"You know, Jack Daniels. Of the Tennessee Daniels."

"Oh. So she's in the bottle."

"You are one quick study, Carlo. Yes, Mrs. Reichenbach is a hopeless alcoholic. You know, in a way I feel sorry for this poor bastard, working his ass off doing round-the-clock surgery, just to keep the country club lifestyle afloat, and he's getting neither love nor affection from the wife, so he turns to the daughter. Unfortunately the inevitable consequence of all this messiness is that our little girl is one serious head case, with a very unhealthy take on the proper way to relate to men.

"So off she goes to college in Tulsa, nice fancy private one with all the amenities, and before you know it she takes up with one of her professors, an older man predictably, the proxy father-figure. Before you know it he has her knocked up. When she tells him about the little bundle of joy on its way he dumps her, being the prince that he is, and refuses to pay for the abortion he insists she have. So she has to dip into the kitty to cover that, cause of course that happy piece of news, her being pregnant, ain't going into the weekly letter home, is it?"

I said, "I believe I'm beginning to get the picture."

"I'm sure you are, and it isn't a pretty one. It gets worse. Now Becky is thoroughly depressed over the breakup and guilty about killing her baby and even more fucked up psychologically than she was when she left home. So what's the next chapter? Drugs, of course. With which she proceeds to get completely strung out. She was reasonably straight the night she died, at least until the Rohypnol hit her, but the autopsy showed traces of Demerol and cocaine.

"So before you know it the allowance from home, generous as it is, just isn't keeping up. Becky needs cash. And this, my friend, is where the adult entertainment industry enters the story and why she found herself living a less than fairytale existence. And speaking of a less than fairytale existence, my young ass is parked in a Residence Inn down here in the sticks for God knows how long trying to show the hicks they have manning our Tulsa office how to run a professional investigation and basically waking up every day and butting my head into an effing brick wall."

I said, "You have no idea how much pleasure your unhappiness affords me. I'm going to hang up now and wallow in it."

"Yeah. You do that, detective."

* * *

The mail came about half an hour after I hung up with Stoner. Stephen's second letter came as no surprise:

Hello again, Carlo, my old friend!

How are you? Another poem to cheer you up:

Roses are red
Violets are blue
Poor Becky's a goner
And that's number two!

I must own up, I must confess
I left her place a bloody mess
Come on, Carlo, use your head
Why do you think this poor girl's dead?

Making any progress on that anagram thing, Carlo? Oops, did I let it slip about that being an anagram? Just as well. Looks to me like you could use the help. Carlo, I like you a lot but what I can find out about this Agent Stoner makes me less fond of him. His public pronouncements have certainly been uninspired. I mean, I'm flattered that the FBI is in on this, it's just that I wonder if they really are up to the task, or are they overrated? Perhaps you have some thoughts on the subject?

Becky was so wonderful, Carlo. I'm just absolutely pleased with the way our date went. You've seen photos, I hope. Didn't she look beautiful? She was a little tiger in bed, my friend, I'm here to tell you. I didn't let her in on my plans for her rather short future until after we made love, which really made it sort of special.

My God, Carlo, the look in her young eyes when I was able to make her realize that she was at death's door! It gets me all excited still, just to think about it. The way she struggled when the anagram was inscribed into her flesh, sweet Jesus, I had to stop twice and tighten the gag, I had to wet it down with water and pull until I thought it would squish her pretty head. We couldn't wake the neighbors, though, could we?

It's an amazing thing, Carlo, when you open the human body up the way I did at her throat. You don't think about how much internal pressure there is and the way the blood is just going to absolutely come gushing out, like a geyser. Exsanguination is the medical term, as you may know. It's such a lovely word, don't you think? It was a blessing for her, though, at that point, believe me. She was really wanting to go, she'd had enough and it was quick and merciful.

You know what, though? I'm sick of whores, and I'm sick of blondes. When I do the next one, and yes, I promise, there will be a next one, she's going to be a nice wholesome girl-next-door brunette, and I'm going to pick her up at a nice respectable night club. Where do you think I should go to look for her, Carlo?

Your friend, Stephen, SAD.

Post mark: Provo, UT
Encl: One Styrofoam box containing small block of dry ice, one vial of frozen human blood, one small toe, left, wrapped in cotton, with tiny shocking pink nail.

CHAPTER 20
MELANIE

Melanie Townsend was a nice, wholesome, girl-next-door-brunette, a mother of one, whose luck such as it was ran out three days before I received her killer's second letter. It was the first weekend of May that she died, a Friday night as it happened. Ironically enough she was a young lady who rarely went out, a working single mom who spent most nights at home with her four-year-old son Christopher. She'd had, what, maybe three dates since the divorce? It was just that, for whatever reason, she needed to get out of the house. One drink, that's it, at that nice quiet little club downtown, across the street from the insurance agency where she worked. Or two, but absolutely no more. Which gets her in a little bit of a horny mood, the alcohol releasing as it will the suppressed desires that all young women, even nice ones, inevitably will experience.

By happy coincidence Melanie runs into a male counterpart, a nice young man who, her feminine intuition tells her, is lonely just like she. One thing leads to another, as they say, and he is invited home for a nightcap or whatever. The babysitter reported to the police, when questioned the next day, that her companion was an average-looking fellow, quiet but seemingly okay as far as she could tell. Followed Ms. Townsend home in his own car, a pretty gold one, Utah plates. Walked her safely across the street to her own house but never said anything to her except good night.

The effect of the evening's encounter on the psyche of young Chris, who found his mother's body the next morning, is uncertain, something we can only contemplate with horror and may not be able to measure clinically for years. Seriously damaging, no doubt. The effect on Melanie is, unfortunately, more well-defined. Stephen has performed his task with cruel efficiency and she has gone with much ado to meet her maker and, we can hope, to life in a new and kinder world.

The final sad chapter of her life, written just two weeks shy of her thirty-second birthday, comes spilling out of an orange and purple FedEx envelope, sent up from Phoenix by my buddy Agent Adam Stoner. Clipped to the stack of photographs is a short note that says "numero tres," and "good call on the car color."

She is lying, as was Mary, on her bed, except that it's a four-poster and her legs are splayed in a vertical *V* and her ankles are elevated and bound to the posts at the foot of the bed with heavy leather cords. Her bottom is thus perched at the very edge of the near end of the mattress, actually overhanging it slightly and her genitalia are inelegantly exposed. A long length of heavy cord is looped several times around her lower torso, at the point where her legs angle up from her body, running just along the top of her pubis and from there the ends are anchored securely to the bed rails on either side, thus keeping her movements well-restrained. Twin ladders of lash marks climb upwards from her crotch along the inside of her thighs.

My eye travels involuntarily to her mutilated abdomen, and the letters are as with Mary burned in with a relatively steady hand, thank God. He waited for her to die first. The experience with Rebecca must have spooked him.

Her arms are stretched above her head and handcuffed, and the handcuffs are in turn secured by ropes leading at divergent angles to both posts at the head of the bed. Her wrists are savagely bruised where in her death struggle she's tried to free her hands from their metal grip. The accustomed accoutrements lie on the mattress on either side of her arms. Her nails are done in a nice Kelly green, to match her eyes, which as expected are open.

He's back to strangulation; no doubt he found all that blood spurting out of Rebecca so untidily to be a little off-putting. The piano wire and dowel remain this time around her throat, which bears multiple swollen rings of trauma à la Mary Bergstrom. Her head is also propped up through her arms by a bolster pillow so that her face is readily visible as soon as her bedroom door is opened. Except that it was easier achieving this posture with her, as subsequent photos taken after she's been moved reveal that her neck has been snapped like a rag doll's.

The odd thing is that her face, arms and upper torso bear multiple scratches and contusions. Clearly there was a physical struggle before she was subdued, and a fairly violent one at that. Obviously Stephen eventually got the better of her, but he couldn't have come out of the confrontation unscathed. This is a curious departure from his normal MO. Walking around with scratches on your face would not be the preferred way to go if you're a serial killer. So why no drugs?

Also, Melanie is much more of a regular girl, it seems to me, by which I mean that she is no stunner. Her face is pretty enough, better than average, but she is certainly no match in the looks department for her two fellow victims. Nor is her body, while again trim and attractive enough, nearly as voluptuous as those of her ecdysiast predecessors. Mr. Stephen is definitely widening his net.

The autopsy report reveals yet another new twist. There is no semen present at the crime scene, though all the other indicia of Stephen's presence are there. Inside Melanie's body are traces of water-based lubricant laced with nonoxydol-9 spermicide, consistent with the use of a prophylactic. Why he would choose to break out the Trojans at this stage of the game is a complete mystery to me, unless he plans to treat me to a sick joke about safe sex in his next letter.

Thank you too much, Adam, for keeping me in the loop.

CHAPTER 21
STONER

He sounded very tired when he picked up. Stephen was really killing his *joie*. "Good afternoon, Adam," I said, "how's my favorite G-man?"

"Starting to feel some heat, Carlo, now that you mention it. The press are pit bulls. Yourself?"

"Yeah, we need to talk about that. But I'm fine. The good people of Prescott gave up on me solving this thing a long time ago."

"You got my package, then?"

"Sure did. Actually it was a big day for me, correspondence-wise. Another letter from our friend came in with the morning mail. I was just getting ready to call when the FedEx truck rolled up."

"Post mark Provo?"

"Correct."

"So you were right. He doesn't post until the latest girl's dead. They're getting nastier, detective. We really need to nail this motherless fuck. This last one, she's a much more sympathetic victim than the other two. One thing when whores are getting clipped. Quite another when somebody out there's creating orphans."

"I feel your pain, Adam, believe me. Looks to me like it's not just the type of victim that was different, but the MO as well."

"That's a fact, Carlo. The Townsend girl didn't go down quite as easily as the other two. Looks like there was a major battle before he subdued her. The bedroom's a mess, and her fingernails had his flesh and blood under them. He's scratched up pretty good, I'd guess. He may have to stick around the house for a while."

"What happened?"

"Clearly he couldn't get the drop on her like the others before. She had nothing in her in the way of drugs, so he just had to take her by force.

You have to hand it to her. She put up a good fight till he got the handcuffs on her."

"So why wouldn't he have used Rohypnol to sedate her?"

"My guess is he just never had the opportunity. In the case of Mary Bergstrom we assume he put it in her drink at the club, right? With Rebecca, we found traces of it in a glass at her place, and of course it was in her bloodstream big time. We figure he gave it to her just before they had sex. Shortly after which she fell asleep and of course when she woke up she was trussed up like a Christmas turkey.

"With Melanie, it was a different deal. He couldn't give her anything at the club, because she was driving her own car home with him following. So he figures they'll have a little nightcap when they get to her place, but guess what? This is Utah, Carlo. The club they met in was a brown bagger...you bring your own bottle and they sell you the mixers. Which she did, the only bottle of booze in her whole house, which they finished off before leaving. He probably tried to get her to have a drink of water or juice or whatever, but she wasn't thirsty and wouldn't cooperate. Therefore, the epic death struggle. It's amazing the kid didn't wake up or the neighbors didn't hear anything. He was one angry dude over it too, I'll tell you. He brought her to within an inch of death with the wire and then he just twisted her head nearly off her neck as payback."

"How's the kid doing?"

"Her son? How do you think he's doing, detective? He's in a very bad state. He's a freaking mess. He's the one who found his mom, in the morning, if you'll recall."

"Yes I know. I don't even like to think about that picture."

"Protective services has him with his aunt, her sister, for now."

"Luckily he's very young. Perhaps he'll get over it, in time."

"Maybe. But my money's on *not a chance*."

I didn't even want to go down that road. I glanced at the map on my wall, now sporting a brand new pin, and asked him, "So, have you got your third marker on the map?"

"Yes I do. Why?"

"Just wondering if we can infer anything about his home base from the three locations, is all. They seem fairly evenly spaced."

"I guess in theory the more pins we get the better our guess about where he's coming from."

"Exactly. For example, say we fit a circle through the three cities. Think he's in the center?"

"I don't know, Carlo. We now know that he's traveling great distances to do these killings, to as far as we can tell randomly chosen towns. Does this mean he sits in his living room and spins a bottle to tell him which direction to go? And then does he always go about the same distance?"

I say, "I would guess near enough. His constraints are the fact that he's driving, at the speed limit I'm sure, and that he probably has only so much time to be away."

"Maybe. Maybe not. Then there's always the fact that he's a clever little bastard and he knows we're going to have this sort of conversation. So he could easily be manipulating us. Hell, face it, he could live anywhere."

"Have you been following up with the Departments of Motor Vehicles to see about stolen plates?"

"Not really. What good would that do?"

"Think about it, Adam. He's probably always stopping short of his final destination, to hole up and rest for the evening. That's when he's stealing the plates, or did in the Prescott case. That tells us the direction of his approach. Find where he stopped before Tulsa and Provo, you have two more lines of approach. Run them backwards, maybe they converge."

"Hmm. Maybe. Maybe not. I'll look into it."

"Would you, please?"

"So what's the deal, detective, you call just to pass the time of day with a little chit chat?"

"No. I have to ask you something. The local ABC affiliate in Phoenix is sending a reporter up to interview me. I'm sure they're looking for a progress report, which could make for an uncomfortable conversation. Anyway, I need to know what I can talk about and what I can't."

"Who they sending?"

"I don't know, some lady with an Indian-sounding name."

"Lolita Redfeather?"

"Yeah, that's the one."

"God help you."

"What do you mean?"

"Lolita Redfeather just happens to be the most hated and feared news correspondent in Phoenix. She's basically your worst nightmare on wheels. She's a nasty combination of attitude and ambition who has a problem with men in general and men in uniform in particular. She's two years out of journalism school and she's looking to build her brand as one tough bitch of a reporter. She's looking to go network, she's looking for scalps and she doesn't care whose she takes. Get the picture?"

"Yes I do. So you're saying don't do the interview?"

"Well, answering the call was your first mistake, that's for sure. But no, at this point wimping out would be even worse. Christ, she'd crucify you and you'd have no chance to defend yourself. No, just be prepared and be damn careful. Watch your step."

"I'll do that."

"You'll be damn lucky if they don't indict your ass when she gets through with you. Anyway, say nothing about the way we found these girls, please, the way they were bound and posed. Manner of death is okay, personal information on them and their families is pretty much out there, so I doubt she'll ask. If she does, tell her. Nobody needs to know we have prints and semen, and nobody sure as hell needs to know about any witnesses we may have, like the babysitter in Provo for example. Obviously, the fact that you and our boy are pen pals goes unmentioned. And for God's sake, whatever else you do you will not tell her about the letters on the bodies. We don't need that being emulated. Other than that, just feel free to talk away. Make sure she pronounces my name correctly."

"Thanks, Adam."

"Don't mention it, Detective Jardina."

"Oh, by the way. I almost forgot. Speaking of my pen pal. He sent me some more souvenirs along with his letter."

"Jesus, why didn't you say so?"

"I was getting to it, Adam, relax. He included some physical evidence, one item of which I believe belongs to victim number two, Rebecca Reichenbach. Or belonged, rather. You might want to shag your ass up here to take a look."

"Yeah, why don't I shag my ass up there to take a look? First thing in the morning. It'll be good to get out of the field office. Phoenix is already starting to get hot."

"I'll count the minutes."

"See, I knew you were missing me. Buy me lunch?"

"Sure, why not. We can do Mexican. I have a great little spot. Just promise not to let word get around that we're seeing each other."

"I'll keep it to myself."

"And don't bring me flowers."

"I guess holding hands is out of the question, then?"

"Not in public, sweetheart."

When I hung up with Stoner I decided to have a quick peek at the computer. Nothing good was shaking. To be honest, tragic as they were the serial killings were beginning to lose their hold on my interest. For all practical purposes I was a bystander in the investigation. Stephen had hit Prescott and moved on to other jurisdictions. Had he not taken a shine to me and started sending me letters I doubt the FBI would even be bothering to keep me in the picture.

The fact was I had two correspondents trying to pull me over to the dark side, and the other was much more intriguing. She was the one keeping me up nights, keeping my mind in a constant state of turmoil, pinning me onto the horns of the most anguishing dilemma I'd ever faced, filling my every waking moment with a bittersweet combination of excitement and dread, and threatening to turn my well-ordered little world completely upside down. At the end of the day it was Jezebel who dominated my thoughts and authored my discontent.

I picked up the phone once more and invited myself to dinner with Amy and Shannon. After reviewing Melanie's package and spending a few moments in contemplation of my relationship with my dark queen, I figured a visit to their sunny little island of sanity was in order. I very much needed to regroup.

CHAPTER 22
AMY

Stoner's comments regarding the weather downstate notwithstanding, in the high country of Prescott we were having ourselves a splendid evening. There was a northerly breeze and the first days of spring were providing us warm sunny days and cool nights. I stopped by the market to pick up a couple of steaks to grill outdoors for Amy and me, plus hamburger patties and hot dogs for the princess.

Amy greeted me with a big hug at the front door and I caught a whiff of the same strawberry-scented shampoo that Shannon used. In the way that familiar smells can sometimes do, the sensation pushed a big emotional button for me. What the hell was I doing mucking around in the sick worlds of Stephen and Jezebel when there was this whole bright and clean and fresh and white-picket world of innocent, guilt-free domesticity? The sort of world where a man could just put his feet up and enjoy the simple but enduring pleasures life without drama offers, the kind of untroubled existence Poppy wanted so badly for me?

In any case, we had a very nice dinner together that evening, punctuated for the most part by the ceaseless babbling of Shannon catching me up on the latest varied and fascinating details of her busy young life, while Amy and I sipped cabernet with our steaks and exchanged frequent glances that hinted at amusement and perhaps something more. Shannon went with the hot dogs.

So the dinner dishes have been cleaned and the trash taken out, the girl is in bed and Amy and I sit down on her living room couch to talk.

I say, "We got us another dead girl, I'm afraid."

"The poor girl in Utah? I heard about it. It's been all over the news."

"Of course, it would be. Our pal's a real star now. Anyway, I received another letter from him, with some...some physical evidence. Stoner's coming up in the morning."

"That's just plain creepy, Carlo, the way he's writing to you."

"You're telling me, kid. If it weren't for that I'd be out of it and I could go back to being just another small town cop."

"Any sense that they're getting closer to finding him?"

"None whatsoever. The analysis that you and I did way back on day one has turned out to be right on. There's just nothing to get a hook into with this guy. It's going to take a lucky break to catch him. Maybe a random traffic stop and they run his stolen plates and find out they don't match his car. Or maybe someone who knows him gets suspicious and drops a dime. That sort of thing. Low probability, though."

There followed a long period of silence, and then of all things, Amy says, "Carlo, you mind if I ask you a personal question?" She scoots her bottom ever so slightly closer to me.

"Of course not, Amy, what do you want to know?"

I'm fully anticipating an interrogation about the state of my affair with Jezebel, so I'm bowled over when she asks, "How come you never made a pass at me?"

My God, Amy, this is going to take some thought. A couple of minutes go by in silence, and then I say, "You want the short answer or the long?"

"How about both, in that order."

"All right. The short. I assume you're enough of a woman to know that I find you attractive, and believe me I do. I've thought about you, that way, many times. I'll be very straight with you, Amy. I've fantasized about you and the fantasies have been very explicit, okay? So your feminine pride is intact; it is not involved here. Additionally I've daydreamed of being Shannon's step dad, and the three of us being a cozy little family. You know how I feel about her. The short answer is that you're too young, and the difference in our ages is just inappropriate. There is also the fact that workplace romances are rarely a good idea."

Another few minutes go by while my answer is considered. "And the long?"

"The long answer, Amy, is about me, and my inadequacies and my male pride, and it's probably not really longer, just more embarrassing. What if I made a pass at you and you weren't interested? I told you I'm not good at reading women, never have been. I was just never sure how you felt. Admit it, you're carrying a very heavy torch for Brian, and if I were to breech that, to disrespect a fellow cop's memory with unwanted attention to his widow, how awful would that be? We work together and we see each other almost daily. How would you like to live with that uncomfortable situation?"

"I might have made an exception for you, Carlo. You are a special man."

"Yeah, well, thanks for saying it but I'm maybe not as special as you'd like to think. Sometimes I think I'm not even a good man."

"Come on, Carlo."

"Whatever. The truth is I'm a coward, I'm a man who saw something good, something worth having, and didn't have the balls to risk his precious ego and go after it and now you've had your unabridged answer and no one is sorrier than I and I can only remind you of what you said in the park that day."

"Which was?"

"Let's not, Carlo, you said. Not today."

At that moment I came within a whisker of simply picking her up, carrying her to her bedroom, undressing her and making passionate love to her. Of proposing marriage on the spot. Of making her my bride, adopting Shannon, and settling down to live the idyllic life of a family man. Of spending the rest of my natural days loving her, playing with Shannon, mowing the lawn, building her a white picket fence and chasing down jaywalkers and shoplifters for a living. Of growing old with her at my side and tottering off into the sunset after a long and blessedly uneventful life.

But I didn't, did I? Part of it was a suspicion that I'd be doing Amy a huge favor remaining on the periphery of her life. She thought of me as a good man, but obviously the validity of that opinion was in serious question. There was a battle raging for my soul, it seemed, and I had come to realize there was a dark part of me that I'm sure she never saw. Maybe Jezebel was wrong, maybe we *are* the product of our childhood and our genetic heritage. If so I was in deep trouble.

Beyond that was a simple fact that no one, not even Amy, could know: I had certain unavoidable obligations.

And, finally, there was Jezebel, wasn't there? Amy was my sun, but Jez pulled at me like the moon pulls the tides. Always, there was her presence.

One of the few things my mother left me was a little piece of Scottish wisdom: *Danger and delight grow on the same stalk.*

CHAPTER 23
ANTONIO'S COYOTE CAFE

My whole life I never knew a cop to be late for a free meal, and Adam was no exception. He showed up at the station right at lunch time, and so I walked him the four blocks to Antonio's Coyote Café and treated him to a local legend, the house *burrito grande*. This particular culinary offering is the size of a regulation NFL football, blue corn tortilla stuffed with every conceivable Mexican food staple you can imagine and a few you wouldn't in a hundred years, seasoned Santa Fe style and smothered in an orange-colored *habanero* sauce, the consumption of which can only be described as a genuinely cathartic experience. I believe Antonio sells them at cost just to drive beer sales. You have one for lunch, you are good for the rest of the day, trust me.

Agent Stoner prefers not to discuss business in a public setting, and so I am tiptoeing around it, just to keep the conversation going as I watch him keep the knife and fork cranking.

"Any progress on that project you were working on, then?" I ask.

Between bites he says, "Nah. Our competitor has a very efficient business model. Can't say for sure which of us goes under first."

"Here I thought you had the best product on the market."

Which remark earns me a nasty look as he takes a swig from his Corona and wipes the sheen of perspiration from his face. I have begun to soften my attitude of late toward Agent Stoner. He has turned out to be a nicer man than I originally suspected, with a lovely wife and three lovely children and a dog. I realize that arrogance is just part of the institutional milieu of the FBI and his should not really be held against him. This does not mean, however, that I cannot take the occasional shot, nor that I cannot derive secret enjoyment from the fact that he's downing his burrito much too fast and the heat is going to catch up with him, with a vengeance. Your *habanero* pepper is a crafty little critter that will sneak up on you.

"No problem with our product, Carlo," he finally answers. "We're just selling to a different customer."

"Fair enough. That does seem to be a large market he's tapped into."

"Virtually limitless. Many, many *emptors* out there failing to *caveat*."

"Amen, brother."

"Christ, what do they put in these effing burritos?"

I laugh and give the high sign to Antonio. "Fire, amigo. Pure fire. I was wondering when you were gonna notice."

Antonio sets a tall cold glass of chocolate milk on the table in front of Adam, and I say, "Drink up. It's the absolute best antidote."

Back at the station we sat down to talk in the war room, a term that was beginning to sound more ironic by the day. Dust and cobwebs pretty much told the story. I had tacked copies of Stephen's letters to the wall with the post-it notes, and added a map of the U.S. to the back wall, with three black pins marking the murder sites. The original of his last letter, along with what I assumed were Rebecca's toe and blood sample, were boxed with dry ice and waiting on the table for Adam.

I said, "So nothing, then?"

"Correct you are my friend. Nada. It's going to take a mistake on his part to nab him. So far he's been perfect."

"If we could just get some idea of where he's going to go next, you know if we could just find a pattern."

"Then what? What if we could? What do we do, put out an alert, scare the holy crap out of half a state, just so he can change his plans and make fools of us? Plus no one ever believes us again."

"Well, just look at the map. I'm seeing Denver as a very likely domicile for him. From there he spokes out to Prescott, Tulsa and Provo."

"Wonderful, Carlo. So now we have it narrowed down to, what, a million men?"

"I know, I know, but what if we look at the remaining directions. We pick the likely ones, we make sure local law enforcement is looking for reports of stolen plates, we get a hit we know where he's headed."

"We?"

"Okay, you. The FBI."

"Which brings us back to our original problem. We put out a warning, he changes plans. It's not just strip clubs he's working now, so anything we do has to be very public and very broadly disseminated. Anyway, he's in and out too fast for the license plates to help. You said yourself he's stealing them from long term parking."

"All right. I give up."

"Splendid idea, detective. I wish I could, believe me. So let me complete the paperwork and I'll be on my way with your package. It'll be winging its way to Quantico by tomorrow morning. And thanks much for lunch. I'm very hopeful that I'll have the feeling back in my mouth by the time I reach Phoenix."

"It was my pleasure. Really. Have a safe drive."

"Hey, speaking of Quantico. I meant to tell you earlier. Our lab boys got a hit on a fiber you gave us, from the Bergstrom scene."

"No kidding."

"Yeah. Turns out it was a special dye lot for a run of knit fabric made in China. It was used exclusively to manufacture a big production of polo shirts in Hong Kong for Target. They're absolutely sure it belongs to a piece the killer wore."

"And so where do you go from there?"

"Oh trust me, it's a big breakthrough. We have agents posted outside every Target store in America, all 1,685 of them, 24/7. They each have instructions to be on the lookout for an average looking white dude in a new polo shirt."

CHAPTER 24
LOLITA REDFEATHER

And so the day arrives for Lolita Redfeather to come calling. She, the avenging angel of the Arizona Fourth Estate, electronic division, point woman for the news department of KPHX-TV in Phoenix, raker of muck, righter of wrongs, inquisitor for the people. Her figure is tall, her bearing noble, her presence commanding. She is surrounded by the seraphim, some of whom bear cameras, lights, recorders and other tools of the trade, and some of whom apply her war paint. She stands confidently and handsomely astride the wide spectrum of the American patchwork quilt, her father the reddest of native Americans and her mother the latterest of latter day south-of-the-border immigrants. It's I for whom she comes, it's my scalp she covets, and my heart is filled with trepidation. A constructive dialogue with a cell of terrorists would be less scary. As far as I have been able to determine, they have nothing like her killer instinct.

"So, Detective Jardina," she asks me, as tape rolls and a pregnant hush descends upon my office, and though I say asks it's really not a question. "One wonders why, as the first official to encounter this dangerous serial killer, you weren't more aggressive in getting the word out. I mean, two more girls may have died needlessly, isn't this so?"

I'm sitting on the corner of my desk, the window a backdrop, and attempting to look casual and, well, vindicated. "I would first point out to you, Ms. Redfeather, in all fairness, that when Mary Bergstrom was killed, the perpetrator of that horrible crime was not, technically, a serial killer. You would need a minimum of two murders for them to be serial..."

"Oh, but isn't that just playing with semantics, detective? After all, I understand that many of the classic signs of serial killings were there with the Bergstrom girl's death. Couldn't a competent professional have picked up on that? Perhaps gotten some kind of warning out to the public?"

"We did in fact observe the signs you refer to, yes, and I'll grant you that we fully anticipated the possibility of more attacks. None of them are conclusive, by the way, the details you refer to. As for warnings, you see, we always face something of a dilemma in cases like this..."

"I've heard rumors that he's even written to you and told you more were coming..."

"I wouldn't comment on rumors at this point, sorry, but I was making the point that we always have to balance whatever good a warning to the public might do with the damage."

"What possible damage could be done by the public having full information?"

"Well, now, I understand that I'm treading on territory that is very near and dear to your heart as a journalist, but the fact is that often publicity in a situation such as this can trigger copycat killings. You would be surprised what you news people sometimes flush out of the woodwork, no offense. Against that is the fact that warnings of the sort you speak of rarely do much good. I mean, shouldn't every woman know already that it's a bad idea to pick up a strange man in a bar and bring him home? Do one or two more incidents in a country of three hundred something million people really make that more true than it already is?"

"Sounds very cavalier to me, Detective Jardina."

"I'm just saying..."

And so it goes for the next five to ten minutes or so, during which my professional competence and integrity, not to mention my all around decency as a human being, are called very publicly and none too subtly into question. Finally the prosecution rests, and her interrogation turns to the details of the investigation at large.

"And now, of course, the FBI is heavily involved and we have three dead young women in three different states, one of whom left a child behind," she says accusingly.

"Sadly so."

"They won't talk to us, the FBI I mean, so I'd like to ask you, in general, how the investigation is going. Has their participation hurried things along? Are you any closer at all to an arrest than you were the day Mary Bergstrom's body was discovered?"

This lady is one to go for the jugular, all right; her reputation is well-deserved. "That's a bit of an unfair question. Briefly I would say yes, of course we're closer. That doesn't mean we're close, however. An investigation like this is never easy. These are random acts against random victims, 'stranger killings' in law enforcement vernacular. They are the most difficult type of murder to solve. As an investigator there's little to sink one's teeth into.

"I can tell you that in the case of the victim here in Prescott our CSI technicians were unable to give us anything to work with. The FBI tells me the two cases they've handled had among the cleanest crime scenes they've ever encountered. The individual we're hunting clearly has more than a passing familiarity with forensic science. Personally, I suspect he may have studied criminal justice or may even be employed in some aspect of the criminal justice system."

"So you're saying he may be a police officer?"

"Not necessarily. I wouldn't want to be that specific. But yes, that's a possibility. I couldn't rule it out."

"God help us."

"God help us indeed. So, we plug along, and we put tiny bits of information on the table and try to make a picture, and maybe one day we get lucky and the right piece comes along and falls into place. You never know where that piece is going to come from, or when. Even the cleverest of criminals eventually makes a mistake. But honestly, it could take a very long time."

"How long?"

"I can't be optimistic. Based on previous examples, we might be looking at years."

"While innocent women continue to die?"

She is getting my back up for me now. "Yes, Ms. Redfeather. Unfortunately, while innocent women continue to die. He could just stop, sometimes they do, in which case we may never catch him. But if he continues to kill, he'll make a mistake. We'll catch a break. We'll get him."

"Really?" This said with the arch of brow and tone of voice that says, boy doesn't that make me feel much better, aren't I relieved? "Do you have any solid clues?"

"A few that we're working on look promising. Nothing I could share with you."

"Any ideas on where the killer may strike next?"

"I'm fairly certain I can name you three towns where he won't, based on what I've seen so far." I point to the map on the wall to my right, the map from the war room relocated for the occasion, and I say, "As you can see from those pins, he appears to be working the western half of the States, primarily. Roughly a thousand mile radius of action so far, but of course that's not a guarantee…he could strike anywhere at any time. Meantime, for the ladies out there, I would have this advice: you want to meet men, go to church mixers or singles' clubs or something. And make your first date a public one."

"Well, thank you very much, Detective Carlo Jardina, for your time and admonition. I know the citizens of Arizona are going to feel much better when they see how diligently you're working on this."

And pull away for the head shot into the camera. "For now, this is Lolita Redfeather, reporting from Prescott. Good night and God bless."

As her entourage ushers her and the truckload of equipment out of my office the thought crosses my mind that maybe Adam isn't so dumb after all, not talking to the press. While licking my wounds I begin to wonder about that unusual first name of hers. Until now the only Lolita I've ever encountered is the sexually precocious title character of the Nabokov novel. It turns out that "Lolita" is a diminutive for "Dolores," which is Spanish for "suffering." So nobody can accuse her of false advertising.

I'm trying to figure a way to get Stephen to visit the KPHX studios in Phoenix when Eric De Leon comes shuffling down the corridor past my door, singing an awful rendition of Roy Orbison's *Crying* in Spanglish. "Hey Eric," I yell out to him, "what did you do with the money?"

"What money?" he shouts back.

"The money your mother gave you for singing lessons."

"Oh, that money. That money I spent for a night with your sister."

CHAPTER 25
LAUGHLIN

In the end, after all the agonizing and equivocating, it was just as simple as waking up one morning and writing out the note to Jezebel, the note that set our next meeting. When opportunity knocks, you open the door, and the fact of the matter was that Jezebel presented an opportunity I just couldn't pass up. Nothing ventured, nothing gained I believe is the current wisdom, moral complications be damned. And so, on an early summer Saturday morning, I saddled up the cruiser once more and headed west.

The Colorado River, living aqueous heart of the American West, begins its long journey just this side of the continental divide, high up in the Rocky Mountains of its namesake state. It then spills down the windward slopes of the Front Range watershed into southwestern Colorado, where it joins the Gunnison at Grand Junction. Sun-warmed and muddy, it wanders in a serpentine path through the southeastern corner of Utah, gathering more volume at its confluence with the Green River. Thereafter it begins to descend into the deep channels and broad canyons it's sawn over the centuries into the stone strata of the high desert plateau of southern Utah and northern Arizona. It flows into Lake Powell, a huge manmade lake that sprawls across the red and brown-painted rock moonscape of the Utah-Arizona border.

It emerges from the base of Glen Canyon Dam a different river, lake-bottom water now, clear and cold, to make a long passage through the Grand Canyon, during which it falls from 2800 feet above sea level to 1200. At times the bed narrows and it runs white in rapids and cataracts. In other places the bottom flattens out and it slows and broadens, with sandy beaches and stands of willows and cottonwoods. At the southwestern end of the canyon it finally empties into Lake Meade.

Pushing through the concrete and steel interior of Hoover Dam it spins the turbines that power the lights of Las Vegas, then turns south toward

Baja and runs along the California-Arizona border. Along the way it's tapped and bled to irrigate the thousand thirsty farms of southwestern Arizona and the Coachella and Imperial Valleys of California. Finally, exhausted, it not so much flows but rather seeps into the marshy northern shore of the Sea of Cortez.

Between Vegas and the Mexican border are two more man-made lakes. More notably, there is Havasu, where the weather is hot but the water and beer are ice cold. "Have-a-few," as it's known to the regulars, is a popular spot for Southern Californians to congregate on weekends and holidays in order to jet ski, wakeboard, sunbathe naked, drink to excess and engage in other assorted unwise, unsafe and impolite activities. Fun in the sun, as they say.

And then, a few miles upstream, there is Lake Mojave. At its southern tip is my destination: the fine little city of Laughlin, NV. This particular community enjoys a felicitous location at the intersection of CA, AZ and NV and has thus grown over the years into a secondary gambling destination, catering to those Californians not disposed to make the longer journey to Vegas. It is no Las Vegas, however. A mere handful of casinos are strung along the west bank of the river, none of which can compete with big sister's glitz, and the clientele are more likely to arrive in buses than planes or automobiles. As it happens, the demographics skew a little more to the AARP-friendly end of the spectrum.

All of which is precisely what recommends it to me for this particular meeting, as the likelihood of Jezzie running into any of her status-conscious, social-climbing little friends is vanishingly small. And all of which is bound to buy me a whole load of grief from her, at least until the good news gets delivered.

Prescott is more than a mile above sea level, and its elevation has thus far afforded us a mild spring. But summer has come in hot and heavy, with dry desert winds blowing in from the west, and today I'm reminded that here in the high country we're just that much closer to the sun. I jump in my car at 0800 but already it's sweltering. I slip my sunglasses onto my face and punch up the A/C. I hit the play button on the cassette. Johnny Cash is falling into a ring of fire, and I know how he feels.

The road from Prescott to Laughlin begins with AZ-89 north to pick up I-40 heading west toward Kingman, where I'm relieved to put the blindingly incandescent sun at my back and pick up some speed on the four-lane. This is not a scenic drive. The winds have raised a dusty haze into the air, foreshortening the horizon. The vegetation is sparse and sickly-looking now that the short rainy season is over and the wildflower blooms are gone. The shimmering asphalt is too hot even for the rattlers. The parched terrain is colored in shades of brown and the animals have all put up closed-for-business signs and are hunkered down in burrows and under rocks. Their day doesn't start until the sun goes down. The lone exception is a red-tailed hawk wheeling high in a cloudless sky to the north and west, free-riding on the hot desert updrafts. The highway is relatively straight, though, and I make good time.

The topography of this part of the country has been corrugated by the relentless pressure of the Pacific tectonic plate pushing against the North American, and so the interstate proceeds across a series of hills and valleys, a feature which affords some visual relief from the otherwise monotonous view.

Past Kingman I pick up AZ-68 and shortly thereafter I am dropping into the Mojave Valley with the Colorado in view in the distance. It's a narrow deep-green band of vegetation, the riverbed, cutting through the sand-colored valley floor, with a black stripe of water running through its center. To the west lies the trackless expanse of the Mojave Desert, stretching from Las Vegas to the Northeast, Death Valley and the Sierra Nevada to the Northwest, and south to the San Bernardino Mountains, the northern flank of the Los Angeles basin.

I pass through the northern outskirts of Bullhead City AZ, cross the bridge into Nevada, the river blue now, and turn south along Casino Drive. It's shortly before 1100. I told Jezebel 1400 sharp.

I cruise slowly down Casino, passing the five or six big hotels strung along the riverbank to my left. They look like so many alien monoliths, dropped improbably onto the earth by some extraterrestrial life form, completely incongruent with the otherwise stark undeveloped landscape. Too crowded for my purposes; I'm headed someplace a little more isolated.

I spot a fast food place on the right side of the street and swing in to grab a hamburger and coke, which I eat and drink sitting in the parking lot, engine running to keep the cool air coming, killing time.

Moving on down the road I finally see the establishment I'm looking for, the Riverside Motel. Here is where I have reserved a room, and here I have instructed Jez to meet me. This is a place of lodging that looks just about like what one would imagine a motel at the very tail end of the strip in Laughlin NV to look like. Fifties architecture. Faded pastel paint scheme. Two story row of rooms with office at one end and balcony with iron railing running the length up top. Refreshing Pool/Free Cable/HBO/ Free Breakfast. No fancy cars in the lot, yet. No well-heeled ladies from Westlake, yet. No false advertising here, though: it truly is by the side of the river, which flows sedately past its rear grounds.

I park in front of the office, check in, swing the cruiser around to park directly in front of my room, as I'd promised her I would, pull my suitcase out of the trunk and let myself in. Turn the window air-conditioning unit to max, flip the TV on and tune into a baseball game on ESPN. Flop onto the bed, tuck a couple of flat motel pillows under my head, and close my eyes to wait for her.

I doze briefly, but awake just before two, and am watching with the curtains pulled back when she pulls up, right on time, in her shiny Benz. Punctuality is without a doubt her finest virtue. I can see when she steps from her automobile that she is way overdressed, and that she is very much less than pleased now she's recognized said fact. She looks splendid, though, and amazingly sexy. I'm instantly struck with a powerful reminder of why I love her so.

She is dressed in black, perhaps in an effort to color-coordinate with her heart. I open the door for her and she steps in without a word.

Today I have decided to skip the opening ceremonies. I really need to get to it as soon as possible and without fanfare. As I anticipated, she is deeply disappointed with the déclassé status of our rendezvous spot. This is evident just to see her face, even before she opens her mouth. For some perverse reason this fact itself amuses me. Maybe my guilt is putting me in a sadistic mood. Needless to say, my enjoyment is short-lived.

"Pleasant trip, baby?" I ask her.

"So, Carlo," she says, ignoring my inquiry. "You really know how to show a girl a good time, don't you? What am I doing in this godforsaken dump, please?"

"Got my reasons, sweetheart. I believe you may approve. Allow me to explain." I sat her down on the end of the queen bed that pretty much filled the room. I grabbed a cassette recorder from my suitcase and sat down next to her. When I pressed the play and record buttons she asked, "What's that for?"

"This, Jezzie, is an insurance policy. Because I said I love you, and I do, but I never said I trusted you."

"Carlo, what the hell are you talking about?"

"I'm talking about the fact that I've decided to do this thing you've asked of me. I've decided to address your Roger problem in a manner that is, let's say, final and irreversible. And this will be a crime the execution of which by its very design will leave you well-insulated, will have to, and yours truly on the other hand rather exposed. So in case you have an unexpected change of heart down the line, or sudden memory loss, I will need to have proof that you have been my co-conspirator from the beginning. That means I'm taping our next twenty minutes or so of conversation, one copy only ever to exist, said copy of course to be in a place of safekeeping chosen by me and unknown to you, from which it automatically surfaces in the event of my sudden demise. Sorry, Jezzie. It's been said that to live outside the law you must be honest, and honest is what I plan to keep you."

Jezebel lights a cigarette and takes a pause for thought. A big smile slowly works its way across her face. She leans across the space between us and gives me a big hug. "Carlo, that's great, baby. I love you. I'm going to make you so happy."

I say, "I hope so Jez. God knows I do. Just don't ever try to convince me that what we're doing is right, or try to justify it. It's wrong, and you can never."

"So what brought you around?"

"Maybe it's as simple as I love you. Maybe I've come to believe that it would be just great for my own sake to have the things I'll never have on a civil servant's salary, the things only money buys, or maybe I'm afraid you could never be happy without them, with or without me. Maybe I feel certain that if I don't do it you'll find someone who will, and he'll probably fuck it up and you'll spend the rest of your life making love to women, which would be an unthinkable waste. The truth is I've had a taste of honey and I want more, and I know that means I must do this thing for you. But Jezebel…"

"Yes, Carlo?"

"This is going to be my operation, darling. I'm calling all the shots, period. Understand? There will be two rules between us from this point forward. Rule one: Carlo is always right. Rule two: If you suspect Carlo is wrong, refer to rule one. I'm putting my ass on the line for you here. I've thought this thing through and I know what I'm doing. So make up your mind right now. This arrangement is either acceptable to you or not. Yes or no. Down the line, if there's a moment's hesitation on your part or failure to follow my instructions perfectly and unquestioningly, I'm out and the whole thing is over, and so are we most likely, but I can live with that, I'm not going to prison for anyone, not even you. Okay?"

"Sure, baby, sure. Of course, that's fine."

She's been puffing away all this time, filling the room with menthol-laden smoke. There is a long period of silence, now, while she finishes the last of her cigarette and grinds it out into an ashtray on the end table. Finally she says, "Tell me more, Carlo."

"All right. The key to me killing someone and getting away with it is, of course, to eliminate any ties between myself and the victim. Which of course means between me and you and explains what we're doing in this dump. This means from here forward we see each other only on an as-needed basis until after it's done, which I figure may be a six month project or more. Never, never in public, it goes without saying. There will be conversations required that can only be held face to face. Also, I'll be needing cash from you. Obviously, when we do meet it's always going to be somewhere far from Southern California or Prescott. Maybe right here again; I like this joint."

"Six months? Why six months?"

"I'll get to that. That's an outside number by the way, just preparing you. May I continue?"

She treats me to a chastened smile, pushes her lower lip out and nods her head.

"The first one they'll look at is you, naturally, and they'll take a good hard look so you have to be absolutely pure and the proud owner of a bulletproof alibi. You can't even be in the same state when I whack him.

"His death will be one of those lamentable and senseless acts of violence we detest so much, a random robbery gone wrong. I'm in a position naturally to follow national crime trends. I'm logged on to the FBI's website on a regular ongoing basis as part of my investigation into the Bergstrom murder. Crime streaks pop up in isolated clusters all the time, across the country. We need the sort of robbery that targets tourists. For example, maybe in Chicago a ring of women posing as prostitutes or lonely tourists on the prowl are working hotel lobby lounges and drugging guests in order to clean out their rooms. Or maybe in Kansas City a guy gets a bug up his ass and starts sticking a pistol into people's ribs on elevators as they're leaving their rooms for a little shopping or nightclubbing, with wallets and purses flush with cash. You get the picture. Sooner or later there will be a city where multiple hotel guests are being assaulted in the hallways or their rooms are being broken into one way or the other and looted.

"When that happens, I'll maneuver Roger to that city, to one of those hotels, and he will be an unfortunate victim of this crime spree, only he will heroically confront the thief and he will be shot, fatally, I'm afraid. Under these circumstances and despite the fact that spouses are always the first to be suspected in the murder of their partners, I feel very confident that there is absolutely no way anybody is going to cast a jaundiced eye your way."

"Why can't it just be a simple case of a random robbery? Why one of a series?"

"Not absolutely necessary, but better. It goes to motive. Your average cop, he has very little imagination. But I don't want us to run into some wise ass detective that starts scratching his head and asking himself if maybe Roger's death was a setup, meant to look like a robbery, in which case he starts looking around for any beneficiaries of your husband's passing. Any idea who might be number one on that particular short list? We want to preempt that sort of thinking, which we do if we fit it into an existing pattern."

"I see. Of course you're right. But we will be able to see one another after today?"

"Yes. But I repeat. Never, and I mean never, do we so much as look at each other in public. Not even if it's a thousand miles from home. That's absolutely vital. The only way either of us gets made for this crime is if we are connected to each other. For as long as it takes me to set this up, and for a decent interval thereafter, we are strangers everywhere but behind closed doors."

"Will we be able to talk?"

"We'll have to communicate, if for no other reason than to set meetings. Mail's too slow and unreliable from now on. Something might come up that affects my plans, or I may need your help with something. I've thought about this, and here's how we'll do it: prepaid cell phones." Two examples of which I pull out of my suitcase.

"Prepaid cell phones?"

"Yes. Burner phones. They're beautiful and they're completely anonymous. You can buy one at any 7-11 and set it up without having to give anyone your real name. They have a fixed number of prepaid minutes. You use 'em up and you can pay cash for a card to replenish the one you have, or you can throw it away and get a new one. No way it can ever be connected to you. We'll use them exclusively.

"So we talk Tuesday nights, if necessary. Any Tuesday night, I'll make it a point to always be home so I can speak with privacy. You get lonely, call me. Something comes up, call me. Just for God's sake always go cell to cell so no call is ever associated with my home phone. This is a very important point. The calls from your cell will be anonymous but there's still going to be a record of the physical location of the nearest cell tower any time it makes a connection. I don't need anybody figuring out that someone in Mrs. Waterhouse's area code has been calling my house, and having to explain who that someone might be.

"Chances of it ever getting to that point are extremely remote, I'll grant you, but why take an unnecessary risk. You'll find that I can be extremely paranoid given the proper circumstances. Never forget this: There are only two motives for murder, really: Sex or money. Between the two of us we have both."

She pauses for a moment and then says, "How about power, or revenge?"

"Hmm…money equals power. But revenge…the dish best eaten cold. I guess you have me there."

You had to hand it to the girl. She always had a knack for touching it with a needle.

"So anyway, we commit each other's number to memory before we depart. And Jezebel, once again, this is important. Never use your home line, never use a cordless, and never call any number but my cell. Understand?"

"Understand, Carlo. It's brilliant. I love you."

"Tell me there's no need to even mention that whatever we say on the phones has to be discreet."

"Of course. There's no need to even mention that whatever we say on the phones has to be discreet."

"Excellent. Also, no names. At least no real names, right? And no mention of anything illegal, say for example jaywalking or, I don't know, murder, right?"

"I get it, Carlo. So how by the way do you intend to get Roger to go to the city you choose?"

"Glad you asked because that brings me to the other thing we need to talk about. You have a rainy day fund tucked away somewhere?"

"Yes, of course. A girl needs to plan ahead."

"Good, because like I said I'm gonna need cash and lots of it. This is going to be an expensive project. I'm gonna need, like, fifty grand upfront, okay? Maybe more later. Almost certainly more later. You take some time and get that together without raising any eyebrows. Make it a bunch of small withdrawals. Then we meet for me to pick it up. Most likely right here, but I'll let you know. It won't be any place where we could run into someone that knows one of us. I'll think of something. As to controlling Roger's movements, I'm shocked you ask. How would you get him to go somewhere?"

A moment's blank stare, and then the realization and the grin. "Of course. A girl."

"Yes, ma'am. I'm going to get your husband a girlfriend, a very beautiful girlfriend who is going to put a little ring in his nose for me and lead him around like an overgrown puppy."

"But she's a terrible risk, isn't she? She's a link between Roger and you. How do you make sure she doesn't talk?"

"Excellent question. Unfortunately, Jezzie, she has to be a victim as well. You want omelets, you gotta break eggs."

Jezebel is nodding her head and attempting to look solemn and a little regretful. It isn't working. I know there's no way she's upset at the thought of one of her husband's playmates getting popped along the way.

She began at that point to undress herself and myself sort of simultaneously, and I was about to get rewarded for being such a good boy. She had a thought. "Where are you finding this girl, Carlo?"

"Lover, there's another California, you know, besides the Valley. It's a magical land where the sun shines faithfully, the skies are pastel blue and the trees are tall feathery palms. The streets are paved with gold. Italian and German sports cars cruise them happily, tops down. Beautiful and pampered women stroll the sidewalks of Rodeo Drive, shop to overpriced shop, poodles on leash. There is a lovely pink stucco and marble establishment called the Beverly Hills Hotel, with a lovely pool where the stars splash and play and sip tropical drinks. All the parking valets are really screenwriters, the waitresses actresses, and the hookers starlets waiting on a break. Here live the most desirable women in the world, and fortunately for us any number of them are readily available for the right price. Here I will find and recruit your husband's next divertissement. I'm going to Disneyland, baby. Or thereabouts."

CHAPTER 26

AMY

I returned to Prescott the next day, Sunday evening, after a very delightful night of romping in the hay with Mrs. Waterhouse. Her attitude had been wonderfully rehabilitated and our love affair instantly reinvigorated by the prospect of Mr. Waterhouse being crossed off the list. Funny how women can be so easy to please, after all.

Looking myself in the mirror Monday morning, shaving for work, I halfway expected to see a big red "M" on the forehead of my reflection. But, no, it was to all outward appearances the same old Carlo we were dealing with.

There were some real problems to finesse, however, now that I was embracing Jezebel's project. The first was the issue of my sudden fondness for travel. In the space of a few months I'd already been to Las Vegas, Sedona, Big Sur and Laughlin. Now I needed to fly or drive down to Phoenix again to catch a jet, or drive all the way to LA. Finding a playmate for Roger was a project I figured would take three days, meaning I needed to ask Max for a duty day off.

Ordinarily none of this would have been a big deal. As a detective I was usually scheduled with weekends off, anyway, barring emergencies. And now that the Bergstrom case was more or less on the back burner, at least unofficially, things were pretty slow for me. The sticking point was that while in the past I'd made the occasional trip up to Vegas, this recent activity represented a change in my behavior pattern. This is not a recommended practice for those planning capital crimes. I could of course have simply lied and told everybody I was spending weekends at home when I wasn't. But, no, this would have violated cardinal rule number one from the murderer's handbook: never tell a lie that someone can easily catch you in. Somebody I know just happens to see me sneaking out of town, then hears I've claimed otherwise, or God forbid something comes up and Max is trying to drum me up but can't, and suddenly everybody is wondering what the hell I'm up to. Not a good situation.

And of course I could not suddenly announce to my coworkers that I had a new romance going, a love affair with the lovely Mrs. Waterhouse of Westlake, CA, the pursuit of which would be keeping me more or less constantly on the road. Any link between Jezebel and me had to be the most closely guarded secret of all.

When I met Jezebel in Sedona and Big Sur I'd had the good sense to tell everyone I was going to Vegas. Going forward, though, that sort of lie was also too risky. Seeing her at all was risky, of course, and so I was determined to keep personal meetings to a minimum in the future. I planned to see her only when I needed cash, and only in Laughlin.

Then there was the Amy situation, which presented an even bigger dilemma. Amy had opened the door to a romantic relationship between us, and was, I suspected, halfway anticipating that I would walk through it. Ordinarily, and before Jezebel, I'd have been a taker without hesitation.

The thing was that I'm sure the one consideration tempering Amy's enthusiasm and leaving me off the hook was the fact that she knew I had someone else. Unfortunately, I now had to convince her that this other woman and I were over, and make her forget that this other woman had ever existed. I simply could not afford to have my love for Jezebel be the object of anybody's idle curiosity, and especially not in the case of Amy.

How, then, to handle her advances without arousing her suspicion? After all, she knew I had feelings for her. She knew, also, that I felt like a father to Shannon. The cynical move, and probably the smart one, would have been to just take her up on it. What the hell, that would have been pretty easy duty. I come up with some story to tell everybody to cover a few more weekends of travel and string Amy along until the Roger project is completed.

That was something I just couldn't do, though. I realized that killing a stranger for love and money was one thing, but that toying with Amy's and Shannon's affections was quite another. It was a frustrating situation, but a relief nevertheless to know that I still had some semblance of a conscience.

In the end I decided that the best thing to do with her was to invoke the very real fact that romance between us would simply be inappropriate. I was in fact a good deal older, I was in fact basically a loner who had never been in a domestic situation, we were in fact coworkers, there were in fact other more suitable men out there for her if she would just open up to the possibilities, and etc. It was a noble and selfless sort of thing for me to do, I let her believe, to let her go for her own good.

As for the other problem, Laughlin was really the perfect solution for the times Jezebel and I would need to get together. It was out of the way enough to make it very unlikely either of us would run into anyone we knew. As a plausible destination for a guy with a known fondness for the tables, I had no requirement to lie about where I was going when I headed out of town. I was going to make it my favorite weekend getaway, with maybe the occasional unadvertised side trip to LA. I let it be known around the shop that I'd had a very good run on my last trip, and believed the cards were friendlier there than in Vegas. So when Friday rolled around nobody was surprised to hear I was headed back. A night drive, this time, to meet Jezebel once more at the Riverside, pick up a bag of cash, and leave from there Saturday morning to drive to Los Angeles. Somewhere in that great metropolis, Roger's last girlfriend was waiting for me. I was most anxious to make her acquaintance.

CHAPTER 27

SUMMER

What becomes of the broken-hearted? Well, if you're a beautiful blonde whose professional name is Summer, who came to Hollywood to be in movies and whose heart was broken by the pitiless tinsel town machine, you've found yourself standing by the big window in my suite at the Beverly Hills Hotel, which is costing Mrs. Waterhouse the better part of one thousand dollars a night. You are backlit by the glow of the City of Lights outside, while inside the lighting is dimmed to serve the romantic mood. You are really too gorgeous to be in pictures; you're working against present trends.

Your face is angelic and your body perfect, your breasts full and heavy, your hips and waist thin, your stomach flat, your legs long and sculptured to ideal proportion. Your derriere is a plump and exquisite work of art, and you've broken a few hearts of your own, haven't you? You're wearing a frilly turquoise lace bra and garter belt with sheer stockings, and matching panties lie on the floor at your feet. The lingerie is by La Perla.

You are a grade *A*, top-of-the-food-chain American beauty, and you have come to me courtesy of Colette, all mine for the evening for the very reasonable sum of $1500, and Colette has come to me courtesy of the bellman, for the very reasonable gratuity of $300. You are the stunning answer to my prayer, you are my third try and you are, I believe, the one.

I sat on the edge of the bed staring dumbfounded at this vision, and after a few moments of polite silence she asked, "So how do you want to do it?"

"Summer," I said, "I don't want to do it. I mean, I would absolutely love to do it with you, believe me, it's just that that's not why we're here." I ache with the pain it's cost me to utter these words.

She frowns and tilts her head, and the look she's giving me tells me her freak alarm is ringing to beat the band. I rush to reassure her. "Don't worry, sweetie, I'm not a pervert or some whack job come to ruin your night. And I'm not a cop. Well, actually I am a cop but not in California, that's not what this is about, exactly."

"I see. And what is this about, exactly, Mr. Jardina?"

"Summer, this is about a business proposition that I believe you may find attractive."

She rolls her eyes to let me know someone's tried to peddle this shit to her before. "You have a role for me, Mr. Jardina? Let me guess, you want to introduce me to the exciting world of pre-recorded adult entertainment, don't you?"

I raise my hand to stop her protests. "No, no, nothing like that. I represent the wife of a very wealthy gentleman, Summer. She would very much like to be unmarried, would my friend, though wouldn't you know it she'd like to take a chunk of his cash with her when she leaves, as a sort of memento of their time together. She's a sentimental fool, this lady."

Summer looks no less skeptical. "Fine, so tell her to get a lawyer. What do you need me for?"

"Ah! You've come right to the crux of the matter, haven't you, young lady? Very good. The thing is, there is a prenuptial agreement in place that my friend fears may prove to be near-bulletproof. I say near, because her advisors feel that if her spouse were to be provably involved in a long-term adulterous situation, pictures and film at eleven, her outlook might brighten considerably. And now I believe you may be able to fit yourself into this picture, am I right?"

She's standing distressingly close to me now; she's delectable, I can smell her wonderful scent and as I've remained seated she looks down at me from the heights. She says, "You want me to seduce this guy?"

"More or less, and based on what I see you are perfectly suited to the task. We want you to knock him over, we want you to become a permanent fixture in his life. We want to be able to control where he goes, and we want to be able to shoot compromising film of what he does when he gets there. And for this service we are offering you $100,000 for one year, payable in quarterly installments beginning tonight."

Summer considered this for a moment. "With Colette I get fifteen hundred a night, any night I want," she complained.

"True. Out of which Colette takes at least a third, I'm guessing. Still, call it a grand. Times five nights a week is five grand. Figure time out for the curse, you maybe average three weeks' work a month. Fifteen thousand. Annualized, one hundred-eighty thousand. However, for this you get to be with a different creep every night, you get to take all associated risks of your trade, be they legal ramifications or complications with the mental stability of your clientele. You have no perks; in fact you spend a small fortune on couture and coiffure and make-up, et cetera."

To which Summer has no reply at the moment.

"On the other hand," I continue, "with our plan you are the very spoiled little mistress of one free-spending dude, free-spending at least where strange trim is involved. I've seen you, and I know the guy. He's gonna give you the royal treatment. Trips, fancy dinners, jewelry, furs, let your imagination wander. And if you want you can probably marry him yourself. I said my friend wanted some cash, I didn't say she needed it all. Trust me, worst case for you she still doesn't make a dent. So you get with him yourself for a while. Not so bad, beats hooking by a mile if you ask me, and he's no gargoyle. He's a decent-looking well-kept clean-shaven individual who's been to school and everything. With your talent you can move up very fast in the organization if you apply yourself, trust me."

She smiles and wig wags her pretty head shoulder to shoulder and looks at the ceiling as if to say, I'm thinking, I'm thinking. Then she asks, "He likes prenups, though, you said, right…that was the whole point of why you needed me in the first place?"

I laugh. "Honey, when he gets a load of you he's going to forget how to *spell* prenup. God knows I would. Now if we have a deal, get dressed before I break down and take your night's fee out in service, and we'll talk details."

After her clothes were back on, I poured us both a drink, sat her down next to me on the bed and explained, "Three things, Summer. First, no outcalls on the side. We need an exclusive on you, business and pleasure don't mix, okay? So call Colette and tell her you're taking a sabbatical."

"A what?"

"An extended vacation."

"Oh. Uh huh. She's not going to want to hear that. I'm one of her most popular girls."

"Don't I know it? Going to be some lonely Johns out there for a while. Nevertheless…second, it's a man named Roger Waterhouse. He owns, among other things, several auto dealerships in the Valley. His main office is the Chevy agency in the auto plaza just off the 101 in Woodland Hills. You apply for a job there. I figure a girl like you, Roger will sniff you out in no time, and from there we just let nature take its course."

"All right."

"Third is communications. We need to be able to talk to you with regularity and security, so that we can get instructions to you. We may want to get him out of town occasionally just so he won't conflict with Mrs. Waterhouse's own social schedule, if you take my meaning. We'll use prepaid cell phones at all times. Here's one to get you started, and you can get another if you need it. They're cheap and readily available. They're completely anonymous and we interpose them between ourselves always and without exception. Use Tuesday nights. Let Roger know that these nights are always taken, you've got a bedridden Aunt Maude in Dubuque you need to call religiously, or you have yoga class, whatever. I'm going to give you my number. It's a throwaway phone just like yours and you're to memorize this number and never ever write it down, understood?"

"Got it."

"520-492-4411. Read that back to me."

She did, faithfully.

"Good. Call me on the nights we discussed, using this cell and calling that number. That way there's no connection between us. And Summer?"

"Yes, Mr. Jardina?" She's smiling big at me now, the cloak and dagger stuff has her amused and she's thinking I'm a little over the top with it, which, from her angle, without the complete picture, I most assuredly am.

"Summer, this is serious. No land line phones, no cordless, ever, promise me. Always use the burner and only the burner."

She laughs, "All right, I promise."

She's standing again, and I give her a slap on her bottom. "Good girl. What's my number?"

"520-492-4411."

"Beautiful." I then handed her an envelope with 25K in it. "There you go, my sexy young friend."

"And I get another twenty-five in three months?"

"You got it, Summer. Plus another twenty-five thousand three months after that, and one more payment after that, as long as you behave yourself."

I watched with some amusement as she riffled through the two hundred fifty crisp bills, her eyes as wide as a kid's in a candy store.

She stuffed the package into her purse.

I said, "Money talks, I'm told, and bullshit walks."

"Not in LA it doesn't."

"Huh?"

"Not even bullshit walks here, believe me. Nothing walks in LA."

CHAPTER 28
PRESCOTT

They say that flying airplanes for a living consists of hours of boredom interspersed with seconds of terror. The surprising thing to me was my discovery that executing the perfect murder could be described in much the same way. Now that I had Summer lined up, it was really a matter of waiting. Waiting until she got my quarry hooked and on the line, and then waiting for the right opportunity to implement my plan.

For a good little while, then, as summer rolled on, I was in lying-low mode. It was an unusually hot few months, and everybody at headquarters and around town spent a lot of their energy bitching about the weather. A massive low pressure system was sitting off the Baja coast and spinning hot moist air over much of the Southwest, including our fair city. For what seemed weeks it refused to budge. To the north and west of Prescott, over the southern Sierra Nevada of California, a high pressure system was pressing down against it, and at the intersection of the two some very respectable thunderstorms were being generated. For the most part they were being carried by the jet stream in a long train passing off to the north of us, over Flagstaff. Every once in a while, though, one would go off course. This was our greatest pleasure, the arrival of a stray over our town, wandering through in the late afternoon or early evening, treating everybody to a spectacle of light and sound and dumping a refreshing load of cold rainwater onto us all.

Jezebel and I kept in touch via the prepaid phones, but there was no point in getting together until Summer had gone through her first installment of cash.

Stoner and I continued to speak by phone from time to time. He was getting nowhere, which of course was my one great source of happiness and I never missed an opportunity to needle him about it. I still had the large map of the US on my office wall, with pins in Prescott, Tulsa and Provo, and he had a similar arrangement so that we had some laughs on one or two occasions speculating on where the next one would go. The FBI wasn't really keen on giving the situation a lot of publicity, as they believed it just encouraged copycat type crimes, and that warning the sort of girls Stephen was killing would fall on deaf ears anyway. They were probably right. So they were mighty displeased when the national media got the story.

Our friend himself remained inactive and uncommunicative as far as I could tell. Waiting for the FBI's interest to wane, perhaps. Following the story in the papers, I'm sure, with great pleasure. Attempting to deduce what he could of law enforcement's strategy, probably, and determine what information we had developed. I had no idea what to make of his quiescence. To be completely candid, it evoked conflicting emotions in me. I and my friends at the Bureau were all pretty much waiting around for Stephen to strike again, not knowing whether to hope he would or pray he wouldn't.

I paid regular visits to the NCAVC database, partly to get a heads up if there was another victim, and partly to look for a hotel robbery that may have gone bad and ended in homicide, just in case. Ordinarily the sort of crimes eligible to be uploaded to VICAP are homicides involving abduction, sexual orientation or those suspected of being part of a series. It was therefore not likely I was going to find there the sort of crime I needed to help me make Mrs. Waterhouse's dreams regarding Mr. Waterhouse come true. Consequently I also started logging onto the websites of some of the leading newspapers of the larger cities around the US of A, and checking the crime reports that way.

I conducted these searches at my home on my personal computer, and used a Tor browser as a proxy server. This setup made it virtually impossible to track my IP address. More than one individual would not be sitting in prison today if only they'd had the benefit of this safety tip and taken the same precaution.

I also made sure to scrub my browsing history from my hard drive with a program I'd purchased for the occasion, with cash, at a computer store in Kingman. Paranoid behavior, probably, but you never know.

Of course I kept up my regular visits to Amy and Shannon. Probably twice a week on average we'd barbeque in her backyard, always steaks for the grownups and dogs for the kid, after which we'd retire to the living room and maybe watch a rental DVD of the latest Disney or Pixar offering.

After Shannon was in bed Amy and I would sit on the couch, have a glass of wine or whatever, and talk. The talk was pretty much always of the small variety. She seemed to have gotten the message that ours was to remain a platonic relationship and had apparently resigned herself to the situation. She refused to look elsewhere, though, and regularly declined offers of dates from the other cops. I felt bad for her in that regard, but Shannon seemed very much okay with our arrangement, and that made me feel better.

I'll be honest. There were a couple of times when I nearly succumbed. Jezebel had reawakened my libido with a vengeance, yet I needed to minimize contact with her, and here was this extremely attractive young lady who had pretty strongly signaled her availability. But though I may potentially be a murderer and may have sold my soul for a shot at the brass ring, I was still a gentleman.

CHAPTER 29

ROGER AND SUMMER

What was left of June and the month of July rolled by slowly yet uneventfully for me, marking time as it were though I was filled with a sense of anticipation and at times of foreboding. The match between Roger and Summer took slightly longer to initiate than I'd planned. She actually had to wait a couple of weeks after filing her application to be called in for an interview. There was a period of time when we were afraid that Mr. Waterhouse wasn't keeping as close an eye on personnel as I assumed he did, and I was beginning to believe she might not get hired. She was making noises on the phone about returning to Colette and I had to work hard to keep her on task. At last he found the bait, however, and having discovered the lovely and talented Summer went at her with a vengeance.

It was enormously entertaining for us, Jezebel and me, to have her recount the story from her side. We were talking most every Tuesday night for at least half an hour, for which I was very grateful. I couldn't have her physically and so the psychological tether our conversations provided became that much more important. The unstated truth between us was, I suppose, that we were steeling each other's nerves.

Roger was feeding Jezzie an unending line of happy horseshit concerning sudden business trips and urgent late night meetings and the like designed to free him up to see Summer. Of course Jez was having great fun pretending to be taken in by his fabrications.

Summer, meanwhile, was sinking her pretty little talons very deeply indeed into his juicy well-heeled flesh, wasting no time inaugurating an ambitious collection of expensive baubles. She stopped mentioning Colette's name pretty quickly after her first liaison with our boy, I'm very happy to say.

General Motors gave a big party at the Four Seasons on the island of Hawaii just before Independence Day. Roger regretted to inform Jezebel that although he would just love to do the trip as a couple, none of the other guys were bringing family and he'd look like a complete wuss if she came along. Diamond bracelet to follow swiftly as a consolation, the intended effect of which Jezebel was happy to simulate. He *was* able to squeeze our girl in, however, his personal secretary you know, and she had a splendid time. Told me all about it, in great detail, the first Tuesday night after they returned.

Summer was apparently beginning to view me as a mentor or father figure. She called faithfully every Tuesday and usually talked my ear off. In reality, we had little need to communicate at all, at least until I was ready to spring the trap. Her only job for the time being was to keep Mr. Waterhouse completely enthralled and malleable.

This was a task she was executing flawlessly. She was taking to life with Roger like the proverbial fish to water. She was adapting to the lifestyle nicely and was working on him to take her to Paris next.

The more her husband dissembled with Jezebel, the more she played the role of the blithely ignorant and contented wife. That fact might have raised a red flag for him in other circumstances, but Summer had the poor guy in la-la land.

I continued to check in almost daily with NCAVC and my news websites, waiting patiently for the right situation to pop up. There were some hotel robberies of the sort I needed, but they were always one-offs, or two. I was looking for more than that. As I'd explained to Jezebel, I wanted a pattern into which the local cops would readily place Roger Waterhouse's tragic death. I couldn't count on any great intuitive leaps of deduction, so I was looking to draw them a picture.

No hurry, anyway. The operation was costing just over eight thousand a month, but hey, it takes money to make money. This was a very small investment considering the potential return, and the sort of thing you really needed to do right the first time. Let Summer and Roger settle in, let the perfect venue and the perfect conditions present themselves. Our day will come, as some Motown poet once promised.

CHAPTER 30
SUMMER

She squealed it out as if she was telling me she'd just been voted homecoming queen. "Carlo, he's taking me to France!"

After my ears stopped ringing I said, "Hey, sweetie, that's great. Sounds like you two are really hitting it off. What did I tell you?"

I was starting to feel like the father of the bride here, which under the circumstances just increased my load of existential guilt. It was good, though, that my plan for her and Roger was working out so well, and these Tuesday night gabfests were actually providing me a welcome break from the grim world of *The Hunt for the Strip Club Killer*.

"It's okay, isn't it? I mean, that fits in with your plans?"

What the hell did I care? Nothing was happening on the national crime front for the moment and I foresaw nothing breaking for the next couple of weeks. "Sure, kid, it's beautiful, it's perfect. We'll have people there with cameras, trust me you'll never see them. Gonna look great in court. When you leaving?"

"Don't know, exactly. He says he has to come up with some story to keep Jezebel cool."

"Yeah, well, he shouldn't concern himself too much, should he, honey? Mrs. Waterhouse is feeling very gullible these days."

"I know. It's sort of weird for me, watching him play all these games and all the time knowing she knows. He won't ever find out, will he Carlo, about me and you two working together? You won't screw it up for me, will you? I'm really starting to like him."

"Like I said, kid," I reassured her. "Not to worry. When Mrs. Waterhouse is done with him, he's all yours. God bless you both."

"Have you been to France, Carlo?"

"Not on a cop's salary, no, but I sure would like to see it someday. Great place, from everything I've heard. I'm sure you're going to love it. They know how to live, the French."

"I'm feeling a little, like, stupid, just now. Roger talks about all these places we'll see and to be honest I don't have the first clue what he's talking about. I majored in boys in high school, and minored in make-up, you know?"

"I understand. So what would you like to know about? Maybe I can help."

"Well, Versailles for starters. He says I have to see it. I guess it's quite a sight, but what is it, exactly?"

I can't help myself, I break into heartfelt laughter. I don't know what to do with this girl. Ordinarily I have no time for bubbleheads, but in Summer's case I find myself going back and forth. She is completely uneducated, unread, shallow, vapid, immature, self-absorbed and clueless. She is the perfect exemplar of every pejorative you may care to use to characterize the MTV generation. She is the Mount Everest of ignorance. There are days when she completely exhausts my patience and I want to kill her immediately. She has a way, though, at other times, of making dumb charming. Sometimes it is good to rub elbows with this sort of adolescent innocence; it's almost like how I feel with Shannon.

In the end, I'm left with a couple of simple facts. It may not be politically correct to say it, but the reality is that there is a direct relationship between a woman's attractiveness and the amount of airheaded nonsense men will put up with from her. Trust me, Summer was about as gorgeous as they come.

Even more important, of course, was the fact that she was a critical player in my plan. She was performing her assigned role splendidly, and that was really all that mattered. So I chose to overlook her intellectual failings. When she really got annoying, I did what so many have done before me. I put a big smile on my face and rolled with it.

At any rate, today was one of her charming days. I said, "Forgive me, Summer. I'm laughing with you, believe me, you are just so sweet. Versailles is a very large palace that was built in the cool suburbs of Paris by King Louis XIV. In his day Paris was crowded, dirty and hot, and so he basically moved his operation to Versailles to get away. Today it's just a short train ride from downtown, and it is absolutely amazingly beautiful. The palace itself is perhaps the most magnificent piece of architecture not a cathedral in Europe, and it's surrounded by the most beautiful gardens, fountains and man-made lakes you've ever seen.

"And of course the interior is completely over the top. There's a room there that's completely covered in gold leaf and mirrored walls, with massive crystal chandeliers. They used it for balls. It's called the Hall of Mirrors, but I'm certain after you've visited they'll call it the Hall of a Thousand Summers."

"Oh, Carlo…"

"It became a major party house for the members of the French court. Wine, women and song. Sort of the Playboy Mansion of its day."

"So did Marie Antoinette live there?"

"She did indeed, sugar. She and Louis XVI, actually, were the last occupants. They partied just a bit too hearty, you know, and lost their heads."

Which bad joke drew a giggle from Summer.

"Let's see if I can get this right. Louis XIV built the place. He was called the Sun King. He came to the throne at four and ruled a long damn time, over seventy years, so he spent decades there. Trouble was, he loved to spend money and between the out of control entertainment expenses and a handful of wars he was running on the side, he sort of ran the country out of cash. But he was a strong king, and so he got away with it.

"Louis XVI was like his great, great grandson I think. Unfortunately his timing proved to be lousy, as he was the poor bastard holding the bag when the French Revolution came along. He was the one married to Marie Antoinette, who was an Austrian princess. She and her Louis were partying fools.

"Trouble was he was a weak ruler, Marie was a foreigner and never caught on with the French public, and despite the fact that France was broke they continued to live extravagantly. Everybody was generally fed up with the monarchy anyway, and all this combined in the end to get both of them dates with the guillotine. End of lecture, my little blonde friend."

"I see. Boy, that's a lot of history. Wow."

"Yep. Wow." And God, don't I love this child just now, an affection that must never be tipped to Jezebel, avuncular though it may be. The horrifying notion of Summer not making it through this story unscathed was something I didn't even want to think about.

"So don't tease me. Have you really never been there, Carlo? Sounds like you know all about it."

"No, I was telling you the truth. Never been east of Philadelphia PA, I'm afraid. Like I said, not on a policeman's salary. I do like to watch the History Channel, though."

"Oh. Cool."

"I've been known to read a book from time to time, also, my dear. That's something you might want to look into. It would be good for you and I think you might even enjoy it. Just because you wasted high school doesn't mean you have to be a bimbo the rest of your life, no offense."

"I guess you're right."

"Girls do not live by boys alone."

"Right."

"Now that I think of it, why don't you pick up one of those tour guides for Paris, next time you're at the mall. You can study up on all the highlights. The Louvre, the Arc de Triumph, the Champs Eleysees, Montmarte…you know, all the touristy stuff. Learn a little something about each of them. Maybe even pick up a few French phrases here and there. Surprise and impress Roger."

"You think?"

"I'm sure of it. Let's face it. You want to marry this dude, eventually, right?"

"Right."

"Well, he's a prominent businessman. He's not going to want a wife that embarrasses him with his colleagues, no matter how beautiful she is. And you said he wants kids, am I correct?"

"Yes. The present Mrs. Waterhouse has no interest in that area."

"Okay, well, whatever else he is he's a smart guy. He's going to want to have smart kids. Ignorance he can forgive…that's not genetic. Stupid is. So if you're smart you will show him you are not stupid, that you can educate yourself. Okay, kid? You hearing my words?"

"I hear you, Carlo. Thanks. I'll do it."

"Good. So make my buddy Roger show you the Louvre, which was once a palace also but is now the main museum. And the rest of the museums as well, Summer. Maybe you can give him a guided tour. And give him a kiss for me at the top of the Eiffel Tower. You do know about the Eiffel Tower, right?"

"Of course. Thanks a bunch, Carlo."

Sadly, this was all just total bullshit on my part. Truth was we were discussing a marriage that was never going to happen. But what the hell, it made us both feel good for the moment.

"No problem, kid. By the way, I'm not certain she ever really said it. Marie Antoinette I mean."

"Said what?"

"Let them eat cake."

CHAPTER 31

JEZEBEL

Jezebel's call followed Summer's by only a few minutes, but her mood was somewhat less jubilant. She started off with, "Have you heard what that son of a bitch is doing, Carlo? He's taking the little whore to France. France! We've been married for six years and every goddamn one of those years I've begged him to take me to Europe, but no, the French are assholes, he wants no part of them, we'll stick with Aspen or Maui for the umpteenth time."

I had to laugh once more. "Baby, don't be petulant. You should be happy she's got him so whipped. Time comes to do it, it's going to make things a whole lot easier for us. That was the point, remember?"

"Speaking of which, when the hell is the time going to come? It's been months. I miss you, Carlo. I need to be with you. Can't you get it over with?"

"In due time, Jez. In due time, and that means my schedule, my way, like we agreed. I get one shot, I intend to take it when conditions are perfect."

She's started to simmer down a little as we've talked. "So guess what load of bullshit the prick is handing me for his reason to go to Paris. General Motors of Europe is supposedly bringing a few US dealers over to meet their French counterparts. A cultural exchange, no less. Believe me, the closest Roger Waterhouse ever got to culture is when they cultured what was dripping from his dick last time he got the clap."

"Jezebel, stop. You're unattractive when you're crude. Trust me, it does not become you. Now straighten up for me right now, woman. I mean it."

"Oh, all right. I went down to the dealership the other day to get a look at this Summer. What a stunner you picked out, Carlo."

I was pretty sure she didn't intend the remark as a compliment, but decided to play it as such anyway. "Thanks, honey. I did my research. We needed somebody your husband would for sure find unable to resist."

"Did you screw her yourself, Carlo? Tell me the truth."

"Damn it, Jezzie, I'm about to hang up on you, I mean it. I love you, I'm out here taking enormous risks for you, and I don't deserve this. Now stop it. If you don't like the arrangement, I can have Summer on the phone in five minutes and terminate it. We'll just call the whole thing off. Frankly it would be an enormous relief to me just now."

Finally I've landed a body blow. There's silence on the other end for half a minute, and then charming Jez comes on the line. "Sorry, Carlo. You're right. I'm just going crazy with the waiting and the not seeing you, and watching Roger's big dumb smile all the time."

"You just keep evil Jez in the closet, sweetheart, and hang in. It'll all be over soon enough, I promise."

"They say she's dumb as a rock, the other girls working at the agency. It's quite an open joke."

"She's okay. A little uneducated, is all. She's actually a very nice kid."

"You're not getting sweet on her, are you, Carlo? You going soft in the head on me? You know she has to go, along with Roger. She has to. She's a fatal link otherwise."

"I know, Jezebel, believe me I know."

"Promise me you're doing them both, Carlo. No ideas. Promise me."

That was the thing about the lovely Mrs. Waterhouse. She always knew where the weak points were, where the chinks in your armor were located. As far as I could tell she had none herself. For her everything in life, and I do mean everything, was a business proposition, with the possible exceptions of gambling and sex. For those two hobbies her love was pure and uncalculated.

For me, on the other hand, things were tougher. For me killing was not something to be done casually, like picking up clothes at the dry cleaner. I'm sure she has to wonder if I'll really be able to pull the trigger. But then, so do I.

"I promise, Jezzie. When the time comes, I'll do what needs to be done."

CHAPTER 32
CELESTE

A bitter February morning of gray overcast sky and black leafless trees. It seems impossible to believe, but it is the tenth anniversary of Celeste's passing. I stand with Poppy at the foot of her grave, neither of us casting a shadow. Next to her an empty plot, where in three years' time Poppy will go to lie beside her for eternity. The mood of course is somber, but the tears in our eyes are from the bitter north wind that whips our reddened faces and carries with it the occasional sting of hard gritty sleet.

It seems appropriate, the weather and the soft blanket of fresh snow that cushions our steps. The scene holds two incongruent elements for my memory, however. The several dozens of bright red roses at Celeste's headstone, a splash of color wholly out of place in this cheerless cemetery, and where in hell did Poppy get those this time of year? The policeman's uniform I wear under my leather jacket, a sight that would in other circumstances be an abomination in Poppy's world, one that might even threaten his continued good health, except that our relationship is well-known and long accepted by his associates.

He takes my arm and guides me down off the ridge and into the shelter of a wooded vale. No other human being stands within a hundred yards of us. "She was one of two good things in my life, Carlo. You are the other. It's been a while since I've told you how proud I am of you, but let me say it now. Don't ever let me down, kid, okay?"

"Don't worry, Poppy. I won't. I promise."

"Your life is like an arrow, Carlo, flying into the future, into a time when I'm gone. Maybe, because I helped to draw the bow, maybe it will carry this old man's atonement. Maybe if it flies true and straight it will carry away my sins."

"No offense, Poppy, but I don't believe salvation can be achieved by proxy. That's something you can and must do for yourself, you know. You're still young. It's not too late. Leave the life. Change yourself."

He shakes his head sadly and pats my shoulder. "Would that it were that simple, my young friend. For me to quit the game now would disappoint a lot of people. The sort of people one doesn't really want to disappoint, if you know what I mean.

"No, the path I've chosen only goes one way, and I say chosen but now that I think of it that's not really the right word, is it? After all, given the world I was born into, wouldn't it be fair to say my only real choice was between success and failure, or between survival and death? Wouldn't any real man have to go the way I did? Christ, it seemed so straightforward when I was young; there was never a moment's hesitation that I wasn't doing what I had to do."

"I think that's fair. I believe that given the context, your actions were justifiable. Hell, they were honorable. It was a war, wasn't it, in your mind I mean?"

"That's a great way of putting it, Carlo. I was born a soldier in an endless war, only what was needed was not another soldier. We needed a real hero, a man who would stand up and say, goddamn it, we're fighting an insane war because the enemy is us, and it needs to stop. God, if only I'd done that, son. But no one did. It would never have occurred to any of us. We all played along, right down to the parish priest. How does such foolishness come to be, I ask myself?"

"It comes from poverty, Poppy, and lack of choices. And being isolated immigrants in a new and uncertain world with your collective backs against the wall. I'll be honest with you, Poppy. There was a time when even though I loved you and was grateful to you, I was ashamed of the fact you were in the life you're in. I mean, it's a world that holds a lot of fascination for people and it's made for a lot of very entertaining movies and whatnot. But it's an embarrassing thing to be in polite company and have to tell someone your adopted father is a wise guy, no offense. You know what I mean. Especially for a cop."

Poppy did not respond, and the two of us stood together in silence for several minutes.

"Obviously, you yourself have regrets. But I'm going to tell you something, old man. I was much younger then, and hopelessly naive. The more I've lived and the more I've learned about the way this world, the so-called civilized world of law and order works, the more I question whether it's really so morally superior."

"What do you mean, Carlo. That's crazy talk."

"Is it? You figure this so-called justice system we've created is the way things are supposed to be? The bleeding heart judges, the half-wit juries, the revolving door prisons? Out here in my world, Poppy, the rights of the criminal trump those of the victim every time. As a cop you're fighting a battle with one hand behind your back and an eye over your shoulder because one misstep and you are the one poor son of a bitch that they will come down on, hard. Meantime the keepers of the system somehow cannot find the will to take animals we know are dangerous off the streets and keep them there. Of course they congratulate themselves on their enlightened compassion, while innocent people pay the price with their lives. So maybe don't feel so bad."

Poppy listens without comment. He fishes a cigar from an inside pocket and lights it up, cradling the flame in both hands against the wind. Nothing reminds me more of him than the sweet aroma of burning tobacco. I can still smell it today, whenever I think of him.

"And then there's the splendid characters overseeing the whole mess. The fucking politicians. Jesus Christ, don't get me started. They wallow around like pigs in a cesspool of corruption, which I guess is only to be expected, but the thing that really gets me is the hypocrisy. A guy like you, you make no bones about what you're up to, and who you are, and you offer no excuses and no apologies. But these sanctimonious bastards, these politicians, it's not enough they have to screw you, you have to listen to them tell you how much they care about you, and the country, and how they spend every waking minute thinking of ways they can make your life better. What bullshit. Meantime the parasites do nothing but get in the way of the few of us left actually trying to do some productive work and maybe make the world a slightly better place.

"I'm sorry, I'm thinking maybe I prefer your brand of crime. At least it's honest crime, if you'll forgive the oxymoron."

Poppy says, "We are a nation of laws, Carlo. Sure the system stinks sometimes, but it's the only one we've got."

"Which is what makes it so discouraging, to see it being so misused. No one appreciates the majesty of the law more than I do, believe me. It's my chosen life's work, enforcing the law. It can only work, though, if there are good men operating the system. Where have the good men gone?"

"Keep talking, kid. I'm starting to feel better."

"I'm not patronizing you here, Poppy. What I'm saying is from the heart. Sure, I know yours is a brutal world, a world of tooth and claw. People are killed. But at least they are people who have entered that world eyes open, knowing the score and the risks and the rules. And they've chosen to break those rules and suffered the consequences. Not a lot of gray areas in your world; it's all black and white. You have a code, and so help you God you live by it. There is a certain appeal to that, a sort of, of primal purity and, I don't know, moral clarity. I am no longer prepared to judge it inferior to the world I live in, where so many rise to the top based on their ability to lie convincingly and abandon any sense of honor or loyalty or integrity."

We have begun very slowly to walk back up the hill, side by side. Poppy draws on the Montecristo every few moments and the smoke is carried rapidly away into the gray sky. As we reach the crest and head back in the direction of Celeste's grave he says, "I appreciate the very able defense you have constructed on my behalf, counselor. Maybe I should fire my lawyer and hire you. You are very eloquent. I worry, though, that you've become so cynical. Not healthy for a man so young. That's for us old bastards. Where is that coming from, Carlo?"

I have to think about that for a while. "I guess it's frustration with this justice system we have today. Everything is set up to favor the lawbreakers, to coddle every criminal that comes along. Makes everybody feel good about how merciful and caring we are. What's forgotten is that by sparing the guilty, you inevitably sacrifice the innocent. In your world, you enforce your own justice, and it's swift and harsh and effective. Guy rapes a young girl in your neighborhood, he's not going to be on the street again in two years to do it again, is he? Let's just say your community enjoys a very low recidivism rate, okay? I like that. That's a real benefit you create, and that needs to be weighed against the bad. Give yourself some credit."

"Well, Carlo, it seems to me that that line of thinking could lead people to take the law into their own hands. It's a dangerous line of thinking for a man in your profession."

It's my turn to answer with silence. This particular discussion has gone about as far as I care to take it for the moment.

After a while Poppy says, "Anyway, thanks for the sentiment, my young friend. Maybe you have a point. Doesn't help me sleep nights, though."

"So change."

"This path I've ended up on by whatever manner, Carlo, it's a one-way trip. You know that. You don't change and live to tell it. I'm afraid I'm just going to have to live with the guilt, and pray that God will give me some time off for the suffering I'm doing now."

"At any rate, Poppy, if it's any consolation I appreciate what you've done for me more than you can imagine, what you both have done for me," I said and nodded in the direction of the grave. "I'm very happy. I look at myself in the mirror every morning, and I see a good man, a man at peace with himself."

"That's beautiful, Carlo. That thought keeps me going. You just keep on doing the right thing, promise me. If you're ever tempted to do otherwise, you think about old Poppy, promise me. You see this big ugly plug in your imagination, and I'm talking to you like a Dutch uncle. Promise?"

"I promise."

"So guess what I was talking about with my Celeste, back there, my boy, for so long."

I smile and say, "I can't imagine. What?"

"I was asking her for special permission to maybe start keeping company with the ladies, it's been so long."

"What did she say?"

"I believe she said she approves. She wants me to be happy. She wants me to go on."

"Anyone special?"

He was not famous for shy grins, but he shoots me one just now and says, "Actually, there is a young lady I've met. Really something. Probably too young for me, but she does make me feel alive."

"That's great, Poppy. Just don't go losing your heart."

"Don't you worry, my friend. Celeste will always be number one with me."

It was, as it turned out, the last time I saw him. I was working then for a small town police department up in Bucks County. I was already thinking of moving west but had been sticking around to be close to Poppy. Once he found himself a new lady, though, I figured he didn't need me to keep an eye on him. I found the position in Prescott shortly thereafter.

The truth was, I had no desire to meet her, the new woman. I understood that he needed feminine companionship and didn't blame him for taking up with her. It was just that for me it was better to keep the memory of Poppy and Celeste together as I'd known them. To do otherwise seemed to me an act of disloyalty. Celeste was like a mother to me, after all.

When he remarried he invited me to the wedding, but my heart wasn't in it. When he died unexpectedly he was in the ground before I even got the news. So it turned out that once I left Pennsylvania I never returned. Sometimes you just have to turn the page.

My memory of that day is completely undiminished by time, the two of us in profile against the flat gray light, standing over her headstone. Although the letters were chiseled into the rose-hued granite of the marker, they may just as well have been cut into our hearts: *Celeste Marie Agnelli.*

CHAPTER 33
LAUGHLIN

She says to me, "You know what's troubling me, Carlo?"

She's lying on her back on one edge of the bed. I'm more or less curled fetus-like facing in her direction, barely fitting on the opposite side of the narrow mattress, with my head resting on her left thigh and my knees tucked under her left arm. In her right hand, which is draped over the edge of the bed and nearly touching the floor, is a cigarette. Virginia Slims mentholated smoke is drawn in coiling strands toward the ceiling by a slowly turning fan. I trace random patterns with my finger onto her belly, which is slippery with sweat.

We have recently finished making love in my grandly appointed suite, room 12 of the Riverside Inn. The high today in Laughlin was north of 115 degrees, and though it's after 0100 in the morning it is still blazingly hot outside. The window unit labors heroically but between its pitiful output and the fan's negligible effect the room is barely livable. On the faux-wood dresser next to the TV are a couple of plastic cups with nearly melted ice cubes, a half empty bottle of scotch and a brown paper bag containing two hundred fifty Benjamin Franklins.

I know what's coming, and so decide to ignore her question. I point to the layer of gray haze trapped against the ceiling and say "Smoking kills, Jezebel."

She says, "I know that. I've been trying to get Roger to take it up for years."

"But with you. It really is a nasty habit. Maybe you need something else to put in your mouth."

"Ha. You should be so lucky. Take care of Mr. Waterhouse and we'll talk. Meanwhile, answer my question. You know what's bothering me?"

"I have a fair idea, but go ahead."

"I'm beginning to wonder if my Carlo really has his heart in this project. I mean, life's pretty good for him right now. This perpetual planning stage we seem to be stuck in is completely risk-free. It's all just talk after all, and meanwhile Carlo gets to have his way with Mrs. Waterhouse, who is spreading her legs for him pretty much on demand. Life's good for Carlo. Not so good for Mrs. Waterhouse, though, who is burning through her rainy day fund at a very healthy clip while she gets to traipse across the state to crappy little towns like Laughlin and be entertained in crappy little motels like the Riverside Inn, a dump by the way in which she would not normally be caught dead, all the while getting very impatient and frustrated with the fact that her piece of shit husband is *A*: still very much with us and *B*: having the time of his life banging his new girlfriend on my dime."

"Ouch."

"Right. Ouch. That's what I say. It's a big no fair, Carlo. You said a couple of months."

"I say a lot of things, Jezebel. Like for example, remember the part where I said we take our time, we take one shot and we get it right the first time on account of this crappy room we're in is gonna look like the Four Seasons to poor Carlo where he's going if we screw up. And I'm not going alone, I promise you. And by the way, when did letting me have my way with you become such tough duty?"

She pats me on the head and says, "Now don't be defensive with me, my pet. No one's attacking your manly skills. Those scratches on your back are real."

"Well, thank you for that. I feel much better. Anyway, you do have a point. This thing can't go on forever. I understand that, believe me I do. The longer we wait, the more likely something happens that forces us to cancel, like we get spotted together by one of your friends is my main fear."

"Not much chance of that in this dive."

Jezebel is still upset with me that I dragged her here rather than meeting her in her room at Harrah's, which of course is a much more civilized environment. Too civilized, is the problem. It's the best property in town and the place any random friend of Jez would definitely stay.

I picked her up in the parking lot of her hotel just after midnight, and we managed to slip into my room when no one was around. This being my third stay at the Riverside they were sort of getting to know me and

I wanted to keep as low a profile as possible. Still, I wasn't too concerned. One thing I've learned as a cop is that people who work in the Riverside Inns of the world have really bad memories. It's part of the job description. Plus I figured if it ever came out that I had a visitor I could just claim I dragged some of the local talent back from the casino for a little *R* and *R*, a girl whose name I never quite caught.

"That's right, not much chance and that's the way I like it."

"It seems to me there's a much better chance of one of the hillbillies working here seeing me with you."

"That's true enough, but they don't know you. You're a hooker, should the question ever arise. An anonymous hooker."

"Gee, thanks. You really know how to make a girl feel special."

"Yeah, you're welcome. No problem. A very high-priced hooker, by the way, if it helps. But getting back to the issue at hand, if you don't mind, and you can get back to your pointless bitching later. I'm maybe being too picky about the setup. I was really hoping to find a streak of robberies somewhere to fit this thing into. That obviously would help sell the story we want everyone to buy. But maybe I'm letting the perfect be the enemy of the good enough. You're going to be a million miles away. As long as I get away cleanly from the scene there's no way to connect me to it. And if I don't we're obviously screwed anyway, so why worry about it. That being the case, what else are the police going to think? Tell you what. If nothing pops up soon, and I do mean very soon, we'll go ahead with it anyway. I promise. Okay?"

This puts a smile back on her face. "That's great, Carlo. Just think how wonderful it's going to be when all this is over and it's done. Then in no time we can be together every day, with enough money to never have to worry about anything. You can turn in your badge and I can get the hell out of the Valley and away from all the spoiled catty bitches that live there that I have to pretend to like. We can travel. You can maybe get me started on that smoking cessation program you suggested. I never want to see Laughlin again, Carlo, thank you, and I definitely want to be through with this motel. I still cannot believe you made me come here, you bad boy. Harrah's is ever so much nicer."

"Remember what I said, Jez. We take no chances. It's a small world, after all."

"Yes, I do know that. I first became aware of the fact on a visit to Disneyland, I believe, as a young girl. Thank you very much for putting that tune into my head."

I laugh. "Don't mention it."

"But Carlo, I need to be serious for a moment."

"Yes?"

"Carlo, you have your concerns. I have mine. My one skill, my one great gift in life, is giving pleasure to men. I believe it's fair to say you've been on the receiving end of this benefit, is that not true?"

"Yes, Jezebel, of course. In spades."

"That doesn't mean you should ever take me for a plaything, Carlo. Don't ever trifle with me."

So there it is. A glimpse of the hard edge that I've seen just once before. I take a few moments to measure my response.

I say, "Jezebel, it would be a foolish man indeed who would think of you as anything other than a serious woman."

"Good."

"But just remember, Jezebel, that street runs both ways. Never forget than I am a serious man."

CHAPTER 34
STEPHEN

Detective Jardina,

I like you, but I simply cannot keep killing women just so you and your feckless friends at the Bureau can have renewed opportunities to catch me. You understand that, don't you, Carlo? The circle has to close sometime, somewhere.

You need to start thinking, Carlo, think! Look at the map, doesn't that tell you anything? Have you still no idea who I am when I'm at home? The anagram, my friend, that's the key. If you could only sort it all out, quickly, you'd have a very decent chance of saving a life, which should make you a real hero. That would be nice for you because right now you are looking like a medium-size goat, if my reading of the situation is correct. Or perhaps I should say monkey, you and your colleagues, a pack of silly little monkeys.

Tell you what. The next girl is going to give you a really big clue, the last major clue I can see my way clear to providing. Study her diligently, my friend. Her body will be talking to you, you have my word on it.

Melanie was a bit of a drag, I have to tell you. I'm going to have to be more circumspect in my choice next time. It was nice not doing a blonde for once. That was getting boring, I'll give you that. But this little brunette was one uncooperative little bitch, I swear. It felt so good to break her stupid neck, you'll never know. That cracking sound was music to my ears by the time I'd done with her, she made me work so hard. I wanted to do her letters while she was still alive, very badly. God knows she deserved it. After all the commotion we'd made that night, though, the two of us going at it, I was just very reluctant to cause any more of a disturbance.

The sex was good, maybe the best oddly enough. I think perhaps the adrenaline rush she caused me actually enhanced the pleasure. But then I'm no expert, perhaps you can consult yours. I saved you a souvenir of the act, by the way, which I hope you will treat with the appropriate respect.

You know, I thought seriously of running across the street after Melanie died and grabbing that cute little babysitter. What is she, sixteen? Very nice little cupcake. What an uproar that would have caused in the papers! But then I thought to myself, don't press your luck, Stephen, maybe she has a daddy and besides, what are you, a child molester?

Now I'm going to tell you something, Carlo, from my heart, and I mean this sincerely. I am very, very sorry about the boy. I had no idea. She never mentioned a kid, which is a shame because I'm sure she was thinking that would queer the deal, which it certainly would have and she would be walking and talking today. I'm looking to have some fun out here, you know, maybe looking to off a few broads that no one will ever miss anyway. But I am not a monster, no matter what the shrinks are telling you. I didn't set out to kill a mother. I just thank the good Lord that the child never woke up, as it would have broken my heart to have to kill him. A miracle, if you ask me, considering the noise the two of us made.

I trust you've seen the glossies? Do you approve of the pose? How about the nail color? Works very well, don't you think? To be honest I went back and forth between the green and the aqua. I just hope that someone out there is appreciative of the artistry I bring to my work.

Anyway, detective, I have to run. Work this next one real hard. I can't tell you who she is yet, naturally. I don't know myself. Maybe she'll be a redhead. This I can tell you, though: she'll be childless, mid-thirties with a thing for strange men, she'll be much more submissive than the last one, and she'll probably have a little something in her to calm her down. She'll be naked and posed prettily just for you, she'll be dead as a doornail, and she'll be coming to a city near you, very soon. Watch for her!

Sincerely, Stephen, SAD.

PS. Tell me if you enjoy this one:

An ode to Melanie

When you wish upon a star
It makes a difference where you are
You come into a random bar
If you get with me you won't get far

Let's just say she made my point
Which is really why I picked the joint
The right place, the wrong day
Now there's a tip, that's all I'll say

Postmark: Sioux City, IA
Encl: One Styrofoam box with vial of frozen milky substance, presumably semen. One belly ring, neatly excised, with minimal naval tissue attached.

CHAPTER 35
THERESA

I could of course have called the police in Sioux City, or the FBI, to alert them. However, it would have been too late to save Theresa Lindholm, who lay undiscovered in her Iowa farmhouse, dead for days, even as I read Stephen's latest letter. I knew this for a fact even before Adam's FedEx arrived to fill in the blanks.

She was thirty-six. Her name was Scandinavian but her features Gaelic. She lived alone in a small house on her family's farm ten miles outside city limits. She was an elementary school teacher. She was off for summer vacation. It was a sweltering Midwest August and outside her bedroom window the corn was high as an elephant's eye. She was a plain-featured woman but she had beautiful red hair and all her friends and neighbors, when interviewed in the aftermath of her murder, unfailingly remarked upon her wonderful smile and the fact that when she lit her face up with one she could be as pretty as a picture. She was a tad zaftig for the fashion of the day, especially in comparison with her three predecessors, she was a corn fed farmer's daughter after all, but she had lovely creamy white skin and as I examined the photo of her naked body I could see that she was not without her charms. No steady boyfriends, apparently, but she never went home without being asked to dance, so to speak. The kids were devastated by the news, her students. She was one of the most popular teachers at her school.

I sit once more alone in my apartment, rocking to and fro in my chair. Tonight the lights are up, to accommodate my perusal of the package Adam sent me. The glass of Johnnie Walker is there, on the floor at my left side. I'm going to need it.

We have a fourth, then. Unlike the case with her unfortunate sisters, one does not gaze immediately into her face upon entering the death chamber. She lies supine on her own bed, but she is upside down, which is to say that her head is toward the foot of the mattress. She is in a posture that mimics Christ on the cross, her legs together and her arms outstretched, and I suddenly realize that she is, in fact, attached to a cross. Her viciously cane-striped body is affixed by rope to a sturdy pair of 2 X 10 pieces of lumber arranged in a cruciform fashion and lying atop the bed. Has Stephen set up a carpentry shop in his trunk? Or did he find the tools and material in her house?

Either way, he's done a thorough job of it. Ropes bind both wrists. Her ankles are crossed and likewise bound. More rope around her waist, her neck and her knees, all holding her firmly to the wooden planking. He wanted no trouble this time, he wanted her very still, and thus the ligature marks cut deeply into her flesh. She has apparently died of manual strangulation. The coroner believes that the killer finished her off while having sex with her, no condom this time, and tied her legs together after she was dead.

Less certain is the question of when the lettering was applied, pre or post-mortem. It's been done in a novel manner, having literally been burned into her stomach. This we know for a fact because lying next to her on the bed is one of those nifty little stainless steel torches that are used to caramelize the tops of crème brûlée desserts, sold in finer kitchen stores everywhere. Theresa has been secured so well to her crucifix that it would have been possible to do it before killing her, though I hate to even contemplate the thought and desperately wish it to be untrue.

Her lips are parted and her open eyes bear the same mute testimony to the horrors she's endured that I've seen thrice before. It's chilling to behold. Stephen decided to go with the aqua this time around.

I need a break. I turn away from the photos for a while and busy myself reading the paperwork. The mystery of how Stephen could have gotten those long boards into a Camry is solved. The local authorities have a witness who saw her assailant and is certain he drove a Tundra, forest green. A medium-size pickup truck, pun not intended. It seems Stephen is a two-car family and a loyal Toyota customer to boot.

I needn't look for any more of Stephen's semen in the mail; he left it inside of Theresa this time. I'm struck suddenly by the monstrous irony and it sickens me, the unspeakable sacrilege, the seed of life expressed as climax to this insane ritual of death.

Also inside of her a small quantity of GHB, Gamma Hydroxybutyrate, another date rape drug. Not enough to knock her out for long, just a little something to calm her down.

When I turn back to the photographs, I notice it immediately. It jumps out at me so readily that I'm shocked I didn't see it right away. On the wall above the head of Theresa's bed is an actual crucifix. It's a very nice one. Christ's figure is rendered in well-detailed brass and the cross itself is a lovely dark-stained mahogany. It's approximately twelve inches in height. It's mounted upside down, as is the young Ms. Lindholm. I wonder if it was there on the wall when he came, to be inverted as part of the tableau he left for us. Or was it something he brought to the party himself?

There is one last item in the stack Stoner sent me. It's a sheet of paper with the handwritten note: *Picked her up in church, if you can believe that. That's to you only. AS.*

Work this one with diligence, Carlo, the man said. She'll speak to you if you listen hard enough. So what do you want to tell me, Theresa? What's the clue you died to pass on to me?

Three new elements have been introduced with this crime. Manual strangulation versus garroting. Is this significant? I put it down to Stephen's mounting anger. Choking someone with your bare hands is a more personal and hostile way to kill.

Then there's the manner of inscription of the letters. What difference is there in burning with flame or with electric current? Perhaps, again, an expression of increasing rage.

This brings us to the symbolism of the crucifix, which must be where it lies, the tip off. But what does it tell us about him? Now we know that he has a problem with Christians or Christianity or maybe religion in general, which makes sense, nobody ever figured him for the God-fearing sort, but so what? How does that help us find the sick bastard, or anticipate his next strike? And what's the deal with him changing his hunting grounds from bars to churches? Somebody looking for women willing to engage in casual sex is going to be much better served by the former, obviously. It has to be yet another way of thumbing his nose at us, or at somebody.

It's late, I'm tired and frustrated and my head is sore from hitting a brick wall. I need some air. I take a walk outside to clear the cobwebs, and before returning I grab a Rand McNally atlas from the glove box of my cruiser.

I pour myself another two fingers, grab a red pencil and sit down with the book. Look at the map, he said. There is information there if you are smart enough to tumble to it. I find a page with the entire US on it and mark the four cities. Christ, it's a square, approximately, of which I am to make what? Does he live somewhere inside that box? Does this simple quadrilateral define his theater of operations, and are all safe therefore who dwell outside it?

There's another girl out there whose life depends upon me finding the answer; I'm certain of it. The FBI will never do it. They laugh at intuition and deduction. For them it's all about modern information analysis, sophisticated lab tests, computer modeling and sheer technological firepower. Stephen has given me what I need to find him. He may be crazy, but this much I believe of what he says. I alone possess it, for I've made a decision not to share any more of his letters with anyone, nor the latest souvenirs he's sent me, obstruction of justice be damned.

Besides, there is a bond between us that goes beyond our mutual but diametric interest in his crimes, a bond he could never have dreamed exists. As it happens, I'm preparing to work his side of the street.

CHAPTER 36
STONER

Unlike my poor Mary, Theresa returned to God with much fanfare. A hellish heat wave had abated just in time. Her funeral was a huge event, mourners spilling out of the small Lutheran church where she'd worshipped and assembling into small clusters of perspiration-soaked whisperers and handwringers trading rumors and condolences under a tempered yet still potent Sunday morning Iowa sun. Sioux City and the surrounding communities are bedrock salt-of-the earth heartland, where friends and family still count for much. Theresa Lindholm was blessed with plenty of both.

Added to this the fact that by now the Strip Club Killer, an unfortunate turn of phrase given the identities of his last two victims but his enduring media label nonetheless, this killer was really achieving critical mass in the marketplace of newsworthiness. His crime spree was gaining more national attention by the day, he inspired a delicious kind of dread from coast to coast, this was a slow news summer anyway as it happened, and the continuing escapades of my pen pal Stephen were number one with a bullet. As far as anyone could tell, it was even money whether, assuming they ever caught him, they'd throw him into prison or give him his own talk show. America after all always has a place in her heart for a true artist.

So it was that the coverage of Theresa's farewell was replete with all the trappings of a media extravaganza. An armada of oversized news vans sprouting satellite antennae from their roofs had lumbered into position along the gravel road leading from the highway to the church parking lot, like so many albino dinosaurs assembled along the shore of some Mesozoic lakebed. Correspondents were speaking solemnly into professional-quality HD video cameras or searching out likely candidates to interview, but among their number I could not find Lolita.

You had to feel very bad for her poor family, sluicing through this turmoil in a gleaming caravan of white hearse and flower-laden limousines on the saddest of missions imaginable. It seemed to me the wrong sort of day to have to lower a beloved daughter's mistreated body into a dark and lonely grave, her face never again to be washed by warm dazzling sunlight such as sparkled off the chrome trim of her coffin. This was the sort of splendid vernal day for a young woman like Theresa to fit herself into a beautiful white flowing gown and be married in this beautiful anachronistic white country church, destined for a certainty to live happily ever after.

I finally had to switch off the TV in disgust, though disgust at whom or what I'm still not sure. I pulled the phone off the end table and punched in Stoner's cell phone number.

"How's it going, Adam?" I asked when he picked up.

"Ah, Detective Jardina. Good morning. Why aren't you in church?"

"My faith is a little shaken this Sunday morning, Agent Stoner. Yourself?"

"Myself is feeling a bit irrelevant this Sunday morning. My masters are displeased, very displeased. I'm afraid I've been relegated pretty much to the role of bystander in this investigation, lately. Washington's assuming the reins."

"You're kidding. Really?"

"Makes sense if you think about it. The Phoenix office was a natural since the first killing was in Arizona, which is why I got the nod. I've always been on a short leash, though. Now that he's spread his wings, and it looks like anybody west of the Mississippi is fair game, the hunt needs to get boosted up to a higher pay grade. Believe me, my feelings are not hurt. It's actually a relief."

"The guys up top are feeling a lot of heat just now, I'd guess."

"And by Christ you'd be exactly right. A ton of it. This latest one was a teacher, for God's sake. That's even worse than a mother. People are screaming for results, from every corner. Our roles, Carlo, are strictly ancillary now and we should both thank our lucky stars. It's going to take a long time to find this prick. He's good, damn it."

"I do feel much better since my chief gave up all hope, I have to admit, but I can't let it go. I just keep chewing on it."

"Got any bright ideas?"

"I wish. I have this feeling I can't shake, though, that there's something in his choice of cities that may tell us more than first meets the eye. I just refuse to believe they're selected at random."

"Don't drive yourself crazy, man. With this guy it could be anything. Since you ask, let's take a look at the venues. What do they have in common? Offhand, I can only think of one. They are all small towns, where he might expect to come up against less sophisticated law enforcement, no offense."

"Interesting. You're right. All small towns roughly equidistant from Denver, by the way. No offense taken at your remark concerning local police, by the way. It's a valid point, except it's out the window once it becomes a Federal investigation, right?"

"Yes and no. Maybe. Christ, Carlo, it could be anything. To tell you the truth, for my money he's throwing darts at a map."

"That's where we part company, but thanks for the encouragement. So speaking of Christ, tell me what you make of the inverted cross thing."

"I draw the conclusion that the man is not a fan of Christianity, how about yourself? A good thing, too, because with his lifestyle he'd make a damn poor parishioner."

"Speaking of which. Were you serious about him meeting her in church? The church where they had the funeral?"

"That's a fact. We've managed to keep a lid on the case with the national media, so it isn't out there beyond the local buzz, but yes, he met her at a parish mixer Saturday night, a week ago."

"That's very strange, to totally change his MO like that."

"Yeah. Tough luck for the girl too. She didn't drink anything stronger than punch and never went to bars. She should have been safe."

"You don't just roll into some town and figure on finding an event like that, right, a church social?"

"Right you are. Two schools of thought there. Maybe he decided to grab himself a church-going lady from the beginning, which means advance planning, to find that kind of opportunity. Since I'm pretty sure he's not coming into town early and staying in a motel or hotel, that means the internet. We're looking at that presently, checking hits on the church website for IP's from out of state. It's a small congregation, so it shouldn't take long to run them down."

I think to myself at this point that if I'm smart enough to use a VPN, Stephen sure as hell is. Needless to say I don't share my pessimism with Adam.

I said, "And the second school of thought?"

"The other possibility is he's rolling into town with the same plan as always, to hit a random bar and pick up one of its better-looking patrons and take her home and do her. But then he just happens to drive by Theresa Lindholm's little white church, St. John's Lutheran. It's situated right on the highway, about five miles from Sioux City limits."

"West of town?"

"Right."

"So on the highway you'd be on if you were coming from Denver?"

"Yes, smartass, as a matter of fact that'd be the one. And on the church marquee is a notice of the church's singles mixer, that very PM. A thought occurs to him. He's already pissed off at church-going types for some reason we have no idea what. Why not really stick it to them by doing one of their own, plucked right from their midst?"

"I like it."

"Me too. At any rate, the party starts at 1800 and up he rolls, right on time, into the church parking lot. Several people who were arriving at the same time remember seeing him, and of course they paid special attention because he was a stranger. He's our guy all right. This is farm country and guys know their trucks here. Green Toyota Tundra pickup. Everybody's pretty sure they would have noticed out of state plates if he had them. He didn't. What he did have was a load of 2 X 10's of various lengths in the truck bed. One of our witnesses who'd come over to his vehicle to introduce himself comments on the lumber, and get this, guess what he says? He's a carpenter, just like Jesus."

I said, "Very cute."

"Isn't it? So in he goes to the mixer and starts introducing himself around. Very nice dresser, well-mannered, good conversationalist. A charming dude, in other words. Not too handsome, not too unattractive. You know, average-looking. Gives everyone some happy horseshit about how he's planning to move into their little community and is looking for a parish and some new friends. Uses the name Stephen Dodd. Stephen Allen Dodd, to be exact."

"You're kidding. S-A-D. You running that down?"

"Of course. All over the western states and especially Denver, but we both know we're not going to get that lucky. Now here's something interesting. One of the cops up there mentioned that the Swedish word for death is död. Spelled d-o-d. So maybe that's another one of his little jokes."

"It fits."

"Yes it does. I do believe our friend is messing with our minds. Anyway, Theresa shows up about 45 minutes later and he proceeds to make a beeline for her. Before you know it the two are joined at the hip for the rest of the evening. Word is she was pretty starry-eyed from the get go."

"And they left together?"

"No. She was a schoolteacher and regular churchgoer with a reputation to protect. Not saying she was a virgin. She wasn't. Saying she was discreet. Too discreet to leave a church social function with a man she'd just met. No, he made his good-byes around 2130. She didn't leave for a decent interval after that, maybe 30 minutes. But obviously they'd made plans to hook up later. You know the rest."

"Unfortunately. Well, he sure made a statement. I mean, look, that was a lot of work getting the planks into Theresa's house, assembling them into a cross and getting her strapped onto it. I just wonder what the hell his beef is. With Christians I mean."

"Maybe he got diddled by a priest as a boy."

"I don't think so. His rage is directed at women. I'm willing to bet there's a mother with poor parenting skills in his past, drug addict or alcoholic or worse."

Stoner said, "That would probably be a very good bet."

"So maybe it isn't anger at Christianity per se, maybe he's just playing for the other side."

"What do you mean by that, he's a devil worshipper or something?"

"Could be. That's where I was going. It makes a certain amount of sense, if you think about it, given that he must be completely insane on some level. Satanism would give him a context for his actions, a justification of some crazy sort for doing what he wants to do anyway, which is to violate and slaughter women."

"An interesting take, Carlo, I have to admit."

"So let's say he *is* a Satanist. What good does knowing that do us? How do we use that information to stop him?"

"Beats the shit out of me, Carlo. I'm going to pop a brew and watch some baseball."

"Fine. But before you go. The Bureau has a ton of resources. You must have people who are up on satanic cults, right? I mean who follow them and monitor what they're up to?"

"Mostly you're talking high school kids with that kind of thing, or wacky burned out hippy types. You know, killing cats and running around in the woods at night with candles and goofy outfits and what not. Not a lot of interstate mayhem going on there that would concern us. Maybe every once in a while some poor kid gets sacrificed or otherwise seriously damaged, but it's rare. Definitely not VICAP material.

"But you're right. We do have resources, and we have some fine academic types on staff whose job it is to keep abreast of the full magnificent spectrum of the behavioral phenomena relating to what we are not always proud to call human beings. Now that you ask, Dr. Misty comes to mind. Mitsuko Nakamura. Georgetown PhD psychologist, very well regarded at the Bureau. She has indeed done some work on the status and habits of various satanic cults around the good old US of A, back when we were concerned they might be networking and organizing into something a little more troublesome. She put together a nice little package. I never read it myself but those who did were impressed. Lots of background on belief systems, symbols, vocabulary, rituals and such. I can shoot you a PDF if you want. Should cover what you're looking for. Might even have a recipe for magic potions in the back."

"Thanks. I'd appreciate that. I'll read up on it."

"You do that, detective. Like I said, I have a beer waiting for me."

"Okay."

"Hey, before I go…one more thing."

"What's that?"

"I've been feeling bad that back when we first met, I came on a little strong with you."

"A little strong? You were an overbearing gold-plated prick. I damn near tossed you out of my office a couple times."

"To be honest, I had a very large bug up my ass back then. The thing is, I had never dealt with a serial killer before, obviously. I had no particular expertise that qualified me to take this case. I was just the poor dumb bastard that picked up the phone. So I was unsure of my footing when I came to talk to you. I guess I was overcompensating. Sorry."

"Apologies accepted. Anyway, now that I've gotten to know you better I've upgraded my opinion of you. You're just a silver-plated prick."

"Well, thank you, you're very kind."

"Don't mention it. Actually, I always figured I was in over my head myself, but I'm surprised to hear you say the same."

"Don't be. The truth is that Phoenix is pretty much a backwater assignment for the Bureau. Not a lot of action down here for us. There's no Muslim community to speak of, for us to keep tabs on. The bank robbers are all in LA, where the freeway system is bigger so the getaways are easier. Plus the pickings are fatter. Thanks to the drug cartels we're the kidnapping capital of the USA, but we rarely get too involved with those situations. Usually the Mexicans work that out amongst themselves. A ransom gets paid and nobody gets hurt. That leaves the internet pedophiles. You can always count on that crowd for some business, but that's pretty much fish in a barrel. So the livin' is easy, Carlo, or at least was until Stephen came along."

"So your one big chance for glory comes along and you run smack into a brick wall."

"Exactly. Lucky me, huh? Washington's not going to do any better, but nobody in DC or Langley ever gets tagged with a loss, if you know what I mean."

"Yeah, I believe I do, Adam. Success has a thousand fathers, but failure is an orphan. Crap runs downhill. Et cetera, et cetera."

"Carlo, you know we may well never catch this bastard, don't you? Let's face facts. He's good. He's real damn good. He's playing on his home field, and he's dictating the rules. We're chasing our tails, and while we do a bunch more girls are going to die."

"Well, Adam, that's a proposition I'm not prepared to accept."

"All right, buddy. Good luck to you, and let me know how it works out for you."

"Okay. We'll talk."

"Indeed we will."

After hanging up the phone I spent maybe an hour sitting in my chair and staring at the wall.

It was tough getting to sleep that night. The *dramatis personae* of my life story was getting to be too long. Dancing in my head as I lay awake in bed were the faces of the four dead girls, Mary, Rebecca, Melanie and Theresa, all rendered by my imagination in gruesome four-color detail recreated from the crime scene photography. Then along came Poppy and Celeste. Steven as I imagined him to look. Roger Waterhouse and Summer. And Jezebel. They wanted something from me, each and every one of them, they clamored for my attention or respect or sympathy or justice or vengeance or for complete and uncontested possession of my immortal soul. The pressure was getting to me.

I needed to bolster my flagging resolve. I needed to pull the trigger. I needed the electric touch of Jezebel's skin against my own, and the galvanizing tonic of her soft whisper in my ear.

CHAPTER 37
PHOENIX

The perfect opportunity for me to make my wish come true presented itself in the morning when Amy popped into my office first thing with a chocolate doughnut and an invitation for me. "Uncle Carlo, good morning. We are going to an antiques show at the Convention Center in Phoenix not this weekend but next, and I am authorized by Shannon and Marley to request your presence."

"You are, are you? And who would Marley be?"

"Shannon's new best friend. You saw her at the park the other day. Little Jamaican girl."

"Oh, yeah, sure. You know, Amy, that would be just great." I meant it with all sincerity. Next to Jezebel, Amy was the one person I wanted to spend some time with, perhaps with an honorable mention for the lovely and thoroughly-spoiled Shannon. Even as I spoke the words of acceptance a plan sprung full-blown into my head. "Tell you what, the Accord's going to be a little crowded. I'll drive us in the cruiser. We can run the lights and siren if we find a lonely stretch of road."

"Super, Carlo. The girls will be thrilled. Marley thinks you're handsome."

"Wonderful. And I think she is one perceptive young lady. Hotel rooms?"

"I'll make reservations. I was thinking Embassy Suites. You can have the couch. We'll leave bright and early Saturday so we just have to spend one night."

"That's great, Amy. Thank you very much. I'm looking forward to it."

I counted the minutes until Jezebel's call the next day.

"Jezebel, my sweet. New plan. We're going to see each other for a few hours, a week from next Sunday." I explained the circumstances to her and asked, "Can you get a reservation, say in Scottsdale?"

"That's absolutely wonderful, Carlo. I will. Why the change of heart? Isn't it risky?"

"Not very, I think. I know I have to see you. I'm going half-crazy here. We can do it with minimal exposure. You get a room, you hang out in the pool area. I'll find you. We don't even have to speak, just put a drink or something on your room with the server and I'll overhear the number. I'll slip up after you. As I think about it, it's really very unlikely that anyone would ever remember seeing us together, months from now. Since we met we've spent, what, all of three or four hours in public with each other? It's always been in fairly crowded settings. The risk is very acceptable. Besides, I'm getting close, now. One way or another, it's going to happen soon, and there are some things we need to discuss privately."

"Carlo, darling, I'm looking forward to seeing you so much."

One thing Jezebel was good at was making reservations. She called me back in thirty minutes. The Phoenician. Scottsdale, AZ.

Marley Mowatt, Shannon's new best friend, is a charmer, a life-size ebony cherub in yellow dress and ribbons in her hair to match, with a soft Caribbean lilt in her voice and an infectious *joie* in her laughter. She's named for Bob Marley of reggae fame, a favorite of mine, and in her honor he sings *No Woman No Cry* from the cassette player strapped under my cruiser's dash. She and Shannon join him in full voice from the back seat, as soon as they get the hang of the lyrics.

Amy is beautiful as always to my right. I can never look at her without thinking what if. My arm is outstretched in her direction along the top of the front bench and every once in a while my hand gives her shoulder an affectionate squeeze and we exchange innocent smiles.

We rocket serenely down highway 17 toward Phoenix, the four of us, with Mr. Marley treating us to his best rendition of all the Wailers' hits while his namesake and Shannon gossip and squeal and laugh and squirm ceaselessly, just as you'd expect a pair of preteen girls to do. A two hour drive, plus a stop for burgers and fries, and in between tracks I check the mirror for company and pull my red light off the floor, set it to flashing and goose the cruiser's siren, all to the great delight of my ladies.

There comes a stretch of long straight highway and a momentary lull in the cacophony in the back, and Amy leans over toward me, scoots her bottom to the center of the bench, and says in a voice calculated to be too soft for the girls to hear over the wind noise, "Carlo, you mind if I ask you a personal question?"

"Uh, sure. I mean no, go ahead."

"This lady friend of yours. It seemed you were really stuck on her there for a while. So did you break it off or did she?"

A mile of asphalt unreels beneath us while I consider how to answer the question. Finally I say, "It was sort of a mutual thing, Amy, but I guess if you had to pick somebody, you'd have to say it was she who pulled the plug. Sad to say, Carlo got dumped. Not that it wasn't for the best, in hindsight. There were just too many…problems."

"I see."

I'm not at all sure at this point what it is she sees, but the wheels are obviously turning inside her pretty little head. I'm fully anticipating a follow up, but thank God she lets it rest.

We pull into town shortly before noon, and by twelve-thirty are checked in and unpacked. I've told Amy that I intend to visit an old friend from the East Coast this afternoon, an unnamed goombah from the hood in Philly who moved to Phoenix for his health. I promise I will catch up with her and the girls in the evening and also that I will spend the next morning and afternoon, Sunday, with them at the show. At this point the visit to the big city and the prospect of new toys for the collection have built the excitement level to a fever pitch, so no one is disappointed that I don't join them as they rush out of the room for the short walk to the convention center.

CHAPTER 38
JEZEBEL AND PHIL

She kneels astride me, gazing down into my eyes, her skin flushed a lovely deep rose with the afterglow. Her hair hangs down her breasts and shoulders, long and straight, my Godiva, and her aureoles play peek-a-boo with me in a manner I find strangely alluring. I am sated, thoroughly.

Outside the room, the fair city of Scottsdale bakes under an incandescent August sun that pours down torrents of heat and blinding white light onto the valley. Dozens of well-oiled guests lie tanning in the lavish and sprawling pool complex that fronts the hotel site and overlooks the city. It was here I found Jezebel lounging, her skinny body seductively on display for all in the most scandalous of string bikinis. Right on cue she announced her room number to a nearby waiter for my benefit.

Surprising numbers of golfers cluster along the links of the hotel's course, inexplicably heedless of the withering heat. The fairways string along the base of Camelback Mountain behind the buildings and spill up onto its foothills and into its arroyos, beautifully tended and expensively irrigated and abundantly landscaped with perfect specimens by the thousands of thriving desert flora.

Inside, however, the curtains are drawn, it is dark and cool and the only sound other than our breathing is the soft rush of chilled air. The bed is capacious and grandly clothed, the décor splendid, the overall level of luxury entirely Jezebel-worthy.

I pull her slender torso down onto mine so that she is lying atop me with her head on my shoulder. She nibbles affectionately at the lobe of my ear. I feel the flutter of her heartbeat pulsing against my chest. My hand glides smoothly down the length of her back, her skin is moist with perspiration, my fingers come to rest on her slippery upturned bottom. I say to the ceiling, "It's going to have to be soon, Jezzie. Very soon, like weeks.

Summer has done too good a job. I'm afraid that any day the bastard is going to ask her to marry him and at the same time serve you with papers. That happens, the game is up. You suddenly have a very strong motive to have him killed. It's not a risk I would be willing to take."

"Good. That's just what I've been waiting to hear. Have you found a good situation, yet?" she says softly into my ear.

"Not really. There've been a number of hotel guests around the country being assaulted or otherwise inconvenienced, but it's all isolated stuff. I haven't found any really good streaks. That's all right. We make it a one-of-a-kind, it still works as long as I bring my end off properly. You will have an absolutely rock solid alibi, and there's no way they put the two of us together. As long as I get away from the scene cleanly, we're good. Trust me, this I will do."

She rolls off me, walks over to the dresser and lights a cigarette, grabs an ashtray and sits at the end of the bed. "So, Carlo," she asks me, "how exactly does it work?"

"I pick a city that looks good, I pick a hotel. I make sure Summer has him in the room at a given time, probably I'm thinking around eight in the evening. Not much hall traffic then. Nobody checking in or out. People going to dinner have left, people out for the evening are still out. I get to this city by car, my own, so that ideally it's going to be relatively close to Prescott, say no more than a day's drive, or two. I believe Summer will be having a high school reunion. She's been vague with your husband about her background, on my instructions, so that we have a good deal of flexibility there.

"So I walk into this hotel, I take an elevator, alone, to a floor below or above their room. I use the fire stairs to their level, and I simply knock on their door after of course making sure the hallway is clear."

Jezebel has been following my explanation with strict attention. She asks, "What if they don't let you in?"

"I've thought about that, Jezzie. Say Summer comes to the door. She'll be shocked, of course, to see me out of context. But her instinct, her natural reaction, is to let me in. If Roger answers, I flash my badge and tell him we have a security problem. He'll never notice I'm with an out of town police force. Either way, the moment I'm in and the door is safely closed behind me, I simply pop them both, without further ceremony. Head shots, one apiece, very close range, they are gone in an instant. No terror, no pain. Then some random shots into their bodies so it looks like they've surprised a burglar, he's shot them as best he can and then applied a finisher to each, execution style. I then go about my business making the room look like a robbery gone wrong. I grab Roger's Rolex, his wallet and his cash. Summer's jewelry as well, including I'm told a very nice new diamond necklace. I find their keycard and leave it in the door, so it looks like that's where it was when they returned unexpectedly and caught me off guard ransacking their room.

"That done, I slip out the way I came. My car is parked within walking distance, but not so close as to tie it to the hotel. I jump in and drive away. I comply strictly with all traffic regulations for the entirety of the way home, it goes without saying."

"Isn't somebody going to hear the shots?"

"Excellent question, my dear. I like the way you're thinking. But no, I have a lovely little carry piece I picked up from a gangbanger a few years ago, when I was on the force back East. Four-inch barrel, single stack magazine. The young gentleman, the gangbanger, had even gone to the trouble of filing off its serial number and adding a screw-on silencer, which was very helpful. I figured he was on probation, his type always are, and I must have figured right because he didn't make a fuss about parting with it; he was just happy that I let him bounce. Anyway, it's just the sort of thing every cop likes to keep in reserve, just in case."

"In reserve? In case your service pistol jams, you mean?"

"Not so much, Jez. As long as you keep them clean and put only high quality ammo through them, modern automatic pistols do not jam. That's pretty much a myth. Sometimes amateurs neglect to rack the first round and are disappointed when their gun doesn't fire, so there is that. But if you know what you're doing and treat it right you can count on your weapon.

"However, you never know as a cop when you're going to make a mistake and shoot some poor asshole who you think is strapped but turns out he isn't. Embarrassing situation, kind of thing you don't really want on your record. So if in these unfortunate circumstances you're in a position to, uh, enhance the scene of the incident, well then it really goes much smoother. Internal Affairs pretty much has to be onboard with it's a good shooting. You see?"

"Yes, Carlo, I see. You boys in blue can be so bad. Anyway, he was guilty of something, right, this late theoretical suspect, or else what's he doing crossing your path in the first place?"

"There you go. Now you understand. Of course, that's a situation in which you've acted in what you believe to be self-defense. There are other scenarios."

Jez looks puzzled. She asks, "What do you mean?"

I think about it for a few moments, whether I should really even get into it. I walk over to the window and part the drapes just enough to peek outside. I squint against the dazzling light of the sun, which has begun slowly to fall into the western sky. The air on the other side of the glass is dry and brittle as September leaves.

Finally I say, "Well, what the hell, let me tell you a little story to illustrate what I'm talking about, okay?"

"Okay, sure."

"As it happens, my first job as a cop was with the police department of the City of Brotherly Love. It's where I cut my teeth, you might say. After five years I escaped to a nice cushy job up in Bucks County, but that's a whole different story. Back in Philadelphia I had this, uh, friend, and let's call him, I don't know, Phil. Now this Phil, he's been on the force two years at the time, just like me. And just like me he's come to the world of law enforcement with very high ideals and aspirations. 'Honor. Service. Integrity,' that was our motto, and we believed it. We were going to save the world.

"Except two years of duty with the Philadelphia Police Department will really change your perspective, I'm here to tell you. It tends to make you very cynical. So to appreciate the story you need to understand Phil's frame of mind. Phil had become very frustrated and disappointed with the great majority of his fellow human beings."

Jez says, "I see."

"Good. So one night my friend is called to respond to a domestic disturbance in a very unfashionable part of town. Neighbors have reported a loud ruckus, lots of yelling, sound of furniture being broken, you get the picture. The apartment in question is in a tenement building, third floor walkup, a very sketchy deal.

"After he pulls up to the address in question, Phil leaves his partner at street level to cover the main entrance and up he trudges. When he arrives at the front door of the apartment all is quiet except for the sound of a television he can just barely hear in the background. He knocks on the door. No response. He draws his service weapon, a Glock nine, and tries the knob. *Voila*, it's unlocked. In he walks.

"To his right is the kitchen area, well lit, and on the floor is an unconscious young girl who clearly has been beaten to within an inch of her life. I mean, she was gonna survive but whether she would ever be the same was anybody's guess. Her face was a pulpy bloody mess, but judging from her body, which was half naked, he figured her for sixteen or seventeen. As it happens she was a street prostitute who had failed to bring home enough cash that evening to her pimp.

"Now this gentleman, her pimp, is seated in a lazy boy chair in the corner of the living area, to Phil's left. He's watching this little, like nineteen inch, television, the one my buddy had heard from the hallway, and which is the only source of illumination in the room. Guess what he's watching, this character?"

Jez says, "I haven't a clue. What?"

"Judge Judy. He's watching Judge Judy reruns. Now for reasons known only to himself, this fact pisses Phil off. Just the whole inappropriateness of it all, maybe. Phil had no daughters, or for that matter sons, of his own, but I suspect the sight of this poor exploited and abused child, lying there bleeding on the floor, evoked a righteous dose of fatherly instinct in him.

"He tenses up, not knowing what sort of reaction he's going to get from the pimp to his uninvited presence, but obviously alert to the possible danger inherent in the situation. But no, the guy is as harmless as he can be. He just sits there in the lounger, both arms outstretched with his hands, empty, in plain sight. After a few moments of the two just staring at each other, the pimp gives him a big shit-eating grin and says, 'Bitch had it comin', man. Little ho was holdin' out on me.' Then he puts the grin back on and just sits there, watching the show.

"At this point, many things go through Phil's mind. He calls in an ambulance for the girl right away, of course. But what about the pimp? He can of course cuff him and arrest him right there on the spot. However, odds are the girl, when she's able to say anything, will say she refuses to press charges. If the PA goes after this piece of shit anyway his attorney will delay the trial until she's completely healed. The pimp will show up in a nice new suit with his mother on his arm, the girl will waltz into the courtroom dressed like a Catholic schoolgirl, the two of them will swear it was all just a misunderstanding, and worst case he gets six months, maybe less, with probation.

"Phil is contemplating the very aggravating injustice of it all when, out of the blue, his Glock, which until now has been hanging innocent and forgotten from his right hand, develops a mind of its own and the next thing Phil knows is he's looking at the pimp and the guy has a nine millimeter hole in his face, slightly to the right of his nose. It's anybody's guess what this young gentleman had been thinking, but we do know the last thing that went through his mind: a standard issue Philly PD soft point bullet. The back half of his head is missing and what was once his brain is now spattered all over the wall behind the lazy boy, which, by the way, is going to need to be reupholstered."

Jez says, "Ouch."

"Ouch, indeed, and you can easily imagine the gravity of my buddy's sudden predicament. The ambulance for the girl is on the way, siren wailing. He's just made a very loud noise in a building with very thin walls, and speaking of thin walls probably put a round not only through the head of the poor late pimp but the wall behind him as well, into the adjoining unit. Neighbors will be gathering in large numbers in the hallway, and eventually in the street below. Now I don't know how this splendid example of humanity was viewed by his fellow tenants. I'm guessing unfavorably. But for Phil's purposes it really didn't matter. A white cop shooting an unarmed black man, that's not going to be well-received in the community we're discussing under any circumstances.

"His partner is no doubt running up the stairway to join him, and Phil has no idea which side of this particular moral dilemma he's likely to come down on, his partner I mean. He's one of only two white men within a radius of five miles, probably, and he's just, well, executed I guess is the word, an unarmed black man. Lots of people, many of them very angry, are going to be asking lots of embarrassing questions. Not a happy situation.

"However, and fortunately for him for sure, Phil is prepared. He's taken the precaution of carrying an unregistered snub nose revolver with him on patrol, which he promptly removes from inside the leg of his right boot with gloved hand and places in the right hand of the inconvenient corpse. Problem solved, and the vital importance of a reserve piece demonstrated."

Jez says, "Problem solved at least as long as the pimp wasn't left-handed."

"Hah! You are a clever girl. Yes, that was one element of Phil's plan that he overlooked. There was that 5% chance. This time he got lucky. Like I was saying, 'Honor. Service. Integrity.' No honor in his actions, perhaps, and certainly no integrity. But he's of the opinion that he has definitely rendered a service to the community, and who would argue with him?"

Jezebel just sits there giving me the eye, with a look on her face I've never seen. Ordinarily she can read me like a book. Not this time, though. This time she's thinking about the story I've just shared with her and wondering, well, you know.

After a while I say to her, "So anyway, I have this piece. Perfectly clean, very quiet when fitted with the suppressor. No guest is disturbed. I'll ditch it the minute I get a chance, throw it in a river or something after of course removing my prints. Also the valuables from their room, I'm very unhappy to say."

"How'd he get in?"

"Sorry?"

"The burglar. How did he get into the room? The police are going to be curious about that part. If they surprised him, so that he reacted in panic and killed them both, if that's the story then they obviously didn't open the door for him, right? So how do you figure he got in?"

I have to give it to her. Jezebel has a natural criminal mind. I have to wonder at the dichotomy. With her girlish body perched cross-legged at the foot of the bed and naked as the day she was born, she looks more the Sunday school teacher than co-conspirator to murder.

"Another excellent question, my sweet. You'd be amazed how easy it is to open your typical hotel door. You just need to slip a piece of stiff paper or a credit card between the door and frame to trip the latch. Of course sometimes these sorts of things, hotel robberies, are inside jobs. People with access to master keycards, for example, find themselves unable to resist temptation. I suppose the police might go in that direction, though I don't really like it. That's small time crime, not likely involving anyone with a gun. Going down that road, too, they'll very quickly hit a dead end."

"So this anonymous burglar is an outsider who just happens to randomly pick the suite of the wealthiest couple in the hotel?"

"Why not? They'll be staying on the concierge level, where one would assume every guest is pretty well-heeled."

She says "I suppose," but only half-heartedly and I can see the wheels are turning in her pretty head, and she's not happy.

She says, "What if he followed them, Carlo?"

"What?"

"The killer. Say he followed them to their room. Picked them up in the lobby, or even outside the hotel, on the street or at a restaurant, maybe. The two of them will look pretty prosperous if I know Roger. He's a flashy dresser from way back, and from what I've heard of the little whore, she'll be sporting more than just the new diamond necklace. She'll be pretty much looking like a friggin' jewel-encrusted European princess. So the attacker notices this, follows them to their room pretending to be another guest, and as they open the door forces his way in behind them."

After thinking about it for a minute I say, "Yeah, Jez, I like it. Roger decides to be a hero, he goes for the guy's gun, he gets a bullet in the belly for his trouble."

"Exactly. Summer turns and tries to make it to the door. She's shot in the back. Then they each get one in the head, just to make sure. He's a pro. Once shots are fired he makes sure there are no witnesses left behind."

"That'll work."

"And another thing, Carlo. You should shoot them like that, in the order we just talked about. Roger in the stomach, first, gun right up against him, like you were struggling for it. Then Summer in the back. Then their heads. The coroner may be able to tell which wounds occurred first."

"Sweetheart you've been watching too much TV. In the real world, trust me, the action is not exactly going to be scripted, and the ME is not going to be that good. But sure, whatever. I'll do what I can."

Jezebel is positively glowing with an almost animal excitement. It dawns on me that we've bonded in the last few minutes, discussing this crime, in a more powerful way than we have during all the terrific sex we've enjoyed. "My God, Carlo, I can't believe it. It's really going to happen, and soon. I can't wait until it's over and we're together."

"Me neither, lover. But yes, the time has nearly come. Only just don't forsake me, Jezebel, after it's done. Don't go forgetting we're partners. Don't go breaking my heart."

She takes a last long drag on her cigarette and stubs it out. Returns the ashtray to the dresser. Walks back to the bed, completely naked and completely delectable. Climbs back on top of me. The soft touch of her hair against my chest. The delicious thrill of her wet belly sliding down my own. Wraps her arms around my neck and gives me a long, slow, deep kiss. Says, "Don't you worry, Carlo. I'm yours. I'm going to make you the happiest man alive."

CHAPTER 39
CHINESE CHECKERS

It turns out the antique show is disappointingly free of antique toys. It's late Sunday afternoon, we've traipsed all over the convention center for hours, and we've pretty much seen it all. No toys. I'm ready to walk to the cruiser, grab my service pistol and put it to my head. Finally we see Shannon, who is ahead of us along the last row of concessionaires' booths we have yet to visit, motioning excitedly. She's finally found one that interests her.

It's operated by an Englishwoman in her mid-sixties, with gray-streaked hair, wearing a rumpled maroon dress, a rumpled face and oversized octagonal spectacles. Her name is Catherine. Her inventory is a disorganized mess, but it's our last chance to score. While Shannon and Marley dig into her treasures she serves Amy and me afternoon tea and keeps us entertained with a surprisingly rich vein of dry British humor.

Her offerings lean toward the occult. Tarot cards, Ouija boards, crystal balls, magician's props, astrological paraphernalia and the like. She also has a fair assortment of turn-of-the-century game sets. Cribbage boards in burl elm with pegs of semiprecious stone, intricately inlaid backgammon boards with hand carved onyx and obsidian markers, elaborate chess sets, the pieces rendered in silver and brass. All these and more are displayed in haphazard stacks surrounding her table.

After much rummaging Shannon drags a prize from the middle of one of the stacks. It's a very well-preserved Chinese checkers board, manufactured London 1902, in its original container with an included wooden box for the marbles. The piece is a circular metal disc with a star-shaped pattern painted on its surface, a six-pointed star, and with holes punched for the marbles. Each arm is a separate color, black with pastel green, pink, pale yellow, baby blue, ivory and faded violet. It's very nicely made with no sharp edges, and the paint is unscratched. After some extended haggling it sets Amy back nearly three hundred dollars.

Amy has never seen a Chinese checkers set, perhaps until today has never realized that such a thing as Chinese checkers exists. It's been way too long for me, like when I was a kid in Philadelphia, and so it falls to Catherine to explain the game to the girls.

"Now ladies," she tells them, "it goes just this way. As many as six, or as few as two can play. As you can see, the game is made with a six-pointed star, a hexagram, or as some call it the Star of David. And as you can also see, each arm is a different color. Each player is given ten marbles, matching the color of one arm of the star, which are then arranged in the holes of that arm. This is the player's home base. The center is neutral territory. Each player then attempts to move all of his or her marbles into the arm opposite his own, before another player does the same. Marbles are advanced by moving from one hole to another, one space each turn, one turn at a time.

"However, one may also hop one's own marbles, or an opponent's. This is where the fun starts. As in regular checkers, multiple hops are allowed and in this case a marble is not limited to moving one space, but may be advanced in one turn as far as hopping opportunities allow. Unlike checkers, mind you, marbles that are hopped by an opposing marble are not removed from the board and eliminated from the game.

"By the way, it isn't really Chinese at all. No one knows quite where the name came from. But quite entertaining, it is, the more so as players are added and everyone is trying to sort out the traffic jam in the middle. Simple enough, then, isn't it?"

This to a pair of solemn affirmative nods by Shannon and Marley, which were evidently sincere because the two girls were thoroughly immersed in the game the better part of the trip home.

We hit a pizza parlor on the way out of town, as a change of pace from hamburgers. Everybody was tired of reggae and so we motored along to the upbeat sounds of Jimi Hendrix and Pink Floyd. I particularly enjoyed the latter's *Money*.

We got a late start and so even though it was the middle of summer darkness had settled in by the time we neared the turnoff for Prescott.

We hadn't heard any noise from the back seat for a while, and up front we'd driven for maybe fifty miles in silence.

Out of nowhere Amy said to me, sotto voce. "So did she break your heart, Carlo, this woman? Is that why you've seemed to shut down?"

I needed to put this to bed, no pun intended, once and for all. I had too much on my plate to have also to deal with this sort of distraction. I said, "Amy, believe me, it's not like that. Frankly, I'm happy it's over. It was a mistake from the beginning. I just fell under the ether. We were very wrong for each other, in every way, from the beginning. I'm completely over it."

"So what does a girl have to due to put you under the ether, Carlo? Not a trick I've been able to manage."

Christ, I thought to myself. To Amy I said, "Amy, you and Shannon have had me under your spell from the beginning. You are without question in terms of physical beauty and intelligence and character, or any other metric you may have devised by which to compare yourself to other women, far superior to this woman, with whom I had a short and meaningless fling."

Another five miles of asphalt under the hood and then, "I see."

"I hope so, Amy, because believe me, and this is the God's honest truth even though you may not be buying today, I am not a man with whom you want to be involved romantically. That is absolutely no reflection on you. It's my shortcomings we're discussing."

There was no response, and so I added, "We have a beautiful relationship, you know? We have a friendship that is deeper and a whole lot less problematic than romance. Let's not screw it up with sex. I understand of course that you also need that dimension in your life. Lucky for you there's a long line of volunteers for that duty, any one of whom would be a far better choice than this monkey."

An hour later we pulled up in front of Amy's house. The girls were out cold and so I carried them into the house and put them to bed, after which Amy and I sat on her sofa and shared a moment and a glass of wine. The subject of romance didn't come up again.

CHAPTER 40
ROBIN

Wednesday evening of the following week. I was just getting ready to go to bed when out of the blue the phone rang. It was Stoner. He said, "Carlo, I have some news for you."

"What's up?"

"I've been doing a little extracurricular research in my spare time. I got to thinking about the whole satanic devil worship thing, and you know, murders with that angle just are not all that common. Then it was bothering me what you said, about the John Doe semen samples and how they should be categorized. I began to realize that maybe I could find something in our back files, crimes where local jurisdictions have sent us samples for analysis. There's a ton of them, and they haven't all been digitized yet, so it's taken me some time."

I said, "I thought you were off the case."

"I'm no longer lead, but I can nibble around the edges as long as I don't step on any toes."

"Jesus, Adam, that has to be a huge job."

"Yes, but I made some assumptions that narrowed it down. We figure Stephen is maybe mid-thirties. If I'm right and he has killed before, he probably would have started in his early twenties, maybe even mid to late teens. So I started at twenty years ago and worked forward. Then I decided to go with your theory that he lives in the Denver area. Doesn't mean he always has, of course, but it's a place to start that keeps the workload manageable. From there it was pretty quick sorting through the cases looking for something with the devil worship angle."

"So how'd you do?"

"Sixteen years ago. Castle Rock, Colorado, which is maybe 35 clicks south of Denver, halfway to Colorado Springs. A fifteen year old high school girl goes missing on her way home from class one afternoon. Of course a major search effort ensues, and after five days they find her body in a clearing in the woods, like about ten miles west of town off a county road leading toward the foothills of the Front Range. She's been staked to the ground and killed in what appears to be a very involved satanic ritual. Naturally, she's been brutally raped. She was a virgin, Carlo, a beautiful innocent little girl. Name was Robin. Robin Cleary."

"Our guy?"

"Well, we didn't have the actual evidence package anymore. It had been sent back to Castle Rock PD. So I asked them to dig it up and forward it to me. Back then we weren't running DNA profiles, and the semen sample was at this point obviously pretty old, but our lab boys were able to run it and compare it to the Bergstrom sample."

"And?"

"Bingo, Carlo."

"So you were right about him having a history."

"Yes, unfortunately. And you were right about Denver. I don't know if this is really going to help us, but it's a piece of the puzzle we didn't have before. At least we have a general location for his ass, which isn't nothing. I sent you a copy of the file. You should get it in the morning. Meantime, I'm taking a real hard look at this case and searching for more. Once I'm done with Denver I'll widen the circle to cover the rest of Colorado, and then the surrounding states. I have a feeling he's always liked to spread his hunting ground out as he goes, which is what kept him under the radar so long. Anyway, maybe we get lucky and find something the original investigations missed, something that will lead us to him."

The FedEx envelope arrived at the station the next day just before lunch. The typewritten investigative report was maybe half an inch thick, and I decided to put my other case files aside and start reading immediately. It was pretty much going to be an exercise in futility, I was afraid, but I still wanted to go through it carefully, just in case there was some obscure little piece of the puzzle waiting to be found.

In addition to the report were a set of crime scene photos and a yellowed copy of the girl's obituary in the local paper. I really wasn't anxious to see the photos, and so I turned to the newspaper article first.

She smiles at me in faded black and white, a beautiful young girl with long blonde hair and a megawatt smile, full of life. She is, was, an honor student and a star distance runner on the school track team. She volunteered at the local convalescent home. She sang glee. She was popular with and beloved by all who knew her. She wore a promise ring on her left hand, signifying her vow to remain chaste until marriage. Jesus, is that why he picked her? Was she, in his sick mind, a virgin sacrifice? Is that why she's now very much dead?

Virtually the entire town of Castle Rock turned out for her funeral and interment.

And then, reluctantly, the photos. The first several show the approach through the woods to the crime scene, and then a partial view of her body, taken through the trees and brush.

The final shot is a close-up of the gruesome aftermath. She lies face up in a clearing covered with pine needles, moss and other detritus. She is nude and has been staked to the ground by her wrists and ankles, legs and arms widespread. A circle has been traced by some sharp object, a stick perhaps, so as to circumscribe her body in a way that reminds me of the famous drawing by da Vinci. Half-burned candles, now extinguished, are placed at intervals on the ground around her. Blobs and rivulets of black and red wax are congealed along and down the sides of her arms and legs. The burning liquid candle wax has been dripped and spattered pre-mortem along the length of her limbs to torture her.

A symbol has been finger painted in what appears to be blood on her abdomen. It consists of a star inside a circle. A dried puddle of what is almost certainly semen has been deposited, probably ejaculated onto, the star. From the symbol a thin line of blood, such as might have been formed by the killer lightly drawing a knife along her skin, ascends along her torso to a point halfway between her breasts. At this point the handle of what looks to be a very large kitchen knife emerges from her chest, where the blade has been plunged a single time into her heart.

The image of the circled star on her belly nags at my memory, and it takes me a few minutes to remember where I've seen it before. Finally it hits me. The piercing Dr. Koz found on Mary Bergen's body. It all adds up.

Robin's eyes are open and staring at the sky in the terror I've seen too many times before. Her hair is carefully arranged in a corona around her head in a manner which is also familiar to me. A gag fashioned from her own panties has been used to suppress her screams. Yes, this is Stephen's work, all right. There is no doubt of that.

Fifteen year old girls, perhaps a number of them. Christ. Goddamn it, I want to scream. I want to put my fist through a wall. I want to stop this sick son of a bitch at all cost. I have to put him out of business, any way I can.

This is part of what I was trying to get at with Poppy, that day in the cemetery. Even if this monster is eventually caught and convicted there is no way he ends up on a table with a lethal IV in his arm. Back in the day, in Poppy's neighborhood, somebody rapes and kills a young girl, they fish his testicle-free corpse out of the Schuylkill River a week after he's caught. So whose world occupies the moral high ground?

I felt righteous anger rising in a hot flush inside me such as I haven't experienced in decades. To be fair, it should have been tempered by the fact that I myself was contemplating murder. There was a difference though. Stephen's killings were cruel and pointless. Mine would be neither.

I took one last hard look at the final photograph, and slapped the file closed. You will be unsurprised to learn that I skipped lunch.

CHAPTER 41

NO. 5

Saturday morning. My radio woke me at 0630 with the splendid news that the Strip Club Killer had struck for the fifth time. I ran into the living room and flipped on the TV. Fox News was doing continuous coverage, and sure enough it looked like Stephen had indeed dispatched yet another victim.

Dateline Denver CO. The screen is a live feed of the exterior of a not particularly prosperous-looking motel, with a facial shot of the murdered girl superimposed in the upper left corner. Every once in a while they run tape of a black body bag being wheeled out of one of the ground level rooms and into the ME's van. No video of the crime scene itself, naturally, but the anchor is building as lurid a mental picture for her audience as propriety allows. No. 5 has apparently been killed in the customary manner, which is to say bound, tortured, raped, strangled and posed.

For what it's worth, the talking head informs us that the poor dead girl is, or was, of mixed race, African-American and Asian. Judging from the photo they're using, which appears to have been a portrait taken from a yearbook, it was a very nice combination. She was gorgeous. I didn't catch her name. She'd been working as a paralegal for one of the larger law firms in Denver, but according to the Chyron crawl there are unconfirmed reports she'd been moonlighting as an escort for beer money. If true, this fact would of course fit right into the picture for Stephen, and rumors to that effect, having surfaced almost immediately, played a key role in attributing the crime to him.

A couple of things bothered me about this one, however, things that didn't seem to fit the pattern. First of all, I'd pretty much convinced myself that Stephen was operating out of the Denver metro area, which would if my theory was correct eliminate it as a hunting and killing zone for him. Also, until now at least he'd always killed his victims in their own homes and left them there. Then there was the fact that I'd gotten no heads up letter from him, though with the USPS you never know.

Finally, there was the issue of the victim's race. Historically most serial killers are white and we certainly know that this is true in the case of Stephen. As a general rule, though not a hard and fast one to be sure, serial killers confine themselves to their own race. Of course, if he ordered her up from an escort agency he might have been stuck with pot luck. Though that, too, would be a break in his pattern. Until now he'd done his hunting in public, in locations where he'd had a choice of women, and his victims had been handpicked.

The thing that bothered me most, I realized as I brewed myself a pot of coffee and scrambled some eggs for breakfast, was the harsh fact that this beautiful child should have ended up selling her body for a lousy couple of bucks, and that she should have paid such a tragic price for that foolish misjudgment. She was, after all, someone's daughter.

But then, so was Summer.

My doubts about the case were resolved as soon as I stepped into my office. The answering machine was blinking and the fax machine had just finished cranking out a color photo. It was from the Denver crime scene and showed the young girl in question bound spread-eagled and nude on her bed, the cord used to strangle her still wrapped around her neck.

Stamped in large letters across the face of the photograph were the words: *FBI Official Crime Photo. Not For Distribution. Eyes Only.* A plain page followed from the fax machine, upon which Adam had scribbled: *Good morning. This is just a souvenir for your collection. Kindly do not share or duplicate. One Tamako (Tammy) Raye. "Professional" name Candy. No letters on her stomach. No DNA. Copycat.*

So at least Washington was keeping Adam in the loop, which of course kept me in the loop, which made me feel good. We both at this point were taking more than a merely professional interest in Stephen's avocational activities.

I returned my attention to the crime scene photograph. She lies face up, her dead eyes wide open and staring into eternity the way I was getting used to seeing. Ropes are tied around each of her wrists and ankles and from there across the mattress and down to the respective corners of the metal bed frame, leaving her totally helpless. Each extremity is severely chafed and bruised where the cords have restrained her futile struggles. It appears that she has sustained a bludgeoning wound to the left side of her head, as there is a substantial though nonlethal amount of blood that has dripped onto the pillow and sheet below her ear. Apparently her killer used some sort of club to render her unconscious, probably when she first came through the door.

She has the slender frame, straight glossy black hair and almond-shaped eyes of an Asian woman, but her skin, which is smooth and mocha-colored, and her high cheekbones are clearly from her African-American parent. Her belly is unblemished, as is the rest of her body. She is entirely clean-shaven and her breasts are small, so that she looks very much younger than her 22 years. I imagine she was quite a hit with those among her clientele with a taste for the prepubescent.

Silver duct tape encircles the lower part of her head and completely covers her mouth. A length of the same type of rope used to secure her to the bed has been wrapped around her throat in a single loop and pulled tight until she died. No multiple ligature marks can be seen. No real indication of sadistic torture, despite the media reports. It's as if the perpetrator was in a rush and had a very simple agenda: get her to the room, subdue her, take his pleasure with her and kill her, quickly and quietly. Clearly the whole operation lacks the sophistication of a murder by Stephen. Whoever did it was not nearly as methodical or pathologically cruel as my pen pal.

The missed call was also from Stoner, and I picked up the phone to return it.

"Good morning, Detective Jardina. How's everyone doing in Prescott this fair morn? You have the double parkers and the taggers under control up there?"

"Actually, no. And the jaywalkers are running wild. We're thinking about asking the governor to call out the National Guard. And so how goes it with the fair-haired boys from the Bureau? Looks like you have a new problem on your hands."

"Yeah, ain't that grand? Exactly what we've been afraid of. The effing media have given our guy so much air it was only a matter of time before an imitator came out of the woodwork. This just makes it twice as urgent we get him and get him soon."

"So there were no letters on her body, I see."

"No letters and whoever killed her was extremely careful to leave behind no personal biological material. Bastard must have shaved his entire body clean and used a double layer of condoms, plus worn latex gloves. Crime scene monkeys are drawing a blank. This one really values his privacy. Maybe his DNA is on file somewhere, unlike Stephen. No question it's a copycat."

"I suspected as much when I first heard about it. I've always believed he's living in the Denver area, and certainly the Cleary murder lends weight to that argument. Also I haven't gotten any letters from him lately. Passing up a chance to taunt me would be unlike him."

"Can't argue with any of that."

"How'd you get all this information together so fast, by the way?"

"The body was actually discovered late Saturday night. Her agency, an outfit called Dream Girls Entertainment if you can imagine, tipped the cops off that she hadn't checked back in from an appointment they'd set up for her. The police sent somebody around to knock on the door of the motel room she'd been sent to and found it unlatched, so they let themselves in. Somebody at the department put two and two together, amazingly enough, and gave our local office a call. We had a team on it before sunrise Sunday. We didn't give it to the media until last night, and as you can see we haven't let them in on the copycat part yet."

"Why not?"

"For one thing we don't want the public knowing we have ways of determining very quickly whether or not a killing is the real deal or not, or asking what those ways are. Anyway, they don't seem to give a shit any more about whether what they report is accurate, so why should we?"

"A fair point."

"Any leads on the new guy, then?"

"Not actually our case, but no, I don't think so, nothing solid right now anyway. The room the girl was called to was paid for with cash, of course. Nobody saw either of them come or go. No security video. Desk clerk gave a pretty vague description of the guy and got no vehicle information from him. Denver PD thinks he's maybe being disingenuous with them and are wondering if he may be involved somehow. He's had some unusual memory lapses and contradicted his own story a few times, but the interrogators have had no luck rattling him. The call to Dream Girls was made from a payphone, it turns out, just a couple blocks from the scene of the crime. They're dusting it as we speak, so maybe they get lucky there."

"Think he'll do any more?"

"Not if history's a guide. The thing is, there are characters wandering around loose out there who go around thinking that this sort of thing, raping and offing some poor random girl, would be kind of fun, maybe just once for a lark, but they don't do it because they can't accept the risk of getting caught. They're cowards, cowards who don't have the brains or balls to break an egg on their own. Then an opportunity like this comes along for them to take one free shot and get it out of their system. They think their crime will just get chalked up as another one for the serial killer and they'll slip away under the radar."

"At least that's what you're hoping."

"At least that's what I'm hoping."

"I have to wonder what the world's coming to."

"What I have to wonder is how your friend Stephen is going to take to having some competition."

CHAPTER 42

STONER AGAIN

Monday evening. The phone rang shortly after I got home from the office. I picked up, thinking it might be the department. It was Stoner.

He said, "Sorry to call after hours, again, Carlo. Hope I'm not interrupting dinner."

"No worries. Living the dream here in Prescott. Just cracked a bottle of five dollar wine and I have a couple of cartons of leftover Chinese takeout in the microwave that's not going anywhere. What do you have for me?"

"I've been working the Denver thing hard this last week. By the way, I've also let Washington in on our theory, so I've had some help on that end. I just got home from the office, and I believe I have a reasonably complete update for you on the early days of Stephen's glorious career."

"Great. I can't wait. Shoot."

"It turns out that Robin Cleary was the last of a series of killings, all centered on the Denver metro area and committed within a two year span. The victims were all taken from smaller towns within a fifty mile radius. There were two others we're more or less certain of and probably four."

"Jesus. You're kidding."

"Don't I wish? Turns out he started eighteen years ago. First was a high school girl in Boulder. She just vanished into thin air one day. They eventually found her body in the woods outside town, up near the base of the Flatirons."

I said, "And was she staked out on the ground with the candles and all?"

"No, it looks like he was just beginning to develop his technique at this point. The Cleary girl was the last of them and his crowning masterpiece. This one in Boulder was two years earlier. She had simply been raped and strangled and dumped. She did have a large 'S' carved into her abdomen. Didn't mean much to the investigators at the time, but it's good enough for me. We're running the semen now, but it's that much older than the Cleary sample, so who knows. Anyway, like I said, it's close enough for me.

"Next one was just about a year later. Girl in Centennial. Another teenager. She was apparently abducted right off the street, walking home from school after cheerleading practice. They found her in the woods after a couple weeks. This one was staked and had a bloody devil symbol dabbed onto her. She got the knife in the heart treatment. No candles, though. No rituals. No black masses. Centennial PD managed to lose track of the crime scene evidence after the case went cold, but here again I'm good with this one being Stephen. I have pics of both crime scenes if you're interested."

"I'm gonna pass."

"Excellent choice," he said. "After the second girl everybody tumbled to the connection, of course. Both cases were sent to us and a file was opened. At that time, unfortunately, DNA testing was unavailable. It wouldn't have been much help anyway, as it turns out."

"And so you mentioned maybe two more?"

"Possibly, but we'll never know for sure, at least not unless we catch the bastard and he confesses. Both were teenage girls that went missing around that time. Same thing, vanished with zero trace. One wasn't found for a couple years. A pair of hunters just stumbled onto her remains, which by then were completely skeletonized, and so we have no useable information on her manner of death. The other girl was never found."

I said, "And then they just stopped?"

"Yes. Naturally, it was a huge story in the area, especially after the second one. These were all attractive young white girls, mind you, and the local media were all over it. Everybody was terrified. Never hit the national wires, but then that was a pretty busy time, news-wise.

"When Robin Cleary was killed, with all the horrific details made public, people just went nuts. Gun and ammo sales went through the roof. Neighborhoods formed their own watch committees and posses and started patrolling the streets. Nobody, and I mean nobody, walked to school unless with a crowd of fellow students. The investigations never went anywhere, though. There were no more victims, and after time it all just began to be forgotten. The cases all went cold and of course were left open but for all practical purposes were shelved."

"So what would have made him stop?"

Adam said, "Any number of possibilities. Maybe it just got too hot for him and he stopped liking his odds of getting away with it. Maybe his family moved away from the area, and he didn't return until later as an adult. Maybe he went away to college. Or maybe he just got it out of his system for the time being. It happens."

"Or maybe he never did stop. Maybe he's been killing all along, just somewhere else."

"A definite possibility, unfortunately. I doubt it, though. The way this guy goes about his business, the signature he leaves on his work, he would have attracted our attention before now, I'm pretty sure. Our information systems are too good these days. Maybe the odd one-off here and there, the sort of thing that might not make it into VICAP, but nothing like what we have now."

I said, "So no strippers in the early days, or mothers or teachers."

"Hell, he was probably only a kid in high school himself at the time. He's just begun to work on his serial killer merit badge. He's not going to want to take on someone older and savvier than he is. He obviously can't get into clubs and he's too young to be chatting up the older ladies, even if he could. So he's going to be picking on girls his own age or younger. Clueless teenyboppers, ripe for the picking, and he's going to just grab them right off the street. He lures them into his car and off they go on their last ride."

"Which explains why he's doing them out in the sticks rather than their homes. They don't have places of their own."

"Exactly. It's also less likely that the bodies are ever discovered that way. He's definitely gotten cockier in his old age. This latest batch, he wants them found and the sooner the better."

"Well, it's nice to see that he's experienced some personal growth through the years."

"Yeah, ain't it grand?"

I said, "And so let me ask you this, Adam. When he's not killing, do you think he's capable of some sort of a normal relationship with a woman? Like do you think he has a girlfriend or maybe even a wife?"

"You mean does he go on any dates that don't end up on the eleven o'clock news?"

"Yeah, exactly. What do your profilers think?"

"Our profilers are agnostic on that particular question. There's good precedent either way."

"Okay. So what do you think?"

"Interesting question, Carlo. I'd have to guess yes. He's a lunatic, but he's a lunatic with a healthy sex drive."

"'Healthy' seems a poor choice of words under the circumstances."

"Okay, a very strong libido, then. He may very well have some semblance of a normal love life. Hell, there could even be a little woman at home who's married to him and totally clueless in regards to his extracurricular activities. Actually I lean that way, now that you ask, either a Mrs. Stephen or a steady girlfriend. I don't believe a woman having a casual encounter with him, without any emotional bond, would be likely to survive the evening. And I don't believe he's been celibate all these years. Come to think of it, it may very well have been a blowup in his domestic life that set him off this time."

I said, "So you think maybe there's a Mrs. Stephen? God, what a thought. What sort of woman would it take to fill those shoes?"

"I'm gonna guess a woman who knows how to mind her manners around the *casa*."

CHAPTER 43

ME

When I hung up with Stoner I realized it was going to be another one of those nights. I had to work in the morning, of course, but I said to myself *screw it.* I was going to have to do the whole bottle of wine. Plus maybe a finger or two of Johnny Walker. I had some serious thinking to do. The Chinese stayed in the microwave, as I had completely lost my appetite.

I settled into my easy chair, the bottle on the floor next to me. I'd dispensed with my glass and tossed the cork in the trash. The television was on for background noise, but I wasn't watching it. My focus was on the photos behind it, and especially the one of Shannon at her first communion. She was much younger than any of Stephen's victims, of course, but still I could imagine the pain and horror I would experience were she to be violated and murdered that way. The pain and horror that God knows how many parents have suffered because of him and his sickness. How do you even retain your sanity after something like that, much less ever pull yourself together and get back to some semblance of a normal life? How would you keep the rage from just eating you up from the inside out? I have no idea.

So now we know that Stephen is an even bigger monster than we imagined, and in my mind the urgency of stopping him has become even bigger. It doesn't really make sense, but I still have the feeling that it's between Stephen and me. As he said in his letter, *mano a mano*. I don't begin to have the resources to compare with Stoner's buddies, but I have something potentially more important: information. I have Stephen's letters and the clues they contain. It's there, I know it is, the answer.

There have been times, I'll admit, that I've regretted keeping the letters to myself. I've even considered giving them to Adam. But the truth of the matter is that that ship sailed a long time ago. No way I can fess up at this late date without admitting to obstruction of justice. Anyway, I doubt very much that anyone at the FBI has the imagination to make anything of Stephen's teases.

No, the reality is that this guy is not going to screw up, and the Feds are not going to catch him. There is at least one girl out there, and possibly more, that are going to be dead in a few weeks unless I can come up with something.

Speaking of which, according to Adam there were presumably five dead girls in Stephen's debut round. A quintet, if you will. Is that happenstance, or is there significance to that number? Will he stop at five this time around? Or is the game open-ended this time?

Now here's the thing: A girl's life is at stake here, or girls' lives, and of course that's the most important consideration. But if I'm being honest there is more at stake for me than just that. For me it's a matter of redemption.

If I am able to save a life, that has to count for something against the taking of life I'm contemplating, doesn't it? There has to be some sort of karmic offset, doesn't there? Or is the whole notion of karma and some sort of cosmic accounting system complete bullshit? Who knows? The fact is I gave up on understanding the workings of the universe a very long time ago. All one can do is call them as they see them and hope for the best. But if I can just figure out a way to stop Stephen I'm going to feel one hell of a lot better. This I know for a fact.

CHAPTER 44
STEPHEN

I returned to work the following morning with a vicious headache and a sense of approaching denouement. As I got out of my car, I noticed that Shannon's new acquisition was left in my back seat and so I brought it into my office with me, thinking to give it to Amy the next time I saw her. I halfway hoped she'd come by with a doughnut for me before leaving for patrol.

The checkerboard sat on the corner of my desk for the rest of the morning as I tossed paper wad basketballs into the wastebasket and arranged and rearranged in my mind the many elements, the risks and the conceivable contingencies of the plan I was preparing to execute. In circumstances such as these, one really needs to attempt to see things from every imaginable angle, to make certain that the planning is sound and that no possibility has been neglected.

And always, hovering in the background, the ghost of Poppy.

A strange thing happened to me as I proceeded. An unexpected and unfamiliar sense of calm fell over me. I came to peace at last with the decisions I'd made, and I was ready to devote my energies to their successful execution. I was going to do it. I was really by God going to do it. My only problem was how.

That part of my dilemma settled, my thoughts turned to the other. Was there a way I could help stop Stephen? The treatise by Dr. Nakamura that Adam had emailed me sat printed and bound in the center of my desk, seventy-five pages of really good material on every possible aspect of devil worship and witchcraft. Her work shed some light on the symbol, the circled star, on Robin Cleary's stomach and Mary Bergen's piercing. It's known as a pentacle and has been used by Satanists for hundreds of years. A more recent variation depicts the star in an inverted orientation, in which case the symbol is referred to as a pentagram. I retrieved my file of autopsy photos to confirm my memory that in Mary's case the star had been placed right side up. Stephen is old school, for what it's worth.

I'd read through the piece twice already but decided to spend the rest of my morning reading it once more. Maybe what I needed was in there and I'd missed it.

To my disappointment, Amy never got in touch. To my even greater disappointment, Stephen did. My heart sunk when the envelope was handed to me, the mid-morning mail. The handwriting was instantly recognizable; the post mark of all places Prescott, AZ. No inclusions this time. Three handwritten pages, which read:

> *Dear Carlo,*
>
> *I am not amused. I will goddamn well tell you that right now. They say that imitation is the sincerest form of flattery, but not for me it isn't. For me it's just some amateur trying to cash in on my efforts. I'm out here trying to create a body of work, an oeuvre if you will, and to do so with an element of style and artistry. You know this already, Carlo, of course. And along comes some jerk-off who thinks he's going to get a free ride to glory? I don't think so.*
>
> *I do love the way you're letting those jackasses in the press hang themselves out to dry, because you know of course the girl in Denver wasn't mine. She was a cute little thing, though, don't you think? Maybe not my taste, but I wouldn't have minded doing her myself. I would surely have done a better job of it.*
>
> *At any rate, I've come to a rather momentous decision, my friend. I'm going to share it with you, since I'd like to give you a leg up here. I'd appreciate it though if you would keep it under your hat. Why give the feds a break? I've decided they're all just a bunch of overpaid bureaucratic bedwetters. Detective Jardina, I am declaring an eight week moratorium on my recreational activities. Nobody dies by my hand for a minimum of sixty days from the date of this letter, that's exclusive to you.*
>
> *Why, you're asking yourself, would my pal Stephen grant such a gift to an undeserving world? There are several reasons,*

Carlo. For one, I want there to be absolutely no doubt as to the authenticity of my work. You can be certain that any murders occurring during this period are copycats.

For another, believe it or not killing women with impunity is a remarkably taxing exercise. There are so many little details to be considered, such elaborate preparations to be made. You'd be surprised. Having this kind of fun is hard work. Believe it or not, but I'll tell you quite candidly that this homicidal maniac (just kidding) is one tired puppy. I need a rest.

There is also the matter of my new found fame. I'm a by God genuine celebrity, and I'd like to take a little while to just enjoy it, to bask, as they say, in the limelight. Do you blame me? You know, Carlo, I didn't get into this business seeking fortune or fame. I did it because I had a real passion. I did it for the artistry. I did it, I suppose, to make my mark on the annals of psychopathology.

Yet now that fame has found me, I must confess that I am thoroughly enjoying it, and I'm going to slow down, smell the roses, and make it last. I'm going to get my money's worth out of my fifteen minutes, in other words. You could be there with me, you know, if you would just cooperate a little tiny bit.

And that brings me to the last and perhaps most important reason for the moratorium. As much as the thrill of the hunt, my friend, I got into this enterprise looking for some intellectual stimulation. It was to be a game of wits between law enforcement and myself. How long could I continue to commit mayhem and elude detection? After Tanya, I read some of the statements you gave to the local press, I looked into your background, you seemed a very sharp man, my hopes soared, I thought to myself, here is a worthy opponent. You know. Small town detective eschews modern crime-fighting techniques, goes with gut instincts honed over years of grappling with the bad guys, uses street smarts acquired during rough upbringing. With this Detective Jardina I will go mano-a-mano, and we will have great fun.

I suppose I needn't tell you how disappointed I've become, Carlo. I expected the FBI to pretty much stand around in stunned stupefaction as my girls went down one by one. But you, Carlo. From you I expected some goddamn imagination, some outside-the-box thinking. I counted on you to at least make it interesting!

Now let me remind you of the stakes, detective. To date four innocent young women have died prolonged and most unpleasant deaths. Families grieve. One small boy is as good as orphaned, father presumably alive but whereabouts unknown. Scores of schoolchildren have been deprived of their favorite teacher, which is bound to have a deleterious effect on their education.

Where does it end? When do you get your act together, step up to the plate, give me a fucking challenge and maybe put an end to the carnage? All by way of explaining why I'm giving you this opportunity. Study the evidence. Work hard. Get your head out of your ass. Because I guarantee that once these next eight weeks have expired another girl will die. She will die horribly, because frankly I'm pissed, even if I did get a page in Time Magazine.

And you can forget putting out warnings. I'm out here on the night club scene in my own backyard where of course I'm never ever going to take prey, and I'm amazed at how easy it is to pick up girls. These dumb bitches have all heard about my killings and yet none ever hesitates to take a complete stranger home to bed. I really don't know what's happened to our society. I think sometimes it must be the schools. Anyway, it really is a shame I can't slaughter more of them, don't you think?

I'll get my share, though, Detective Jardina, if you don't stop me. Ergo, look alive, so others may stay alive. I promise you, if you can get inside my head you'll be a star. One final clue for you alone: "D" is for death. Hah!

Your faithful correspondent, Stephen

PS: I do hope you've had the opportunity to review and enjoy my work with the lovely Theresa. I believe I may have outdone myself, though the beneficiary is regrettably unavailable for comment. Another little ditty for you:

Theresa struggles to stop the pain
I laugh aloud, I wield the cane
She begs for mercy but it's all in vain
Sometimes I wonder if I'm insane

She really is a sweet young gal
It's just she's picked the wrong locale
She gets to see my bag of tricks
She ends up dead on a crucifix

She made such a lovely sacrifice
I'd love to do the same thing twice
You understand it's love not hate
It's the golden rule of real estate!

It is a fact I won't deny
I do love watching women die
But lately it's begun to dawn
The killing can't go on and on

Don't you have to wonder, friend
When and where it all will end?

So Stephen was taking a breather. We, or rather I, had eight weeks to find him and stop him. Eight weeks to save the life of the next girl, whoever and wherever she was. The clock was running on her, whether she knew it or not.

As I sat contemplating this splendid news, Max knocked on my door and came in for a chat. Nobody had been murdered in Prescott since Mary Bergstrom, but the sign on my door said *Robbery-Homicide* and there were a number of liquor store holdups, muggings, home break-ins and the like that I was investigating when the mood took me, and when I wasn't too busy staring at the cover of the Mary Bergstrom file or thinking about Jezebel and Roger and Summer.

I gave a decent accounting of myself with the open cases, the chief seemed satisfied, and it seemed a good time to broach the subject of vacation. "You know, Max," I said, "I've got some time off coming. Would you be able to live without me for a couple of weeks? I'm thinking of going back East to visit the old gang."

"No problem, Carlo. Things are as quiet just now as they ever are going to be. Everybody has forgotten about Mary Bergstrom, thank God, and it looks like our friend has moved on to greener pastures. Sarah and I have been talking about getting away ourselves, but we're looking at October. I'll be wanting you to stand in for me then, so if you go now it's perfect. When do you want to leave?"

"Next Monday, I'm thinking."

"Check in with personnel. Tell 'em I okayed it. It'll be good for you. While we're talking..."

"Yes, Max?"

"You okay, Carlo? You seem distracted lately. You're not taking this Bergstrom thing personally, are you? Because I know I was maybe a little hard on you with it when it first broke, but you know nobody blames you that it's still open. Chrissakes, the FBI has done squat with it."

I said, "Thanks, Max, it's kind of you to say. It's not that. I'm just tired, I believe."

"Well, I just wanted to say that you're appreciated, kid. You do good work. You get more done around here in an hour than most of the chuckleheads I have on the force do in a day. So go have some fun."

This was exceptionally kind of the chief, to tender me these generous words of encouragement, and I felt good as he left my office. Except that when he was gone I remembered the letter I slid into my top drawer when he came in, and was knocked instantly back into a funk.

So, Carlo, I say to myself, Stephen said think. Let's do that. If I can get inside your head, you wrote, I'll be a star. What the hell do you mean by that? And if *D* is for death, what does that make the *S* and *A*, and how would knowing help me catch him? I stare at the map on the wall, attempting for the umpteenth time to divine some critical piece of information from the disposition of the pins stuck into it. What's the pattern? What are you trying to tell me, you sneaky bastard, when you hop into one of your Toyotas?

My feet are on the desk, my hands behind my head, I've been in this posture for thirty minutes, the map is blurry to my vision and I have yet to advance the cause a single step. My right foot slides off my left inadvertently, and in so doing knocks Shannon's checkerboard onto the floor. It hits the thin carpeting with a metallic noise and rolls around in ever-diminishing loops on the floor in front of my desk, until it runs out of energy and falls in on itself, coming to rest face up.

Stooping to retrieve it, I fixate on the pattern painted on its face for a moment. Stop. I notice for the first time its similarity to the symbol drawn in blood on the belly of Robin Cleary, the dead girl in Castle Rock. I glance to the wall. Back to the board. I am hit by a moment of clarity such as I've not experienced in years. I grab a marker and draw five straight lines on the map. Of course. My sudden insight gives me an adrenaline rush. My girl Shannon has inadvertently handed me the piece of the puzzle I needed. I'll be damned. Both ends of my dilemma have finally come together into one single resolution.

CHAPTER 45
SUMMER

Later that same day, Tuesday evening. I sit in my living room, awaiting her call. The cordless lies in my lap and the TV remote is cradled in my right hand. I'm finding the continuing coverage of Stephen's supposed latest victim enormously entertaining for some reason, what with the total bullshit that's being peddled all over the cable channels.

She checks in right on schedule with me. Her mood is effervescent. Things with Roger have exceeded her wildest dreams and she is one happy young girl. There have been times, lately, when I've hated myself for even entertaining the thought of bringing her party to an end. I listen to perhaps ten minutes of her elliptical babbling, however, and I'm ready to reconsider.

Finally I decide to interrupt her monologue. "Summer, sweetie, okay, I get the picture. I'm very happy you and Roger are getting along so well."

"You bet Carlo. It's, like, so great. Better than anything I ever imagined. I cannot thank you enough for getting me out of the life."

"My pleasure, kid. Speaking of which, have you heard from Colette lately?"

"She's given up. My boys are heartbroken."

"As well they may be. So has he talked marriage?"

"Roger?"

"No, Louis XVI. I thought you might be moving into Versailles."

"No need to be sarcastic, Carlo."

"Sorry. Has he?"

"Not in so many words. He's very careful in that area. I guess you have to be, having all that money and all plus okay looks. I have noticed that he's sort of begun talking about Jezebel in the past tense, though, you know? Nothing obvious. It's more subconscious like. He's bringing the jewelry on, though, I'll tell you that. He's even talked about children, if you can believe it. Jezebel didn't want any, but I've told him I always wanted to be a mother. So I'm thinking it's only a matter of time."

"Excellent. Listen, Summer. I have very important instructions for you. *Muy muy importante*, okay?"

"Sure, what do you need?"

"Weekend after next. September 16 through 18. Friday to Sunday. I want you and Roger in Minneapolis."

"Minneapolis? Why Minneapolis?"

"No questions, Summer, remember the deal? I'm paying you a hundred grand a year plus turning you on to the setup of a lifetime in return for no questions. Just say it's important to me and Mrs. Waterhouse. The present Mrs. Waterhouse, that would be. Check into the Four Seasons or the Ritz Carlton if they have one. Otherwise, the Hilton. Something nice. Plan to be in your room at eight o'clock on Friday night. Without fail, my dear. Understand? This is crucial, what I'm telling you."

"All right, all right," she says. "And I'm supposed to get Roger to take me to Minnesota how?"

"The usual time-honored way that girls get men to do the things they want."

"But what's my excuse for wanting to go there?"

"Tell him you just got news of your high school reunion. Tell him it's on that Saturday night. You haven't told him where you're from, right? So tell him you grew up there. You look Scandinavian, so it fits nicely."

"Fine. And if he wants to go with me to the party? What's he gonna say when I have to tell him he can't, on account of there is no reunion?"

"Tell him you're embarrassed to take him because he's old enough to be your father. Tell him you're afraid the other girls will find him so scary irresistible that they'll all hit on him and you'll have a jealous fit. Tell him whatever the hell you feel like. You'll manage, I'm sure. He's wrapped around your little finger, isn't he?"

A long and loud and melodramatic sigh. "Okay, Carlo."

"Get right on it. Time is short."

"Okay."

"Where are we going?"

"Minneapolis."

"When?"

"September 16 to 18. Weekend after next."

"Beautiful. And we'll be where at eight o'clock Friday night?"

"In our luxurious suite at the Four Seasons. Or maybe the Ritz."

"Good girl. Call me next week and fill me in on the details. Ciao, beautiful."

"Ciao."

And so we're off and running.

I must admit that at times I find myself bemused by the blossoming of the relationship between Roger and Summer. But then I guess I shouldn't be. After all, wealthy men and beautiful women have been getting together for a long, long time for mutually beneficial companionship. I suppose that in this world that's constantly changing it's nice to see that some things remain eternally the same.

At any rate, in a week it won't make a dime's worth of difference.

CHAPTER 46
JEZEBEL

And then, my Jezebel. She called not long after I hung up with Summer. I had a fresh glass of Johnny Walker on ice in hand when the phone rang, by this point an absolute necessity.

"Jezzie," I said to her, "you're just the girl I need to talk to. I believe I've got a firm schedule on that project we've been discussing. I want you to meet me in Barstow."

"Barstow? For God's sake, Carlo, have you decided that Laughlin is too good for me?"

"Don't complain, Jezebel. It's a much shorter drive for you, and this is going to be a short meeting. We are coming to the end."

"Oh my God that's wonderful news."

I hear the undertone of excitement in her voice. God help me, she's actually enjoying this. I can't tell her why I've decided against Laughlin this time, but the truth is that the prospect of doing what I'm committing myself to do has put me out of the mood for sex. I don't want us to share a room for the night and I don't want any expectations on Jezebel's part. I just want to get it started and get it the hell over with.

"So listen. There's a Mexican restaurant about ten miles off the 15. Take the Blue Star Highway exit, California 58, and just head west. It's called Las Brisas. North side of the road. Pull around the back of the building and park next to me. I'll be there at 3:00 PM Saturday afternoon. I just need, like, a quarter hour. Can you do that?"

"Sure, baby, of course. I'll see you there."

"Good. Bye."

"Bye."

I found this particular little dive when I took a short tour of the town on my way back from LA, after recruiting Summer. I was originally looking for a motel suitable for Jez and I to use as a rendezvous, though eventually I decided Laughlin was a better choice. The food is actually decent and the beer is cold, but we wouldn't be going in. I just needed a secluded, anonymous spot for Jezebel and me to have a final conversation, one I didn't want to put on the air.

Barstow is a popular stop for people traveling across the Mojave Desert between Las Vegas and Southern California, for gas and a quick bite to eat. Nearly everyone ends up right off the highway, at In-N-Out Burger or McDonald's for the most part. But even if you're looking for sit down you would have to drive a long way and pass half a dozen much nicer places to get to Las Brisas, so I figured there was no way we could possibly run into any of Mrs. Waterhouse's acquaintances.

I was halfway afraid that as the rest of the week went by my resolve would weaken, but when I rolled out of Prescott Saturday morning my only emotion was one of relief. This time when I hit Kingman I took I-40 and dropped south of Laughlin, crossing into California at Needles. Friday night and Saturday morning most of the traffic is eastbound, and so I made good time to Barstow.

Las Brisas is on the western edge of town, close to where development ends and the desert begins. It's a one story adobe structure, with a pair of massive date palms in front. Garish murals painted along the front depict a red-tiled city on a large bay, presumably Acapulco, flanked by a pair of Mexican flags fluttering in an imaginary sea breeze. The restaurant's name is bannered across the top of the front wall above the door in green, red and black neon letters.

A couple of cars are parked on the street out front, but I pull around to the rear of the building. Three more cars and a pickup are lined up along the back row of the lot, probably staff. I take a spot on the opposite side of the dumpster enclosure. It's 1430, the lull between lunch and dinner. There is very little sign of life, as I'd hoped when I set the time for our meeting. A half dozen tumble weeds wander across the glass and paper-strewn asphalt. A scattering of Joshua trees dot the distant desert landscape to the north and west, their branches raised to the sky in mimicry of their biblical namesake.

I roll down my front windows. Tejano music thumps out the rear door, which hangs partially open. The air is hot, and laden with the aroma of cilantro and cooking lard.

Her Mercedes slides into the spot to my left at 1510. I leave my car and hop into her front passenger seat. She immediately pulls me to her, gives me a long, deep kiss, then pushes me away and with a whirl of her hand indicates her surroundings. She says, "So, Carlo, very classy. You've really outdone yourself this time." There is no irritation in her voice though, and she says it with a smile and a wink. She's a happy girl.

I say, "Yeah, nice place, huh? Your friends come here?"

"I'm sure they don't know it exists. Where I come from Barstow is for gas and burgers."

"Precisely. So, Jezebel. September 17 is going to be it. There's been some stuff up in the Minneapolis-St. Paul area that more or less serves our purpose. It's not a perfect fit, but I don't want to wait any longer, for reasons we've already discussed."

"Yes, for sure. It needs to happen now." She's looking straight ahead, out the windshield, but I can see her face in the mirror and that scary gleam is back in her eyes.

"I have Summer working on getting him there. Meantime, Jez, here's what I need you to do. I want you to go to Rapid City, and wait there while it goes down."

"South Dakota? Why the hell would I go to South Dakota, Carlo?"

"Because, goddamn it, Jezebel, I asked you to. Remember our deal? Because I want to see you as soon as it's done. Need to, I mean. Must."

"Isn't that awfully risky? I thought we agreed to remain apart for a while."

"Jez, work with me here, please, okay? I'm begging you. The thing is, this is not easy for me. It's going to be the hardest goddamn thing I've ever done, all right? You seem almost to be having fun with this. You have this animus toward Roger. I don't, sweetheart. I have not a thing in the world against Roger Waterhouse. I don't even know him. I know Summer, and I like her and obviously I have nothing against her. Actually, I think she's an exquisite creature and the thought of destroying her sickens me. How's that for candor? I'm the guy, nevertheless, Jezebel, who gets to look them in the eye, who gets to put a gun to them at very close range and blow them away and get his clothing spattered with their life blood. Who gets to carry that image around with himself for the rest of all time. Can you understand what I'm saying here, woman? Am I getting through to you?

"I'm going to need some comforting. I'm going to need somebody to take me in her arms and hug me and make love to me and say to me that's all right, Carlo, it was worth it, you are now going to have a wonderful life and you have committed an act which is ultimately good. Good because it was for us. And to reassure me once again that there is an *us*."

She says, "All right, Carlo. I get it. But I see two problems. It's really very unlikely that I would ever travel to South Dakota. I mean, it's just not my style. More importantly, if my husband is going to be…if it happens in Minneapolis it's going to look more than a little strange that I just happen to be hanging out in some hick town a couple hundred miles away, for reasons I'd be hard pressed to explain if anybody asked. And I'm pretty sure when the authorities come to notify the next of kin, they will ask."

"I do understand the problem, Jez, I do. I picked it because it's close, but not too close, to Minneapolis, and because it's big enough to get lost in but out of the way enough for us to be inconspicuous."

"So why am I there?"

"Try this. Roger told you he was going on a business trip to Minnesota, although he neglected to mention that he planned to cut down on expenses by sharing a room with his secretary. You asked him to take you with him. He gave you some bullshit excuse why that would not be a good idea. You threw a hissy fit. You told him you didn't really care about Minneapolis-St. Paul but that all your life you've wanted to see Mount Rushmore, which as you may know happens to be in Rapid City. So in order to pacify you he agreed to meet you there after he was done with his business."

"All right. That would work, I guess."

"Good. Now look, I want you in place no later than Friday morning. Thursday night would be even better. Book yourself into a downtown hotel. I've checked and the Hotel Alex Johnson is probably going to be it. It's part of the Hilton chain. Sorry. It's what passes for a full service high rise property in Rapid City. It doesn't appear to be too bad. Make a reservation for Mr. and Mrs. for four or five days, and tell the hotel your husband will be joining you later."

"Sure, Carlo. I'll be there."

"Good. Now on Friday evening…"

"Yes?"

"Hang out in the lounge. Just an hour or two, after dinner. Find yourself a drinking buddy, one who will be sure to remember you. Conversation only, but make an impression, all right? Leave him wanting more and leave him in the bar. Think you can do that?"

She laughs. "Do you think I can?"

"I'm afraid I know damn well you can, baby. So retire early, Jezebel, alone..."

"Carlo, stop it."

"All right. Anyway, just in case I should need to get in touch it would be nice if you were available. It goes down, I'm thinking, the thing with Roger and Summer, like I said before, around eight. Speaking of which, when you get your room, leave the number on my answering machine in Prescott. Just the number, say nothing else. I'll call and pick it up from on the road, and then erase it. Are we clear?"

"We're clear. By the way, how are you getting the time off to do this, so far away from home? What did you tell your boss?"

"Told him I needed some vacation time. He gave me a couple of weeks. Told him I'm visiting my old gang back East. Works out real well, because I have a dozen guys in the old neighborhood who will swear on their mother's graves that I was with them the whole time."

"Okay, so I'll see you in South Dakota after...it's over."

"Good. I've rethought the part about leaving the keycard in the door, by the way. No one would do that. I'll lock the door and hang out a *Do Not Disturb* sign. With luck the bodies won't be found for at least a day, maybe two or three. That will give us time to spend at least a night together, maybe more if I'm lucky. I'll drive over and check into a different hotel, and if we're careful we should be able to hook up. I'm going to need some serious stress release, if you know what I mean. Once we hear they've found them, I'll bug out and you can wait here for them to deliver the bad news. You can start shopping for a new black dress and we can begin waiting out the decent interval until it's safe to reconnect publicly. I figure six months should do it."

"Carlo, I can't wait, believe me. It's going to be so good. When you get here we're going to have the best night ever."

"Maybe in a few years we can come back here and we really can visit the monument, for old times' sake. We'll scramble around on those stone presidential heads like Cary Grant and Eva Marie Saint."

"What?"

"Never mind."

CHAPTER 47
ME

So it begins. Or ends, hard to say which for sure.

Late Monday evening, and it is neither clear nor starry. A lowering sky is pressing down on us, foreclosing our options. The cloud deck nearly touches the mountaintops and the glow of the lights of Flagstaff reflect off its smooth lead-colored belly. No moon to be found anywhere. Jazz in brass and woodwind, mournful evocations of exotic Spain. John Coltrane's *Olé*. Miles Davis' *Sketches of Spain*. As I climb into the foothills, desert plants and creatures give way to pine and mesquite and the occasional deer leaping across my headlights.

I am a somnambulist. No philosophy this night, no thinking or feeling of any sort, not mine to question why. Carlo Jardina has had quite enough of that for a lifetime, thank you very much; he believes he will resign his fate to the gods. Only staring dumbly out the windshield while the miles unroll effortlessly and my automobile takes me unbidden toward my destination. Turn off your mind, relax and float downstream, Lennon said. It is not dying.

I've slipped out of Prescott unheralded. The stage is set. The players are taking their appointed places and my preparations are complete. Mine now to do and die. I spend the evening in Flagstaff. The hotel is anonymous, but I'm not. I check in using my real name and write my actual license number on the register. I pay with a credit card. Anonymity is not yet a requirement, for this city is on the route to my alleged destination. The room is reasonably comfortable, but I sleep only a little.

I'm up with the sun. Quick breakfast and a thermos of coffee and I'm cruising along the great cross-country artery of the southern tier, highway 40, heading with renewed confidence toward New Mexico.

As I descend through the mountains to the east of Flagstaff the cloud cover diminishes and eventually I find myself driving under an unblemished blue sky. It vaults above me, luminous and unbounded and once again my sense of limitless possibility is restored. Surrounding me the pink and red layer-cake mesas and windswept monolithic rock formations that spike the landscape south of Four Corners like so many giant tombstones, and then the trackless brown and gold desert and hills west of Albuquerque.

The afternoon shadows lengthen as I approach the outskirts of the city, sprawled haphazardly between the Rio Grande and the Sandia range of the Rockies. Here I intend to turn to the north, along route 25, climb back into the mountains toward Santa Fe and thread my way along the spine of the continental divide all the way to Denver. Here too I will depart my announced itinerary and will therefore need to travel in anonymity.

Behind me the sky to the west is streaked with orange and pink, while ahead, beyond the peaks, it begins to shade to indigo and black. I stop in town at a roadside restaurant for a quick dinner. Call my apartment phone with my cellular and hear Summer's voice. Before I hit the road I instructed her and Jez to use my answering machine for voicemail, a risk I judged acceptable and necessary since I would be intermittently out of service range on my phone. She's telling me that she and Roger would be leaving Thursday for Minnesota, first-class nonstop on Delta. Hotel particulars to follow. A moment of relief that the last minute arrangements didn't leave them flying coach, after which I erase the message. I finish my club sandwich with coleslaw and fries and wash them down with more black coffee.

Back in the saddle, I realize that I'm out of tapes I haven't listened to since leaving Prescott, and so I try the radio. The good thing about Albuquerque is that you can listen to just about any kind of music you like. Assuming you like either country/western or Mexican, I mean. I select the former, figuring that as I near Santa Fe, which like Sedona aspires to sophistication, I'll be able to tune in some jazz.

Darkness has fallen, I'm back among the conifers now, my ears are popping every once in a while as the roadway winds upward and the altitude increases, and a vast panoply of stars is once again on display above me, startling in their white intensity. My fingers twirl the tuning knob, they connect with a jazz station as I was hoping, and the present hour is dedicated to the work of the New Age fusion group Hiroshima. A colossal irony, this, it occurs to me, considering that not more than forty miles to the north is Los Alamos and to the south a couple hundred miles lies the Trinity test site. Trinity for the Hindu Trimurti: Brahma, Vishnu and Shiva. Brahma, the creator. Vishnu, the preserver. Shiva, the destroyer. I refuse to close this particular metaphysical loop, there being no profit in it for me. Rather I relax and allow the music to lull me into a dream state.

I cruise at speed down the twisting Amalfi coastline behind the wheel of a spanking new Ferrari Modena Spyder, black. Top is off, exposing me and Jez and our luxurious new aniline leather interior to the warmth of the southern Italian sun. Fat low-profile Pirellis sing shrilly against the pavement as I throw her into the corners while busily working the six-speed gearbox. The highway is carved out of the very rim of a vertical stone cliff, so that at the apex of every outside curve we are treated to a dizzying view of the sparkling blue Tyrrhenian Sea, what looks to be about a thousand feet below. Jezebel is beside herself, she shrieks incoherently with a mad combination of terror and delight that puts me in mind of my Shannon on some wild carnival ride.

She asked me, after we made love at the Phoenician, "So, Carlo. Where shall we go first, after our time of waiting is up and we can be together? I want to show you the world, baby. Where shall I start?"

I answered her without hesitation. "Italy, Jez. Land of my fathers. I've always wanted to go. I want to swim in Lake Como. I want to feed pigeons in San Marcos Plaza. I want to pick olives in Sicily. I want to walk the ground of Tuscany and see Florence. I want to climb Brunelleschi's Dome, I want to see Michelangelo's David. I want to go to Pisa and see the Leaning Tower. I want to see Rome, the Sistine Chapel, the Pieta, the Colosseum. I want to eat good Italian pasta like my mother never made, and drink Italian wine. I want to eat gelato.

"Then Naples and the Amalfi coast. This, most of all. There's a town down there, Jez, called Positano. Heard of it?"

"No, I honestly haven't."

"Well, let me tell you. I have. I've seen pictures of it. Movie stars and other jetsetters vacation there. It's beautiful. You are gonna love it. If there is a more romantic spot on the planet I'd love to see it. We'll stay at a hotel just north of there, the San Pietro. It's built into the solid rock of a sheer promontory so that you enter through a lobby at the top and then work your way down to the sea. The view of the Med is spectacular. We'll get a room that looks west toward Capri. We'll eat wonderful Italian food all day and make love all night under a big white moon."

I decide to call it a night when I hit Santa Fe. I pay cash for what are decidedly less deluxe accommodations than the San Pietro, using an assumed name and fictitious license plate number. It's the middle of the night by the time I hit the sack. No new messages on my machine. Tonight I sleep very soundly.

Wednesday is a very long day. I crawl down the back side of the mountain. I push through Las Vegas, NM, up into Colorado, through Pueblo and Colorado Springs, running all the time along the eastern toe of the front range so that the great plains stretch off to my right and the day darkens early as the sun dips into the peaks to my left. The Sangre de Cristo mountains. The blood of Christ. The last wedge of sun glows a soft blood red.

In Denver I pick up route 76, headed away from the Rockies and across high flat terrain, northeast into Nebraska. Past midnight I cross a long steel cantilever bridge that spans the Rubicon River, though the highway sign claims it's the S. Platte. It looms up at me, the bridge, like some overgrown child's erector set creation, black spider work in the waning moonlight that seems at once large yet surprisingly fragile. My tires hum pleasantly on the surface of its roadbed. Its twin lies in shadow a quarter mile downriver and a long freight train crosses it in the opposite direction. Two o'clock and I am exhausted. I can drive no farther. I check into a very forgettable little motel in North Platte.

"And you, Jezzie? Where would you like to go?" I asked her.

"Hawaii's my favorite. The Four Seasons on Maui or the big island, either way."

"Excellent choice. I've never been, not even to Waikiki. They tell me it's very nice."

"Except that Hawaii reminds me of Roger."

"A serious drawback."

"That really sort of spoils it for me."

"That makes two of us, then."

"No kidding. I know, even better. Tahiti. Bora Bora. Moorea. Oh, Carlo, I've heard it's awesome. The water is perfect there, clear and blue and warm. We'll go native. We'll get one of those places on stilts that they have built over the water on some lonely lagoon. You'll be just like Gauguin. You'll paint and I'll sip Mai Tai's. You'll gawk at the topless island women and I'll have to work overtime to keep you coming home. We'll speak the language of France by day and the language of love by night."

Only I'm about as far away from the Society Islands this Thursday morning as one can be. I'm in cornhusker country, harvest time approaches and I'm drilling down a highway that runs straight as a bullet flies, clear to the horizon. It slices cleanly through endless expanses of tall green corn that run as far as the eye can see in all directions. One really needs to see it like this, from the ground, to appreciate the scale and fecundity of our farming industry. It really is quite amazing. Though when I break into the open and see the small communities with their farmhouses and barns and silos and picturesque white churches that dot the gently undulating landscape I'm reminded of poor Theresa, which makes me sad.

Tomorrow is the day and a buzz of excitement mixed with dread is building by slow accretion inside the back of my head. Late in the afternoon I stop for gas, and when I get out of the car the air is still and hot and humid. The sound of distant swarms of insects floats in the air, along with the smell of ozone that in the plains of the Midwest presages the coming of a thunderstorm. A flock of crows passes overhead, winging north to some faraway rookery, their cawing loud and urgent. To the south a line of thunderheads is building, grayish black on the eastern faces but backlit gold and silver by the sun as it falls slowly toward the western horizon. Diaphanous wisps of virga trail in coils from the bases. Lightning races across the squall line lacing cloud to cloud and cloud to ground but I'm too far away to hear the report.

I decide to spend my last night of travel in Sioux City, IA, less than a hundred miles south of the Minnesota state line. The idea is to knock off early and get a good strong start on the final couple of hundred miles. This will allow for a nice leisurely pace and give me time to recover from last-minute problems such as flat tires or mechanical failures.

It occurs to me of course how nice it would be to visit Theresa Lindholm's flower-strewn grave while I'm here. Sadly, I'm unsure of its location and for obvious reasons I'm in no position to ask.

Approaching town from the south, I pass an airport and can't resist the opportunity to borrow a page from Stephen's game book. What the hell, it's dark and uncrowded and a slam dunk grabbing a set of Iowa license plates from the car park, which are the next best thing and should not be nearly as conspicuous in a neighboring state as the ones from Arizona.

I spend the evening in an extremely mediocre establishment; I'm pretty sure I'm the only patron that's neither a trucker nor an adulterer. I'm annoyed by the sound of Roger and Summer in the room next door, having at it one last time. It's without regret that I anticipate the end of this particular road trip.

Jezebel is on my answering machine. "510," she says, nothing more. I listen twice, to be sure, and erase her voice. Then, Amy with Shannon chiming in from the background, wishing me a safe journey and pleasant visit with my old friends. A request from the mother to give her a call sometime and from the daughter to keep a sharp eye out for new old toys.

Friday morning. I put on a pair of dress slacks for the day, dress leather shoes and a sports shirt open at the collar. I throw a blazer into the back seat of the car. I want to be dressed suitably enough to wander around the lobby of a nice hotel without raising any eyebrows, yet unremarkably enough that nobody remembers seeing me. I'm looking to fade into the background today, just like my pal Stephen.

I treat myself to a nice leisurely breakfast at a coffee shop the motel clerk recommends to me. Eggs Benedict, my favorite. What the hell, who's to worry about cholesterol at a time like this? Hash browns and orange juice and about half a gallon of black coffee. Gas up the cruiser and hit the road around 1030.

I'm leaving corn country. I drive through vast inland oceans of alfalfa and barley, hay and oats, rye and spring wheat, rippling like water under a heavy northwestern wind. Past enormous green pasture lands dotted with herds of cattle and sheep. Behind the passing weather front the air is cooler and dryer. It smells of rain and wet grass. The sky is clear except for a high shredded layer of cirrus.

I come to a small farm town where the highway runs close by an elementary school, and because I have an extremely sharp eye today I'm able to spot Shannon and Marley moving up and down on the opposite ends of a teeter totter and laughing as if this were just another day. I'm loathe to spoil it for them by telling them the truth, but I decide that because I'm ahead of schedule I have the time to pull over for a little while and enjoy the sight of their innocent play.

I watch until it's time to continue the lonely drive to my destination. I stop short of the city to have an early dinner; it is perhaps 1700. I enter downtown around 1830. It is late summer and the latitude is of course much farther north than I'm accustomed to in Prescott, and therefore the sun hovers well clear of the horizon and the sky is still surprisingly bright.

I have now to locate the ideal parking spot. This is a crucial detail. As I remarked to Jezzie, the trick is to be close enough to the hotel to make it an easy walk; I don't want to stumble into the lobby huffing and puffing. I want also to be able to reach my car quickly in the event of a problem. On the other hand, I need to be far enough away so that no passerby would ever connect my vehicle with my destination.

After perhaps ten minutes of cruising around, I find the perfect spot. It's an underground garage next to a mall about five blocks from the hotel. I drive down to a level which is relatively uncrowded but not so isolated as to be suspiciously so. I don't want to draw attention from some over-eager rent-a-cop security guard. I find a spot that's inconspicuous and poorly lit. I check my watch. I'm early. I have time to kill. I listen to news on the AM for half an hour. I learn that the world is still going slowly to hell. Smile and nod to a young mother who walks by with two toddlers and an armful of shopping bags.

It is time. The mini Styrofoam cooler sits next to me on the front passenger seat. It's secured by a band of shipping tape, and when I unseal its lid gray-white vapor streams off a block of dry ice. I pull the blazer off the back seat and put it on. Smooth my hair. Open the trunk.

When I emerge to street level the sun has disappeared and the city is recast in crepuscular light. I put a friendly grin on my face and stroll toward the hotel, just another self-satisfied citizen with no particular agenda other than to enjoy a fine Midwestern summer evening, do some window shopping and admire the lights that burn brightly now in the deepening night.

The lobby is fairly crowded, for which I am thankful. I manage to wait for an empty elevator without it being obvious that I'm doing so, and ride alone to the second floor. I walk down the hallway to the stairwell door. Checking over my shoulder that I'm unseen, I open the door and step in.

The sickly sweet banana smell of damp concrete. The dim glare of a single naked bulb on the wall of the landing below me. The soft metallic resonance as the door closes itself behind me. Then empty silence. I begin the climb, accompanied only by the faint echo of my footsteps.

My feet so damnably heavy. Must I ascend the whole way to the heavens? Is that where I find peace? Suddenly I notice that I'm no longer alone in the stairwell. There are Poppy and Celeste, hand in hand. How are you two? So good to see you together again. Poppy, you have such a troubled face. Please, Poppy, don't look at me like that. It isn't vengeance, I swear it. It's justice. It's your kind of justice, old man.

Perched above them, Amy and Shannon greet me with innocent smiles. Good evening, my loves. You've been much on my mind. Perhaps we were meant to be after all.

And around the corner, a bunch of the boys from back home. South Philly hoodlums, how's it going? Save some cheese steak for me, you silly pricks. I'll be there soon.

Sprawled out along the next flight of stairs are the dead girls, all four of them. Lovely tonight, my sweets, I'm not certain I still remember all your names. No matter. Sorry I wasn't in time to save you. Don't worry. No more innocent girls will be coming to lie bleeding beside you. You may take that comforting piece of news back to your graves with you, when you're ready to return.

Hello, Stephen, there you are! AKA Satanic Angel of Death, am I right? Are you happy now I've tumbled to your game? Like you promised, I'm a star. Actually, I am the final tip of the star you've been describing by your fatal wanderings, am I not?

Or is pentacle a better word? Five sides to the Devil's logo; a dead girl to mark each point. Take the rest of your life off, pal. Your work here is just about finished. This one's on me.

Hey, Stoner, don't look so glum. Not the first time some rube cop has shown you up.

Finally, here comes Thumper, sitting all alone on the last landing, his foot tapping busily on the second-to-last step. Your night, my man, really. You are the guy who made it all possible. Tonight, Thump, I could believe in a vigilant and proactive God, for how small must the odds have been that our paths would cross by chance?

Your story put it together for me. When Poppy was murdered, the papers never said a word about his young bride's involvement. Or that Rochelle was given a new name and identity by the Feds. And without your telling me she loved to gamble, how could I have ever known where to start looking for her? Might have been a perfect ending, kid, had I been able to keep my heart out of it.

I'm here. The fifth floor. I peek around the corner to an empty hallway. Attaché case full of party supplies in my left hand. With my right, I check underneath my left shoulder. The Beretta's there, safe and sound and reassuringly heavy. I pull a pair of nitrile gloves from my blazer pocket and slip them on. I tap my shirt pocket. The vial you sent me Stephen, the last one, it's there. Defrosted by now. Walk quietly. Knock ever so softly on the door. Room 510, Rapid City Hilton. Good evening, Jezebel.

If you enjoyed reading
DANGEROUS PLAYTHINGS,
please leave a review to recommend it to other readers.

CPSIA information can be obtained
at www.ICGtesting.com
Printed in the USA
BVHW091143020223
657731BV00015B/393